Her hair fell below her waist, ripped free of its ties and weighed down by the warm, lashing rain. The sky-blue dress, so carefully chosen for this night and tried on so many times in her bedroom, was ruined. One strap had torn from her shoulder and dangled down her back. Mud splattered the hem. Sweet Cantaloupe lipstick, a lovely coral that heightened the green in her eyes, was smeared like a bruise on one cheek.

She ran.

The high school gym behind her, decorated in crepe paper and curtains, vibrated with electric guitars and teen-aged hormones. Couples gyrated on the dance floor and then disappeared into dark corners. It was late and the Spring Dance was in full throttle. No one would miss her for hours.

In front of her, trees dripped in moss, barely visible in the darkness. She envisioned the moss brushing her shoulders, low branches snagging her hair. The possibility of snakes both at her feet and over her head, made her hesitate.

One scream, one gasp, and he would find her.

Wild Crime

by

Julie Howard

Wild Crime Series, Book 3

Wild Crime

Cover Art by *Abigail Owen*

The Wild Rose Press, Inc.
PO Box 708
Adams Basin, NY 14410-0708
Visit us at www.thewildrosepress.com

Publishing History
First Mainstream Mystery Edition, 2019
Print ISBN 978-1-5092-2863-8
Digital ISBN 978-1-5092-2864-5

Wild Crime Series, Book 3
Published in the United States of America

Dedication

This book is for those who try,
and then try again, again and again.

Prologue—The Beginning

*Her hair fell below her waist, ripped free of its ties
and weighed down by the warm, lashing rain. The sky-
blue dress, so carefully chosen for this night and tried
on so many times in her bedroom, was ruined. One
strap had torn from her shoulder and dangled down her
back. Mud splattered the hem. Sweet Cantaloupe
lipstick, a lovely coral that heightened the green in her
eyes, was smeared like a bruise on one cheek.*

She ran.

*The high school gym behind her, decorated in
crepe paper and curtains, vibrated with electric guitars
and teen-aged hormones. Couples gyrated on the dance
floor and then disappeared into dark corners. It was
late and the Spring Dance was in full throttle. No one
would miss her for hours.*

*Before her, trees dripped moss, barely visible in
the darkness. She envisioned the moss brushing her
shoulders, low branches snagging her hair, the
possibility of snakes both at her feet and above; this
made her hesitate. It would take one scream, one gasp,
and he would find her. To her right was the even more
daunting, murky swamp filled with alligators and
snapping turtles. Impassable. Unthinkable.*

*The only choice was to turn left into the open. Not
far off were the sand dunes where hills would offer
shelter. Panting heavily now, she glanced behind her,*

blinking rain from her eyelashes. A shadow shifted and her vision blurred. How many drinks had there been? Only two, maybe three; four if you counted the one she gulped in the parking lot before the dance, to get the party started. She drew in a deep breath, the thick air oppressive and smelling of rot.

She wanted nothing more than to lie down and rest, to give up this unending pursuit. Some animals did that, didn't they? Finally admit defeat and submit to their fate.

She once wrote a paper on "pursuit predation" for a high school English class and became fascinated in how various beasts engage in attacks and counterattacks. Honeybees, for instance, conquer hornets, their primary foe, by swarming a lone hornet. Clustering around, the honeybees vibrate their abdomens to create heat, thereby cooking their enemy to death. Cheetahs win by speed, lions by ambush, ants by swarm.

Dragonflies, she discovered, are among the most strategic and successful hunters. Instead of heading directly toward a target, they predict where their prey would flee and adjust their flight pattern in advance. They almost never lose their prey. Her teacher gave her an 'A' for the paper, the only one she received that semester.

The shadow behind her grew larger until it took on the shape of a man, growing closer and closer. He'd angled to intercept her. The dunes were within reach; she was nearly there. The ocean's steady roar hid the whimpers now surfacing with each of her breaths. She stumbled and fell. In a flash he was on her, gripping her loosened hair in a tight fist.

"Little rabbit," he crooned in her ear, the hateful nickname he gave her when she was twelve.

She screamed but the sound was carried away by the wind.

Chapter One

High above the rooftops of downtown Fifteen Palms, Florida, the attorney's office faced the cityscape and offered a view of the cluster of seaside businesses catering to tourists. At the street far below, statuesque palm trees lined up in a row like sentries guarding the entrance. A stone fountain gurgled cool water amid the blinding white concrete. In the distance, the sea was still, a sheet of slate blue stretching to the horizon.

Meredith Lowe turned from the floor-to-ceiling windows. She'd arrived early, nervous for what was to come. Today, she would learn the identity of her father. Perhaps her grandmother would have left a clue why she banished her daughter—Meredith's mother, Laura—twenty-five years earlier, leaving her to die without making any attempt at reconciliation. Perhaps, her grandmother's death might lift the veil on a few of their family mysteries.

Arriving a half hour early didn't mean Meredith would discover the identity of her father any sooner. The lawyer said eleven a.m. and the clock now read ten fifty-eight. The door from the waiting room to his inner sanctum remained shut. Apparently, this was a man who stuck to a schedule.

Her heart thumped heavily in her chest, and she regretted the sundress she'd chosen for the day. A sundress at Christmas was a luxury, especially since it was snowing back home in Idaho. But this was Florida, where a hot December sun warmed the beach sands and reflected the heat off the sidewalks, making it feel warmer than eighty degrees. Pure heaven. Regardless, a day of revelations wasn't the time to go sleeveless. Damp splotches already formed under her arms, and she needed to wipe her palms against her sides more than once. Her ash-brown hair, pulled into a low messy chignon that morning, was already falling apart. The receptionist at the waiting room desk frowned at her in disapproval. Whether it was for sweaty palms, her choice of dress, or just her in general, she didn't know.

There was a low click behind her.

"Mrs. Lowe." The lawyer materialized in the doorway. Tall and stoop-shouldered, his suit jacket hung loose on skeletal shoulders. A few wiry hairs weaved an odd circuit over the top of his head, seeking to cover its bony surface.

"Mr. Holt?" There was no doubt it was him, the firm's senior partner. Who else would be behind the door emblazoned with: Therald F. Holt, Senior Partner?

"Please come in." His thin lips barely twitched. "We'll get started." A nearby clock chimed the hour. Meredith felt relief that he didn't offer to shake her hand in greeting.

She wiped her palms one more time, glanced at the still-frowning receptionist, and followed him into his office. Her grandmother, Leila Brittan, had been here, in this grand office, treading upon the same deep plush carpet. The old woman who sat by and let her only child die without a word of comfort or a goodbye, who wanted nothing to do with her only grandchild—Meredith—had sat in this same leather chair the color of dark umber. Even when Meredith's former husband, Brian, sent Leila a note, informing her of their wedding and also later when she'd become a great-grandmother, there had been no reply.

Meredith swallowed a lump that had formed in her throat as she glanced around the room. On one wall was a series of black-and-white photos of palm trees, and on another were three framed diplomas vouching for the capabilities of Therald Holt. A floor-to-ceiling bookshelf took over a third wall, filled with thick leather-bound tomes ostensibly chock full of laws, regulations, and statutes. The final wall consisted of large floor-to-ceiling windows tinted dark against the relentless Florida sun.

The lawyer settled himself at a massive mahogany desk in a tall wooden chair twice the size of hers. His seat didn't appear comfortable, but nothing about this man emanated softness. He offered no condolences for her grandmother's recent death and apparently didn't believe in small talk. He cleared his throat and spoke as the clock finished its eleventh chime.

"As you are already aware, my client—your late grandmother—tasked me with contacting you regarding two items in her will." He peered at her, eyebrows raised, and once she nodded in acknowledgment of this fact, he continued. "First, there is a sealed box she assured me is of little value. Secondarily, there is a letter you may not take with you or copy or take notes from. I am to read the letter out loud and then destroy it in your presence. Do you understand and agree to these terms?"

She fidgeted in her seat. She'd traveled more than fourteen hundred miles from her home in Hay City,

Idaho to Fifteen Palms, Florida to hear the contents of this letter. Long-held secrets revealed, for there would be no other reason for this meeting. The information was the key, not the printed words. If the lawyer wanted to make confetti out of the letter afterward, what did she care?

"Yes, please read it."

The lawyer sniffed and didn't budge. There were no papers before him on the desk. It was a blank surface, smooth and glossy, with no family pictures or knick-knacks from grandchildren, or anything at all that indicated a life outside the office. The self-important man was all business, and he clearly had more to say before a letter would appear.

"As for the sealed box, you'll want to open it here in the safety and privacy of these walls, and I'd be happy to advise you what to do with the contents. Of course, if you choose, you may also take it and open it elsewhere." From his tone, it was clear he believed the best option was the first one. Therald Holt's gaze burned into her. Still, he didn't stir.

"Yes...I don't know...I'd like to hear the letter." She wished he'd get on with the business. There was a gentle whoosh as the air conditioning clicked on and goosebumps popped up on her arms.

"You are aware my client left you nothing of value." His lips pursed together. If he were a judge, she was getting the maximum sentence. "She spelled that out specifically. She said this to me directly, sitting before me, right where you are now. If you have a notion of contesting the will, be assured—"

Meredith broke in. "I haven't considered contesting anything. I don't want any of her money. I just want to hear the letter. Now." Her breath came fast. In case it would help, she added, "Please."

A small smile crept to his lips as he opened a drawer near one knee and brandished an envelope. This is it, she thought. This is what I've waited twenty-five years to discover.

Without any other preamble, Therald Holt opened the envelope and withdrew a single page. Chilled and hot at the same time, she wiped her palms once more against her sundress as he began to read in a monotone:

"Dear Mrs. Lowe,"

Mrs. Lowe. Her throat tightened in irritation. The woman couldn't even call her granddaughter, not even in death.

"Now that I am gone, I'd like to correct any falsehoods your mother may have told you about your father. It's unfortunate she carried so much anger in her heart, anger that separated a mother from daughter for a lifetime. A person reaps what they sow. It should be clear to you that while I have reaped good fortune, your mother only effected misery onto her life."

Fury rose in Meredith's chest. How dare this woman lecture her from the grave. Her mother was the most honest person she knew. Laura struggled with alcoholism, that was a fact, but illness and some type of decades-old quarrel wasn't a reason for a permanent estrangement and these final cruel words. Fists clenched, it took everything she had to stay seated and to not storm from the office. The lawyer paused, appearing almost to enjoy her discomfort, and then went on.

"It must be terrible to have a dishonest parent, but we don't get to choose our relations. Let me set the

record straight about who your father is. There is no doubt on this matter. His name is David Givens and last I knew, he lived in California, although there was no reason for me to keep track of these things."

David Givens. David Givens. David Givens.

Meredith chanted the name in her mind, her fingers itching to write the two words down, terrified she'd forget. After all this time, here was her father's name. He was in California, where she'd lived nearly all her life until recently. She could have passed him on the street, ridden next to him on a train, waited impatiently behind him in a grocery checkout line. The name echoed over and over in her mind, and she had to force herself to focus as the lawyer continued to read.

"Your mother was my only child. A child's wicked impulses are daggers in a mother's heart, but I found solace in doing good works for others. I encourage you to do the same, although I suspect you have followed in her path. Turn from her vindictive lies and believe the truth I've written here."

It was a moment before Meredith realized the lawyer had stopped speaking. Her grandmother's last words to her were both a revelation and an insult.

"What does she mean about my mother lying?" The words burst out. "She never said much at all about my father. She refused to name him. What did he do?"

The lawyer sat back in his chair, staring at the letter. Indecision worked at his lips, his jaw twitching. "It's hard to believe that Laura never said anything."

Her mother's name prompted tears to spring in Meredith's eyes. Since her death, no one spoke of her. In a voice barely above a whisper, she said, "All my mother said was he did something…terrible."

The lawyer's humorless chuckle startled her. "I knew the Givens family, and did some work for them once. Saw the boy around town. He was a good-looking young man, fair-haired, clean-cut. I doubt he got into much trouble. Things happen, you know. Teenagers."

"Was?" she asked, trembling inside. "You said '*was*.' Is he. . .my father...dead?"

The quarter hour chimed once. An echoing chime came from the direction of the reception room, the two clocks ever so slightly out of sync.

"I wouldn't know." His voice was tight, the brief joviality gone. "I said 'was' because the Givens family moved away years ago."

"But...how do I find him, my father?"

The hard chair creaked as Holt shifted. "I deal in estates and trusts. Not investigations. If I were you, I'd let it go." He cleared his throat and ran his tongue over dry lips. "As I mentioned, your grandmother also left a box for you."

Meredith watched bewildered as he opened another desk drawer and set a small, plain cardboard box on his desk. The container was about two-thirds the size of a shoebox and wrapped round with yellowed, cracked packing tape. The unassuming package didn't appear to promise riches inside. He slid it across the smooth surface toward her. Now that she was in this room, after three days of hard driving with two kids in the back seat and weeks of wondering what the lawyer would reveal, the moment passed too swiftly. She stared at the box, her mind still on her father.

David Givens, she repeated silently.

He slid a pair of scissors forward to lay next to the box. "You can open it here." The statement emerged from this unfriendly lawyer as an order. His voice was stern. Any indecision she might have had disappeared. She would open it away from his cold, judging gaze.

Meredith stood and grasped the box, feeling the contents shift slightly. The package was light. Whatever was inside didn't weigh much. "If that's all, I'll just open this later."

The lawyer's gaze lingered on the box; he appeared to be making up his mind about something. He retrieved the scissors and, studying them, his Adam's apple leaped. She took a step back with a frown. Silly, she thought, there's no threat here.

With a huff of annoyance, he replaced the scissors in their drawer and then rose. "One last thing."

Taking up the one-page letter, he strode to a machine at the side of his office. He flipped a switch at the side of the machine and then fed the letter through a slot. There was a whir and then a light buzzing sound as the letter was sliced into thin strips.

David Givens, Meredith repeated in her mind. There was an ache in her chest, knowing his identity had been shredded, with no other testament to his patrimony than the words stored in her memory. She clutched the box to her chest, wondering if more clues about her father were inside. The lawyer scowled at her, his eyes darting to the box as if he had the same idea.

"I suppose that's all," she said.

He laid a piece of paper on his desk along with a pen. "Sign here for receipt of property."

Her hand shook as she signed. As she entered the elevator, the clock chimed the half hour. David Givens, I'm coming for you.

****

Double doors whisked open automatically as she approached the building's exit. The full force of Florida's late December heat hit her. Perspiration sprang from her forehead, the back of her neck, under her arms, behind her knees, between her toes—all at the same time. Eighty degrees and ninety-five percent humidity with the sun fully overhead. The fountain spouted a series of cool streams, and she stopped before it to adjust to the sudden change in temperature.

Back home in Hay City, Idaho, the temperature was twenty degrees at high noon and getting colder by the day. People there told her the depth of winter wouldn't arrive for another month and that below-zero days weren't unusual. As a relative newcomer, she didn't ask about the nights. Already, icicles were dripping *inside* her house, from the kitchen ceiling where a leak had developed, and along the interior edges of all the windows. It was a good thing she and her children were living thirty yards away in a trailer, the one they'd been living in ever since the ceiling in her daughter's bedroom collapsed a month earlier. There was nothing she could do about her deteriorating house until spring. Each day, she stared across the yard, wondering what new horrors had developed overnight.

"Mom!" Five-year-old Jamie ran up, mouth agape and ringed with purple. She stuck out her tongue to show off its matching color. "The sheriff bought us snow cones."

She lifted her gaze. Tall, solid, dependable Curtis Barnaby approached with nineteen-month-old Atticus perched on his shoulders. Blue drips stained the front of Curtis' white polo shirt and the top of his head, signs of the remnants of Atticus' berry snow cone. The knot so tightly coiled in her stomach loosened at the sight of his steadfast easy-going presence. Thank God he's here.

Curtis, Hay City's sheriff, was more than a steadying influence on her life. He'd literally saved her life, more than once. Without him, she could be in prison for murder and her children taken away forever. She could have frozen to death on a mountain road. Who could have predicted they'd be together now, traveling across the country in the dead of winter?

"That was fast. Everything okay?" He swung Atticus down to the ground and ran a hand through his hair, wincing slightly at the stickiness on his fingers. The children wandered over to the fountain's edge.

"I have his name." Saying the words was a relief beyond measure. All the way across country, she'd worried her grandmother's letter wouldn't name her father and that the long trip would be for nothing. She gestured with the box. "The lawyer, gave me this."

Curtis nodded, a somber expression on his face. He didn't pressure her for any details, and she was grateful he allowed her to decide what to reveal in her own time.

"I haven't opened it," she said, her fingers touching the packing tape. "That lawyer was terrible. He was so impersonal…and unkind. I just couldn't open this in front of him."

She suspected the box contained items once belonging to her mother, for nothing else made sense. Her grandmother cut her mother off years ago, and the lawyer made it clear nothing of value was passed on. For Meredith, though, any fragment of her mother's childhood would be invaluable. All she had left of her mother were a few pictures and a secondhand game of Life, one missing all the male characters.

"Story of my life," her mother would always say with a laugh when they played it at night. Meredith cherished the game for the memories it evoked. Her mother had no jewelry, no knick-knacks, no dishes or furniture—nothing to pass along when she died. They'd been drifters, vagabonds, free spirits, homeless. "'Wild thing,'" her mother would sing, and grab her up to dance along. "'You make my heart sing.'"

Whatever you wanted to call them, it meant they had precious little other than the clothes on their backs.

Giggles erupted by the fountain where Jamie was leaning over the side and splashing at the water. Atticus stretched over the edge, trying mightily but failing to extend a hand to the water.

Curtis glanced down at the box. "Want me to take the kids to the beach so you can open this alone?"

Her fingers were already picking at the brittle yellowed tape, stripping it across the lid flaps, which were stuck together with glue. Whoever sealed the box had wanted to make sure it stayed closed. She pried at the lid, and there was a pop as the glue released. Curtis shifted next to her. His tall frame shadowed her from the harsh sun and acted as a shelter.

"Come over here." He put a gentle arm around her shoulders and led her to a bench facing the fountain. Her legs gave way, and she collapsed onto the seat as her heart beat faster. She'd glimpsed a photograph as she lifted the lid; a younger version of her mother, barely recognizable but her, all the same.

She lifted the picture. Laura Brittan had been impossibly young, with creamy blonde hair French-braided away from her face and falling behind in a long heavy rope. No lines of hardship or age marred her face. Wide emerald eyes stared straight at the camera, clear and luminous. It was her mother and yet not her mother. This was a girl filled with promise and dreams, before life swept her away to another future.

What happened to you?

Meredith set the picture on the bench, ready for the next discovery. Her breath caught in her throat. In this next picture, her mother again, a few years older—or perhaps she only appeared so much older from the makeup and the way she'd pinned her hair. It must have been prom or some formal school dance, because her mother wore a baby rose corsage on one wrist and a powder blue dress with narrow straps at the shoulders. She noticed all this in an instant. It was the boy next to her that captured her attention. *Fair haired. Clean-cut.* The words of the lawyer echoed in her mind. David Givens. Her father. There was no doubt this was him. The two were an ideal match. Goosebumps prickled on her arms despite the heat.

"Meredith." Curtis studied her, an expression of worry on his face. "Are you okay?"

She handed him the photo. "This is him. I know it."

He flipped the picture over and studied the back. "There's no name."

"I just know," she insisted.

He simply handed the picture back to her, not protesting. She studied the photo for another moment, trying to find something in the boy's face that resembled her own. His crystal-blue eyes stared back at her. He was tall, with silky blond hair and one arm looped around his date's shoulders, a perfect fit. There was no sense of gazing in the mirror as she studied his picture. There was no shadow of her in him—no turn of the lips, the shape of the jaw, the way her right eyebrow arched higher in the middle than her left. There was nothing. Her own hair was ash brown and her eyes the lightest tawny with flecks of green. Her father was absent in her life in more ways than one. She tucked the photo in the pocket of her sundress and then, worried it would get bent, took it out and placed it on the bench atop the other picture.

Next, she lifted out a small jewelry box and popped it open. Inside was a pair of silver teardrop earrings on long stems. She touched them gently, wiping away a few grains of sand in the jewelry case. It was as though her mother was with her.

The next item puzzled her as she drew it out. A roll of fine yellow thread, tied through the middle with a ribbon. It struck her suddenly; the thread was actually several strands of her mother's fair hair, so long in the photos, wrapped over and over. At some point between the dance and her leaving home, she must have had it cut short. She raised the looped hair up to her cheek and cherished its softness, a most personal keepsake, and then laid it back down.

She lifted a small piece of black cloth and her fingers touched something hard wrapped within it. Unfolding the material, she uncovered a ring. A large diamond-cut stone, pale violet in color and in an oversized gold setting, sparkled in the sunlight. It didn't appear to be a diamond, which wasn't remarkable since a young girl was unlikely to own a diamond of this size or wear something quite so gaudy.

She rolled the ring around in her hand and tapped the stone with a fingernail. "Tanzanite, maybe." Her mother always spoke highly of the gemstone, frequently stopping to admire it in store windows. "They're more than a pretty face," her mother would say. "They have healing, transformative properties."

Meredith recalled seeing price tags in the hundreds of dollars, with darker colors bringing the highest prices. A pale-colored stone this big, though, could be worth even more. It would be something to cherish and pass down to Jamie someday. She'd tell her daughter how tanzanite was her grandmother's favorite stone. It would be a family heirloom, the most expensive piece of jewelry she owned.

Not something she would ever wear. The stone was too big; the setting bordered on ostentatious. A valued keepsake, nothing more. She wrapped the ring carefully back in its black cloth and replaced it in the box.

The bottom of the container was lined with several folded pages from what must have been high school yearbooks. She tugged them out, the old paper sticking slightly to the cardboard box. On each page, there were photos of her youthful father and mother together in various school clubs: building houses for the homeless, in art class, planting trees in a park. Her mother was laughing or smiling in each picture. She'd been captured in a time before life's cares and worries caught up to her. Next to her, David stood tall and confident. He would be a boy who promised to stay by her side. Their story wrote itself in her mind. Her parents were high school sweethearts, both with promising futures, and then something went wrong.

Was it me? Did I come along and ruin everything?

Jamie stood before her, hand in hand with Atticus. "Mom, I want to go to the beach." The front of the girl's shirt and shorts were soaked from the fountain's waters, and Atticus' hair was wet as well. Her five-year-old had kept them cool and entertained in the afternoon heat.

Curtis raised his eyebrows. "The beach might be good for all of us. When you're ready."

Three questioning faces gazed at her.

This was it, then, packed in one small box, all her grandmother kept of her own estranged daughter. From all appearances, the box had been sealed away for years, perhaps never opened at all since her mother left home in her teenage years. For some reason, her grandmother severed the relationship, discarding her daughter. Why, then, had she kept this box of memories at all? She returned each item to its place and started to close the container. Somehow, shutting the lid felt as though she were closing a casket. Her hands hesitated.

"Wait," she said, and reopened the jewelry box.

She took out the earrings she was wearing, tiny blue crystal studs. She dropped them in the jewelry box and removed the silver teardrop earrings, fingering them lightly before inserting them in her ears.

"Okay." She gazed up at Curtis and nodded firmly. This was better. "I'm ready."

Chapter Two

Screaming at a full-throated pitch, Jamie ran straight into the surf. To each side of her, waders edged away and gave her plenty of space. Her five-year-old danced in the shallows, drawing her legs up high and stomping them back down to cause maximum splash. The purple one-piece bathing suit with a sequined neon green dragon on the front shrieked nearly as loud. In one package, child and dragon, they were indomitable.

"Like the parting of the seas," Curtis murmured, the corners of his eyes crinkling as he smiled.

Meredith winced, and took a sip of her iced tea. "It's her super power."

White sand stretched far to the left and right of them on the long, narrow band of beach. Dotted along the shoreline, several other families, numerous couples, and groups of friends had spread their own colorful blankets and towels, creating a vibrant checkerboard on a white sand backdrop. Occasional laughter drifted their way and her tension melted.

She slathered more sunscreen on her toddler who did his best to wriggle away, and then applied more to her own bare pale shoulders. Their former year-round California tans had faded after their first full winter living in Idaho, and already the ridge of her nose was turning an angry shade of pink.

She'd debated over buying a bathing suit. This

wasn't a vacation, not for her anyway. And besides, she was shy about her body. She browsed through stores on their long drive across country, half-hoping she wouldn't find one among off-season goods. There was none to be found at home, of course; a bathing suit in Hay City was a luxury since there was no ocean, few lakes nearby, and a short summer season. In California, her former-and-now-dead husband, Brian, never liked her to show too much skin so she'd always gone to the beach in shorts and a tank top. The last bathing suit she owned was a one-piece when she was thirteen, still despairingly flat-chested and narrow-hipped.

This one was the cheapest one to be found, a simple, hideous-looking two-piece discovered on a clearance rack. It was a solid maroon except for thick black edging as though someone designed a bikini for mourning. Somehow, the bathing suit took on a different nature once she tried it on, uncovering her gentle curves and flat stomach. She'd stood in the dressing room staring at her new self until Jamie banged on the door and demanded entry. The maroon color shifted to a deep burgundy under the Florida sun, contrasting against her pale skin, a startling combination that drew stares. On the beach, her cheeks burned when they passed a group of rowdy teenagers. One shouted, "You got a fine wine there, yeah brother."

Curtis glared at the group, not sure which boy spoke, and they continued on to a spot farther down the beach. Blanket spread and their turf declared, they headed to the water's edge. She peeked at Curtis' hard stomach and broad chest, noticing the light-colored hair trailing down to the upper edge of his tropical-colored swim trunks. She imagined touching him there, her lips trailing along the hairline, and breathing in his musky, earthy smell. With some effort, she forced her attention away from his lean, hard body. She was grateful when he dove into the waves so she could concentrate on her children. Her kids demanded her attention for a while as they played in the surf, and she cautioned Jamie not to wade in too deep.

Her daughter pointed far beyond the surf where Curtis' powerful arms cut through the water in easy strokes. "The sheriff's way out there."

"He's a grownup. Anyway, he probably took lessons." She didn't know this for sure, but this extra point was a good way to keep her adventurous daughter from heading out to sea. Atticus had little interest in the ocean, intrigued instead by digging his hands in the wet sand at the water's edge.

Jamie's eyebrows knitted into a thin furrow. "Can I take lessons?"

"We'll see, when we get back home."

Satisfied, her daughter agreed to return to their black-and-red plaid blanket. She then proceeded to ask about building a giant sandcastle, what was for lunch and why she had to wear sunscreen.

Meredith dug in her heavy canvas tote for what she thought of as 'tier one' toys: small books for Jamie, and old spoons for Atticus. In other words, toys for when her kids weren't too bored, but needed something to keep their hands and minds busy.

'Tier two' toys, such a coloring book or a wind-up gadget, emerged when boredom set in and tempers threatened to flare. Saved for desperate moments were those 'tier three' toys: brand new items purchased at discount stores. She hoped to save these emergency amusements for their long cross-country drive home.

Water sprinkled them all as Curtis reappeared. He shook his head over them, aiming the salty sea water from his hair at her children, and elicited delighted squeals and laughter. He then collapsed face down and full-length on the blanket. Atticus leaped up at the spray of water and clambered onto Curtis' back.

"I'm starving," he gasped, eyes closed, behaving like someone who hadn't eaten pancakes, bacon and eggs for breakfast, along with two iced doughnuts, and a snow cone two hours earlier.

"I want to eat a horse," her daughter shouted.

"You *could* eat a horse," he corrected with a laugh. "You probably really *want* to eat a hamburger."

The girl jumped up and hopped on one foot and then the other, kicking warm sand up on the blanket. "With ketchup. And fries."

"Hamburgers all around? There's a stand over there." He edged Atticus off his back and sat up, then gestured toward the road where a row of food trucks lined up, selling a variety of cuisines from fish tacos to shrimp po'boy sandwiches. "I can carry it all back."

The water and sun did make one hungry. Meredith's stomach growled, as though in agreement. "Extra mustard on mine, no fries," she ordered, tucking a strand of ash brown hair behind one ear. "Plain, no bun for Atticus."

He rolled his eyes comically. "Not mustard." He tugged his polo shirt over his head, covering his bare torso, and grunted as he rose to his feet. "I'm disappointed in you."

"What's wrong with mustard?"

He only gave her a sad shake of the head and

headed off, beckoning Jamie to follow.

"No one likes mustard," Jamie said, tossing her wild black curls as she mimicked his shake of the head, and then ran after him across the sand.

"Make it extra *extra* mustard," Meredith called out, giggling and falling back on the sandy blanket.

****

Hamburgers consumed, mustard and all, they scooted their belongings into the shade cast by a palm tree. She shook the blanket clean, re-laid it neatly on the ground. One by one, they sank down and found their own spot. They lolled with full bellies and little desire to move. Atticus promptly fell asleep and Jamie, in a slow-moving food coma, dug for pirate treasure in the dark sand. Waves of conversation from nearby beach-goers rose and fell, softened by the constant hum of the Atlantic Ocean. A welcoming breeze kicked up and tossed about scents of salt air, fish tacos and wet towels.

"Did your mother talk about what happened, why she left home?" It was the first time Curtis broached the subject. Even when he made the extraordinary offer to drive them across the country and provide moral support in this journey, he'd been delicate about discussing her family. He knew the basics: alcoholic mother, unknown father, unapproachable wealthy grandmother. She'd had a life far from his idyllic country upbringing, as foreign and confounding to him as the surface of the sun. His "normal" life, with two rational parents who'd stayed together, was equally alien to her.

"She told me for years that we had no other family. She made it out to be fun, you know, like we were pioneers." Meredith gave a short laugh, remembering.

"You'd think I would have wondered why other kids had uncles and aunts and cousins, but I never did. My mother made our life normal to me. We were different and this was okay." She considered this for a moment before adding, "I asked about my father every once in a while and always got a different answer. Mostly, she told me he was dead. In the end, she told me he was a terrible person and not to search for him. I didn't know what to believe."

Her toddler stirred in his sleep, his pudgy hands gripping and releasing in some childish dream, before heaving a sigh then going still. She rubbed his back absently. Her satisfied belly was suddenly too full of a greasy hamburger and too many fries. The extra mustard may have been a mistake after all.

She slurped at her drink to cover the tears that threatened. Her mother had been gone for nearly a decade, but the heartache persisted. "She told me about her childhood, with ski trips to the Alps and horseback riding and that they had a cook because her grandmother didn't know how to boil water." Meredith smiled wryly at this, her eyes distant in remembering. "My mother always laughed at the fact we had cooks, too. In the homeless shelters."

"And your grandmother?" he prompted, bringing her back to the original question.

"Just that they never spoke. And nothing about why she left home."

"What about your grandfather?"

A good question, but also a dead end. "He died when my mother was young. No father figure there either." Her hard laugh fell short of being genuine.

Sand sprayed them, kicked up by a herd of loose-limbed teens racing by, calling to each other in shouts and shrieks. They circled down to the clear blue water and splashed through the surf and around again in the other direction. Atticus' eyelashes fluttered and then settled closed again.

Curtis closed his eyes too, and his breathing became heavy. His chest rose and fell, a strong pulse beating at his throat. It was a miracle he was there at all, with her, on a Florida beach in the middle of winter.

Just two weeks earlier, Meredith learned her grandmother had died and left a letter and box for her. A stipend from the estate had been left to enable travel to the attorney's office in Fifteen Palms, Florida, from her home in Hay City, Idaho. Instead of using the money to fly and stay in a hotel, Curtis offered to drive them out, saying he was overdue for a vacation. It was Jamie's winter break from school and, so, why not?

She didn't consider the intimacy of such a trip until it was well underway. Even though they had separate motel rooms—and once, Curtis slept in the bed of his truck, complaining he missed the stars—being traveling companions brought them closer than ever. Of course, they were already lovers. That happened weeks earlier, but opportunities for being alone together were rare. The presence of her children hindered any serious romantic activities, although their hands touched at every opportunity, drawn to each other. He would touch the small of her back or brush a strand of hair away from her face—actions her children wouldn't regard with any meaning—but the light touches carried the weight of a caress. But no further than that. Her children had gone through too much change in the past year, and she worried about introducing one more change in their lives. How did single parents date? How did they explain a new partner to their young children?

The road trip across country took three long days, the terrain gradually changing from the winter snow and high mountain peaks of Idaho and Utah down to the vast desert stretches of Texas and across the drenched southern states to the lush sub-tropical semblance of Florida. The truck grew stuffy with the waxiness of her children's crayons and window markers, and by mid-Texas they all had memorized the words to every sing-along cassette they'd packed. Once they arrived in Fifteen Palms, they tumbled out of the truck in relief the long drive was at an end.

Meredith studied Curtis as he chatted with her children on the long journey, and couldn't help imagining him as their stepfather, coaching her young son into boyhood and directing her daughter's high energy into productive avenues.

As for the two of them...they'd come a long way since her husband was murdered and Curtis pursued her as the prime suspect. Their path didn't begin in an auspicious manner, but she no longer doubted him. His judgment came from a generous heart and a solid belief in the goodness of people. He admired what he called her "grit" and encouraged her to be strong, even when she disagreed with him.

He makes me a better person, she thought. This was a new idea to her; Brian had diminished and abased her through their five-year marriage until she was very nearly nothing at all.

Curtis spoke, startling her out of her reverie. She realized he'd been thinking all this time and not asleep after all. He opened his eyes and she colored, caught staring at his bare torso. "Did your grandmother ever remarry?"

Strange, she'd never considered this possibility. "I don't think so. Who would marry a wretched old woman like her?"

"Rich," he said shortly. "And not terribly old back then. She couldn't have been more than, what, in her late forties or early fifties when your mother left?"

A step-grandfather had never been mentioned by anyone. Perhaps her grandmother remarried later in life. Then she realized why this couldn't have happened.

"If there'd been a husband, he would have inherited everything."

Another dead end in her anemic family tree. Deficient in men for yet another generation.

Curtis rolled on his side and gazed up at her, his expression somber. "When I investigate and try to figure out what happened, I explore all angles. Even if...the scenario is unpleasant. Sometimes it shakes loose the truth." He hesitated and his voice lowered. "Like in your case."

Her case. When her husband, Brian, was murdered the previous spring. Curtis, in his role as county sheriff, first considered her the prime suspect. As their personal attraction grew, her desperation to absolve herself led them to the murderer.

"Could your mother be at fault in leaving, not to do with your father or grandmother at all? She was a teenager then, and sometimes teenagers aren't entirely rational. They get into trouble of all sorts."

Her mouth opened in protest and then snapped shut. Hadn't some version of this crept into her mind too? Her mother wasn't always reasonable, even as an adult. "I've wondered the same thing."

To be honest, she'd wondered more than that. Viewed as a child, her mother's behavior was normal because she didn't know anything else. Now as an adult, she had to contemplate whether her mother had a mental illness or some other affliction in addition to the alcoholism. Why else did she insist on living at the fringes of society, dragging her daughter from motel rooms to tent camps along the riverbank to homeless shelters? This possibility was painful to acknowledge.

"It still doesn't answer where my father is." She heaved an exasperated sigh and gazed out over the water. Her family issues were so wide and deep; she needed to focus on the most important one, the one that prompted her to travel to Florida to learn the name of her father. "How do you find someone?'

Curtis grunted as he rose to a sitting position and started digging absently in the sand next to him. "In the case of such a common name, I usually start with someone they knew and go from there. One person usually leads to another."

She had a feeling he'd say that. David Givens relocated from Fifteen Palms years earlier, back when the seaside town was dominated by low-slung motels and winter condos. The place was now a burgeoning city with several impressive skyscrapers, a boardwalk lined with tourist shops and a raft of construction cranes hard at work. A new generation lived in the city, none of whom would know the good-looking, congenial teenager from twenty-five years ago.

The only link she was aware of was the lawyer, Therald Holt. Her gaze lifted above the sand dunes toward the downtown skyline and picked out the soaring glass tower in the middle of the city. The lawyer could be scanning the beach right now from his lofty office window. She would just be a dot in the sand to him, just another tourist sunning on the beach. Her life and problems were nothing to him. She'd have to return to the lawyer's office to ask some questions. It wouldn't be easy getting answers out of the prickly, terse man. He had no reason to cooperate.

"The lawyer's the one. But I doubt he'll say much," she said. "He wasn't very chatty."

Curtis packed wet sand into his empty soda cup and upended it next to the blanket. It formed a miniature gray tower with crumbling edges. She shifted around to work next to him, shoring up the tower's sides, and packing more wet sand around a growing castle. Their hands worked together efficiently. Without saying a word, Jamie scooted over and began excavating the hole to expose more wet sand. The three of them dug and formed towers quietly for a couple of minutes. Small white clouds drifted across the sky and the sun's relentless presence softened as more clouds billowed up on the horizon.

"Sometimes a trade works, information for information." Curtis focused on his creation, building more towers, one by one, until a circular fortress was formed. "He was interested in the box."

Her hands went still. The only genuine emotion the lawyer displayed was when she refused to open the sealed package in his office. On reflection, the man had been intensely curious and perhaps even…worried. Curtis' suggestion of a trade could shake some information out of the man. Her bargaining chip was her mother's box of memories.

Chapter Three

This time, all four of them rode the elevator up the glass-sided building. Jamie jumped up and down in the confined space, making Meredith queasy as the rising booth trembled each time the girl landed. The building intimidated her, as did the lawyer and the idea they were there to pry information out of him. Without thinking, she slipped her hand into Curtis' and they exited the elevator this way, shoulder to shoulder, with the kids following behind.

She wore the same blue sundress as before, the only nice clothing she packed, and the kids in their second-to-last last clean shorts and T-shirts. Curtis wore neatly-pressed khakis and a maroon long-sleeved shirt, with the collar open and sleeves rolled up. Somehow, he'd traveled across the country without wrinkling his clothes into a thousand lines. Having him next to her side gave her confidence that all would be well.

The box of memories she clutched in one hand, snug against her middle. It was their key negotiating chip in the meeting ahead. Curtis was right about the lawyer's curiosity about the box's contents. The man who'd been unwilling to tell her much the first time around, responded quickly to a request for a second meeting—once she laid out the terms of a trade. The contents of the box unveiled for details about her mother's life and her father's possible whereabouts.

She supposed it made sense. The lawyer was privy to all the details of her grandmother's life for fifty years or more. He was intimate with the family secrets, including her grandmother's net worth, the details of her mother's leaving and the name of her father. It was obvious he took pride in knowing the private pains of one of Fifteen Palms' most illustrious citizens, one who bequeathed the majority of her fortune to the local hospital and nothing to her only blood relative.

The one thing hidden from Therald Holt was whatever had been sealed inside the box. The prospect of this one secret must have infuriated the man—he, who had been trusted with everything else. And he must be truly worried about something, for simple curiosity wouldn't have garnered her an invitation to return. Pictures, earrings, ring and high school yearbook pages. Which of these items—if any of them—concerned him? Of course, there was her mother's hair, but he already knew she had long, blonde hair.

A rush of cool air hit her as they filed into the lawyer's waiting room and she released Curtis' hand, not meeting his eyes. This time, she was prepared against the air conditioning and her nerves, bringing a light tan sweater that she now shrugged on. Questions buzzed around in her mind. The evening before, Curtis helped her prepare a list of questions. It boiled down to basic information: who, what, when, where and why.

"Five questions," he advised. "Keep it simple and stay focused. Don't get distracted."

She already discovered the *who* was David Givens. She also wanted to know *what* happened to cause the rift between her mother and grandmother, *when* her mother left, *where* her father was now, and *why* her mother hated David Givens so violently. There were any number of questions she could ask, of course. Anything really was more than she knew now, which was slightly more than nothing. The most important answer was where her father could be now, so she could track him down. California was a vast state with millions of people, and he could have ended up anywhere in the previous twenty-five years. He could even be back in Florida somewhere or living anywhere from Australia to Zimbabwe. There must be hundreds of David Givens in the country and more throughout the world. The lawyer was the only link she had to the story of her vanished, ruptured family.

Again, the receptionist made them wait under a disapproving stare. And again, it wasn't until the stroke of the hour that Therald Holt appeared in his office doorway. His gaze traveled to Jamie and Atticus, who stood at one of the tall windows with their noses, mouths and fingers flattened against the glass. An expression of distaste flickered across his face before he addressed Meredith.

"Would you care to come in now?"

She gestured toward Curtis next to her and waved toward her kids. "This is my friend, Curtis, and my children, Atticus and Jamie." She couldn't help adding, "Leila Brittan's great-grandchildren."

The two men nodded acknowledgment of the other.

"We'll wait out here." Curtis spoke softly, touching her arm. "So you're not interrupted."

A twist of fear swept through her. He was the experienced interrogator. She hadn't anticipated facing the lawyer without him by her side.

"You'll do fine." He leaned to murmur, "You're

tougher than you think."

She gave him a grateful smile and entered the lawyer's office for a second time. Once again, they settled themselves into the same uncomfortable chairs and faced each other across the vast mahogany desk. The sweater was a bad idea; perspiration broke out above her lip and gave a light sheen to her forehead.

His tone was cold and brisk, one of an important man who had more demanding matters to attend to. "Let's see what you have there."

She took a deep breath. Over a dinner of fish tacos the night before, Curtis coached her on how to approach the meeting.

"Slow," he instructed as they sat close in the restaurant booth, Meredith aware they appeared like a typical, everyday family. The waitress praised them for their cute kids and neither of them corrected her. "Don't show your hand all at once. Make him give you what you want first. Keep him guessing. Seems to me, he's worried about something. Let him do the talking."

Now, she stared at the un-embellished cardboard box on her lap and opened the lid, aware the man across the desk was sitting forward in anticipation. She drew out the first item, the photo of her mother. She paused for a moment and then slid it toward him.

"She looks about fourteen," she said, unable to stay quiet and wait. "I never knew her to have such long hair. She always had it cut short. She was…so beautiful back then."

The lawyer's face softened just a fraction as he gazed at the photograph. "Your mother was going to be a debutante. She could have married the son of any wealthy family in this city. In the county." His lips twisted in disapproval. "But she had a bit of a wild streak. Your grandmother did her best, gave her everything. When your mother ran off, it broke Leila's heart. She went away for a few months and returned a changed woman."

Meredith didn't care about her grandmother's heartbreak. *When,* she reminded herself. "How old was my mother, when she left?"

The lawyer's jaw tensed and loosened. "Fifteen, sixteen maybe."

In the photo, her mother appeared relaxed and happy, just a typical teenager lucky enough to be born into abundant wealth and privilege. Something changed between the time this picture was taken and when she ran away. Something happened during the next year. Her earliest memory of her mother was of a loving, fragile woman trying to hold pieces of herself together, relaxing only when she drank. She didn't know her mother ran away quite so young and she tucked this information away to think about later.

The lawyer's gaze settled on the box and she cracked it open to withdraw the next item: the picture of her mother and father, frozen in time, and dressed for a formal event. They made a perfect pairing, these fair-haired children from affluent families. They should have married, settled in a beach house and had a handful of tow-headed children of their own. She placed the photo on the desk. When the lawyer stretched forward in earnest to grab it, she remembered Curtis' words: *He's worried about something.*

She gripped her tongue between her teeth, and forced herself to wait while he studied the photo. "It's amazing what people will say if you're quiet," Curtis told her the night before. "They'll fill the silence with their secrets."

The lawyer cleared his throat. "That's David Givens there, with Laura. I suppose that's your question, although you could have figured this out on your own. A nice enough boy, though Leila was concerned about how much time they spent together. A young girl needs to be careful."

"My grandmother talked to you about them?" Meredith was surprised. They must have been close enough that he would know her grandmother's frustrations in raising a teenager.

He cleared his throat again, an obvious stall for time as he considered how to answer. "Leila changed her will, after Laura left. I doubt that surprises you."

What happened, she thought. "Just for running away? She never tried to find my mother? Never called the police to bring her home? She was underage."

Therald Holt's blank face was hard to read. She barely breathed. He owed her an answer. This was the deal. A look at the box's contents for information.

"Everything went wrong for Leila, your grandmother, that year. First, Anthony left. Then your mother. It would have killed a lesser woman."

Meredith frowned, searching her memory for mention of this name. "Anthony? Who's Anthony?"

"Leila's second husband. Anthony Noble." The lawyer blinked at her in surprise and slight dismay rippled over his features, likely at volunteering information for free. "You didn't know about all that? Probably for the best, a story done and gone."

"What do you mean?" Another *who*. Another story untold. Curtis had been right to wonder whether her grandmother remarried. Anthony Noble would be another link to her family narrative, someone with information to share. She tucked his name away to follow up on later. More questions bubbled to her lips, but she needed to stay focused and seek specific answers. Otherwise, she would run out of items in the box before all her questions were answered.

His lips twisted as though he was deciding how much to divulge. "Leila married a younger man, an obvious gold digger, with unpleasant family connections. He ran off one day and, as luck would have it, we never heard about him again." He waved a dismissive hand as though that chapter was closed, and returned to the main issue. "A few months later, Laura took off. Now with Leila passed, an entire family is gone, just like that."

"I'm here, and my children too. Not an entire family gone. Not at all."

He blinked at her as though at first he didn't understand her point. "Ah yes. Of course, but you weren't here. You were never really part of the family."

She let that go. "No one searched for my mother after she ran away?"

"David, your father, posted 'missing' signs around the city, but your grandmother had them taken down. The Givens family left the next year."

"This doesn't explain why my grandmother never tried to find her."

His tone sharpened. "It's pretty obvious, isn't it? Your mother was pregnant with you and argued with your grandmother over it. As I said, Leila had other plans for her daughter. David was a fine boy, but your mother should have done better. And a teenage pregnancy..." He trailed off, his meaning clear. There would be no debutante ball. No grand wedding. No lofty alliances forged. No daughter to be bartered off for family gain, just like the good old medieval days. Just an embarrassment to the family name.

Meredith shook her head in disbelief. "So she just cut her off forever. Her only child?"

"Some people still care about doing things in the proper order," he snapped. "Marriage first, *then* children."

She'd never cared about all that. Times had changed for the better. For generations, so many women's lives were ruined by babies born out of the "proper order." Those so-called loose women were cast off from families and society—not the fathers, of course—and thereafter struggled against poverty, loneliness and despair.

Two more questions: why and where. With three more items in the box, she was ahead of the game. The jewelry box emerged next and Therald Holt blinked.

His spine stiffened and he sat straighter in his seat. "What's this? I was expressly informed nothing of significant monetary value was to be included. Whatever this is belongs to the estate."

She hesitated, and turned the box over in her hands as his eyes narrowed. It wasn't fair he would take the earrings away from her. Now she was doubly glad for the one small deception she'd decided to make at the last minute. The ring was safe in her pocket. She felt no guilt at hiding it from him even if this was some sort of breach to her grandmother's will. The lawyer would only take the ring and sell it so more money could go to expand the hospital in her grandmother's name. Or the proceeds would go toward funding a plaque in tribute to her grandmother, or toward a statue of her in the middle of town. Her mother would have wanted her to have this; otherwise, why pack it away? A trickle of sweat ran down her back and she fought the urge to remove her sweater. She didn't want him to see her nerves.

With regret, she handed the jewelry box over into the lawyer's outstretched hands. He boosted the case up close to his face, with an eagerness akin to a child at Christmas. His face fell when he saw the silver earrings. "How do I know this is what was in here?" He slid the box back at her. "How do I know you're telling me everything?"

"How do I know you're not giving me false information?" she shot back.

Meredith tried not to show relief he wasn't interested in stealing the earrings away from her, after all. Even if he didn't place much worth on them, the teardrop earrings had great value to her. She set the jewelry case back in the cardboard box.

They stared impassively at each other, continuing their game of chicken. The lawyer inspected his watch and she understood it to mean he was losing patience with their deal. Through the wall she heard Atticus laughing, one of his full belly laughs she loved so much. Meredith forged ahead, aware time was short. "Why did my mother hate my father?"

"I suppose he didn't want his future ruined too." He raised his eyebrows at her. "I suppose he wanted Laura to have an abortion. They were in high school, with bright futures ahead. So she ran away."

The explanation fell flat on Meredith's ears. This could be the reason for going separate ways, for being angry and feeling betrayed, but not for the lifelong hatred her mother bore her old high school boyfriend. If she realized one thing about her mother, no one could force her to do anything she didn't want to do.

He straightened his shoulders and leaned back in his chair. "Let's move on. I have an appointment coming in."

Her fingers trembled as she lifted out the yearbook pages and unfolded them on the desk. The most important question was still to go: *where*. "Where did my father's family move?"

"I couldn't say." His tone was clipped as his gaze scanned the pages. "I didn't have dealings with the Givens. They weren't clients."

Tears sprang to her eyes. Behind him, through the large tinted window, the sun disappeared behind a fast-moving cloud. More of the same hurried across the sky. A quick storm was moving in.

She drew out the lock of hair tied with the ribbon. This was one item she couldn't let him touch; her mother's hair was too intimate. He leaned forward and squinted to see what she held. She lifted it up and twisted the lock around in her fingers. "Why did she cut off her hair?"

The lawyer sat back, shrinking away from the hair as though it were something rotten and distasteful. A series of emotions fluttered across his face before closing into its original stony expression. "Seems to me young girls change hairstyles once a week."

She waited for more, heeding Curtis' advice to let her adversary fill the silence. He was right; if she peppered questions at the lawyer, he'd clam up.

"It was a shame," he muttered to himself, but the

words were clear enough.

"What was a shame?"

He glanced up, as though startled he uttered the words out loud. "You're chasing ghosts," he said, and then gathered up the yearbook pages and handed them across the desk. "Leila understood what she was doing. Everyone you're searching for is gone. My advice to you is to leave this alone."

She took the pages and, folding them carefully, set them back into the box along with her mother's lock of hair. She folded the top shut. There were no bargaining chips left and a million questions still in her mind. Across from her, the lawyer breathed in and out audibly, clearly unsettled by the hair.

She took advantage of his discomfiture by slipping in an extra question. One other person ran away from her grandmother's house that year. "Do you know where I'd find Anthony?"

His lips thinned and he cleared his throat. "That one's a dead end for you. Not even real blood family. He never fit in and, frankly, people were relieved when he left. Dredge up memories of those days and you embarrass your grandmother's legacy. She worked hard for decades to compensate for those few bad years." He leaned forward over the desk. "I'd advise you not to ruin all the good work she did."

"I'm not here to create trouble. I'm here for one reason—to locate my father."

"You might talk to David's sister. I suppose she'd be your aunt." He breathed the words out in a rush. "She's still in town, far as I know. Came back and married a local boy."

"My aunt?" Meredith was stunned, not anticipating

other relatives. "What's her name?"

His mouth clamped shut as though he'd said too much and nothing more would be allowed through his lips. There was nothing left in the box to lure him with. He rose, indicating the interview was over. She'd played all her cards and there was nothing left to pry out of the lawyer. She fingered the ring in her pocket, considering using it as bait for a few more answers. But, no. He would certainly take the ring away. She could find her aunt without his help. It was time to move on.

To chase my ghosts, she thought.

Chapter Four

"I have an aunt."

The words burst from her as soon as they exited the building's glass doors. They'd ridden down the elevator in silence, Jamie again jumping up and down during the descent, and her own mind swirling and trying to process all she'd learned.

"Here, in Fifteen Palms. I have to find her. She can give me my father's phone number. I'll be able to call him and talk to him, maybe go visit him, get to know him. I can ask my aunt what happened, without bribing her for every little detail."

Curtis put a hand up. "Slow down. One thing at a time. You have an aunt."

"Yes." Impatience built, turned her strides long and fast; she tugged Jamie along by the hand. "I need a computer. We have to get to a library."

He stopped, Atticus tucked in one arm, and it took her a couple more steps to realize he was no longer at her side. When she glanced back, he was waving his phone at her. "Smart phone."

She was back at his side in a flash. Her own phone was a cheap prepaid model, and she forgot most people owned phones that were veritable mini-computers.

"Search for Givens, Fifteen Palms."

"First name?"

"He didn't tell me."

He was already typing. It had been twenty-five years. Her aunt had probably married, changed her name, relocated, died. The lawyer could have lied or been mistaken. There could be twenty Givenses, all unrelated.

He handed her the phone. "Here."

She squinted in the sunlight at the small screen. Sarah Givens-McHenry. Her aunt had hyphenated her name, making the search ridiculously easy. There was a series of photographs alongside her name and there was no doubt. One of the pictures was of her wedding and David had been a groomsman. Even a few years older, he appeared much the same as he had as a teen. Blond, clean-cut, all-American. A face that could do no wrong.

"Is there a phone number?"

He took the phone from her. "Wait a minute."

"What are you doing?" Her voice was high and broken. "Give it back."

"Meredith." He nodded toward Jamie, who was staring at her open-mouthed. "Let's think about this for a moment. You can't just call her out of the blue, standing here on the street, and announce you're her niece. She might not know any of this."

"Mom? Mommy?" Jamie tugged at her hand, her expression anxious. "You need to slow down."

Meredith closed her eyes and inhaled deeply. When she opened her eyes, she directed a calm smile at her daughter despite her emotional turmoil. Curtis nudged her shoulder and chuckled an "all is fine" laugh. Her daughter gazed between the two of them, and apparently satisfied all was well, proceeded on to a more important subject.

"I'm hungry."

"Most people only have three meals a day," Curtis informed her. "Not five."

Jamie tilted her face up and stared at him with a serious look. "I'm a growing girl. My teacher says 'trishun is very important."

Meredith sighed and pointed to a food truck down the street. Nothing more would be accomplished until her daughter's belly was satisfied. "I bet they have nutrition over there."

"Fries?" her daughter asked hopefully.

Meredith nodded and the five-year-old skipped toward the truck.

"Any time I call my aunt, it's going to be 'out of the blue.'" She returned to her annoyed state of mind, needing to unleash her anxiety on someone. "There's no preparing for something like this, for any of us. I may as well call her right now."

Curtis tucked the phone in his pocket and gestured toward the food truck. Annoyed, she wriggled out of her sweater, far too warm for the day despite the overcast sky. He put his arm around her shoulder and they strolled as one to join Jamie at the food truck, where the girl chatted with the cook through the window. Her heart was still jumping inside her chest from the meeting with Therald Holt. His answers rolled around her mind and she could barely focus on her daughter's order.

"I'm having an alligator sandwich." Jamie announced with pride at ordering on her own. "He's making 'jun fries special for me, too."

"Alligator? Are you sure?" Curtis peered at the handwritten menu board, trying to figure out what Jamie ordered. "*Cajun* fries? They might be spicy."

She wrinkled her nose at her daughter's adventurous order. There was no way her own stomach was in a condition for food, and certainly nothing spicy and exotic, but between her daughter and Curtis, one or the other was always hungry. Their trip had been dotted with frequent stops at cafes, supermarkets and delis for munchies and meals. It was a toss-up which of them could consume the most.

"I suppose I could have something too." Curtis handed her toddler into her arms before stepping to the counter and having his own consultation with the cook.

The casual way he'd put his arm around her, holding her close against him, added to her confusion. *Of course* they were a couple now. They journeyed all the way across the country together. He dropped everything in his life at a moment's notice to join her on this trip. What else could this mean except they were a couple?

It was silly but doubt continued to linger. Her self-confidence was painfully wounded after a five-year marriage to an abusive man who diminished her at every opportunity. It was difficult for her to believe this kindhearted, handsome man wanted to be with her, putting up with her prickly nature, and with two kids in tow. More likely, he felt sorry for her and wanted to atone for the fact he'd investigated her for Brian's murder. This won't last, she cautioned herself. Enjoy it, but don't get used to it.

Curtis and Jamie rejoined her, their hands full of deep-fried victuals in greasy cardboard containers.

"I saw a picture of an alligator at school," her daughter announced through a mouthful of food. "It had giant teeth like a monster. Mom, watch me. I'm eating a monster."

"With ketchup," Curtis added.

She let her toddler have a taste of alligator, but kept the spicy fries away from him. Instead, she gave him a few crackers she always kept in her handbag.

The four of them lingered near the truck until Curtis and Jamie finished their late morning snack of monster and fries, her daughter un-fazed by the peppery seasonings. A light breeze kicked up, nudging around the warm air and doing nothing to cool the humid day. More people strolled up to the food truck and the aroma of fried alligator nuggets and aromatic spices filled the air. She set her son down to let him run around their legs. There was nothing to do except wait and breathe.

Her deal with Curtis had been this: She would pay for gas on the trip and he insisted on paying for most of their meals. They would each pay for their own separate accommodations. In this way, she could stretch the meager stipend the lawyer offered for her travel to cover expenses for the week-long excursion. This was one reason she didn't feel guilty about withholding her mother's tanzanite ring from Therald Holt. The lawyer had been so stingy about both the stipend and information.

Jamie, re-energized after finishing what she called her "first lunch," started chasing her brother. She motioned to Curtis that they needed to keep moving. Her children needed a playground or the beach. The break at the food truck had been a good idea. Her breath now came easier, and her heartbeat slowed from its furious pace.

"It was good advice, staying quiet and letting him talk." She bided her time until she could again broach the topic of calling her aunt. Her own cell phone wasn't a smart device and didn't have internet access. She eyed his pocket which contained his mobile and, thus, her aunt's information. At one time in the past, she'd heard, phone booths with phone books were on nearly every street corner. These days, people had to carry their own expensive personal device with them. There were computers and portable tablets, and even watches that did more than display the time. As a single mother earning little more than minimum wage, these were luxuries she couldn't afford. Mostly, she didn't miss those electronic extras—but times like this filled her with envy.

Curtis scooped up her son and set him on his shoulders. They strolled along the downtown sidewalk, and she related details of the interview. He listened without asking questions, and allowed her to explain what the lawyer revealed: her grandmother's gold-digging second husband, her mother as an unruly pregnant teenager, and a possible location where her father might be. She told him how her father put up missing signs after her mother ran away, and how her grandmother took them down.

"Twenty-five years is a long time," he finally said, zeroing in on the most important detail. "David Givens could be anywhere now. He might even be…" He stopped himself and restarted, "He could be anywhere."

The words he didn't say echoed in her mind. Her father could be dead. After all this effort, it could be too late. She grew up believing he was dead, with her mother telling her wild stories about his demise. He died while abalone diving, in a car accident, falling off a fishing boat. It happened in Ohio, in Nevada, in

Mexico. Finally, right before her death, her mother all but admitted none of those stories were true. But she kept his identity a secret, declaring only that he was a terrible person.

Clouds blanketed the sky now and an occasional drop of rain foretold more to come. Their destination was a city park a block away, crowded with primary-colored play equipment where the kids could be released to burn pent-up energy. Rain would spoil these plans and she eyed the clouds with annoyance and increased her pace. Halfway up the block, her daughter spotted the park and squealed.

"Go on," she encouraged. Jamie trotted ahead, and launched herself at the rambling play structure featuring a tower, slide and swings. Curtis set her son down at the edge of the playground and he toddled after his sister. A warm breeze gusted carrying an undercurrent of something cooler to come.

Other families were in the park, and her children made instant friends as only kids can do. Curtis steered her toward a bench shaped like an elephant at the edge of the play area, and they sat facing the play structure.

"Is that what you do in all your cases…stay quiet and let the suspects betray themselves?"

"I suppose. There aren't too many serious crimes in Hay City."

She examined her short, unpolished fingernails so she didn't have to meet his eyes. His advice worked wonders with the lawyer. If she had charged in demanding answers, she wouldn't have been as successful. When he investigated her for the murder of her husband, Curtis' approach was slow and subtle. Most of the time he kept quiet and let her talk. All the time she believed she was somehow betraying her guilt, when in fact she'd betrayed her innocence.

She peeked at him and felt her way carefully with the next question. "With me, for instance, and...well, the case up in Twin Lakes?"

The Twin Lakes case nearly tore their relationship apart. Three people died by poisoning, with Curtis ruling two of them accidental, the third a suicide. In her heart, she believed all three people had been murdered and she knew exactly who the killer was: The man's too-beautiful wife. He disagreed by officially declaring the case closed; he'd put it behind him without a further word. She'd been furious, accusing him of not understanding the true wickedness of human nature. Privately, she suspected the woman's beauty played a role. What man believes a beautiful woman is evil?

"I find people generally want to talk. Keeping a secret is a burden. You just have to give them the opening and they'll spill everything," he said. "The method's served me well most of the time. In some cases, where evidence is scarce, a confession is all I have to go on."

Meredith blinked up at him, startled. "Twin Lakes," she whispered, afraid he would be angry at her persistence. She'd pestered him incessantly when the deaths occurred. She wanted the man's wife arrested and dragged to trial.

His tone remained matter-of-fact. "No prosecutor would have touched the case. There was no proof of murder. No proof of motive. No witnesses to anything suspicious."

"Jacob told me..." she started, then bit her lip. They'd been through all this before. The man she'd met only briefly, Jacob Burns, was the first one to die from mushroom poisoning, with his death occurring soon after he told her his wife was going to kill him. There was no use arguing over the case anymore. The people were dead. All except for the beautiful wife.

"Meredith." He stretched out and squeezed her hand. "Do you understand what I'm telling you? The law doesn't care what I believe; my job is to collect evidence. If there's no evidence to discover, or no confession, there's no case. In Twin Lakes, there wasn't even proof any murders took place."

She recalled how she'd rushed in with questions and accusations toward Jacob's wife, confronting the woman and stumbling around like a junior investigator. Brooke Burns, guilty or not, wasn't a stupid woman. Her guard went up and she'd covered her bases. At the time, Meredith believed Curtis was incompetent at his job for not interrogating the woman, but in retrospect, he'd been the clever one by staying watchful and quiet. Could it be that *she* was the reason Brooke Burns got away with murder? Her mouth opened in a round 'oh' of understanding, and tears sprang to her eyes.

"I spoiled the case with my interference. Without me, you might have tripped Brooke into a confession."

"Maybe. Look, it's not your fault," he said as she crumpled against his shoulder. "Your intentions were good. We may have been wrong anyway."

She heard the "we" and understood he, too, had believed in the woman's guilt.

"People don't like to hear this, but sometimes murderers aren't brought to justice," he added, his voice steely. "Sometimes, murderers go free. I'd like to think, though, their crime haunts them the rest of their days."

50

They sat on the bench until the rain started and cleared the playground of other families. She lifted her head and wiped at her nose. "I should get my kids out of the rain. Are you ever going to let me call my aunt?"

****

In the end, she didn't tell Sarah Givens-McHenry her entire identity, saying only, "I'm Laura Brittan's daughter, Leila's granddaughter."

The woman jumped in with the rest, offering condolences for her grandmother, then again for her mother once Meredith informed her she'd died as well. Sarah hesitated when she asked to visit, then gushed an invitation as if they were old friends.

"It's such a busy week, but come by tomorrow at two-thirty. I'll have to dash out right at three-fifteen for a hair appointment, but at least we'll have time for a quick cup of coffee while you're in town."

She wrote down the address on the back of a receipt, and then sighed in relief. She was getting somewhere, bit by bit. Curtis was right about gathering her wits first and not charging in with a startling announcement over the phone. She'd find out soon enough if Sarah already was aware of their relationship. There was every possibility her father never told his family about the pregnancy. The main thing was getting David's phone number and address. Her father was the one who needed to know she was alive and searching for him. Surely, he would want to know his former girlfriend, her mother, was dead. She was more resolute than ever about tracking him down.

With a rainy afternoon ahead of them, they drove to her grandmother's sprawling estate and parked outside the gated driveway. Through a lush canopy of trees far back from the road, sat an imposing house. Tall wrought iron railings guarded the drive, while low leafy palmettos and soaring magnolias filled the front grounds. She knew there were stables in the back, along with riding trails circling five acres of manicured landscape. The grand home and property was the backdrop of her mother's unhappy childhood. For years, one vile old woman lived on the estate by herself, alone with her riches and self-estranged from family. In Meredith's imagining, her grandmother was a modern-day female Scrooge, turning down the heat and counting dimes.

"Nice place," Curtis said.

She envisaged her mother running over the front lawn as a child, and having pretend picnics with stuffed animals under the trees. Her mother would have watched the magnolias set their broad blooms, and called this place home.

Her father had driven through these gates, anticipating another date with the pretty blonde girl and knowing he'd have to make awkward conversation with the mother while he waited. It wasn't supposed to turn out the way it did. Her mother should have stayed here, had her baby—*me*—and lived a different life. Longer, cared for, loved.

Only one person was to blame.

One person who set her mother on a path to self-destruction. He'd gotten her mother pregnant, then turned his back on her. Something else must have happened as well, something that would have kept her mother from ever returning. She was going to hunt her father down if it was the last thing she did. He would finally have to face up to his actions.

Her teeth clenched, and she turned her face from the estate. "Let's go. I've seen enough."

Chapter Five

Sunlight streamed around the edges of the motel room's heavy blackout curtains, cajoling them into a lazy wakefulness.

"Last day," she whispered to herself as her eyes blinked open. She stared at the motel's yellowed popcorn ceiling, stained by years of old cigarette smoke and who knew what else.

One more day in Fifteen Palms before they needed to start the long trek home. A new job as assistant city clerk waited for her in Hay City, a full-time position paying just enough to support her and her children. The job materialized just as she considered selling her property and moving to a larger city where she could find a decent paying job. She owed the position to her friends, Honey and Crusty, who wielded significant power in the county. They'd been good friends to her since she arrived in the small town the previous spring.

Tomorrow, back to Hay City they would go. She would transition from tropical warmth into icy winter as they drove back across the country, racing from the country's southernmost state to the far north. She had to rate the trip a remarkable success, with her main goal to find out her father's name. Not only was this accomplished, but today she would find out where he lived, perhaps even speak to her father on the phone. It would have been too much to ask to find him on this trip, to expect he'd be in Fifteen Palms just waiting for her to show up and claim him as her father. Her grandmother gave her the only gift she ever wanted from her: knowledge of whom she belonged to. Beyond this, she had her mother's boxed up treasures and she would prize them forever.

But one mystery led to another. She wanted to know the full account of her mother's life. She'd never be satisfied with half a story.

"Can I watch TV?" Jamie's sleepy voice piped up from under the covers in the next bed over. Her five-year-old was elated over finding cartoons airing at any time of day, and would have been happy staying in her pajamas all day staring at the flickering screen. A television with twenty-four-hour cartoons was a big change from home, where the only shows available were the DVD movies she memorized by heart.

"Just until breakfast," she agreed. "Remember, we're having strawberry pancakes today."

As she rose from bed, Meredith rapped three times on the wall behind her headboard, the agreed-upon signal to Curtis they were up and moving around. Sleep came difficult knowing his bed was just inches away from hers, separated only by a thin wall. She held her breath from time to time in the night, trying to hear whether he snored, or was a restless sleeper, or watched TV at night. No sounds filtered through the wall, and she imagined him listening too, trying to hear the quiet murmurings of her settling her children into bed and later, her own deep slumbering breaths. She hoped she didn't snore.

Their courtship had edged along, cautiously punctuated by a rare embrace, a stolen kiss and frequent brushing of fingers. Four times they'd slept together. A single handful of private, delicious hours. She worried about the romance's effect on Jamie, who had adored her father, but her daughter exhibited amazing resilience at the recent changes in her life: moving to another state, losing her father, starting kindergarten. Atticus was still too young and adaptable to be confused, but she stayed watchful, not wanting her children to suffer for her mistakes. Her own childhood haunted her and her children deserved better.

But how long was long enough? She ached to slip out of her room in the darkness and quietly tap on Curtis' door, slip into his bed, and stroke every inch of his firm physique. But, of course, she would never leave her kids alone like that. Her responsibility to them would always come first. She would break the chain of chaos running through her family and give her children a stable upbringing. If she needed to wait a little longer for her own life to sort out, it wouldn't kill her.

A return rap on the motel wall sounded in acknowledgment and quickly enough, they were off to find breakfast.

****

Jamie plowed through her pancakes in record time, strawberries, whipped cream and all. Somehow, she managed to keep a chatter going nonstop even as she chewed. "Can I have a dog when we get our new house? One with golden hair."

"Dogs have fur, and the answer is no. No dogs." She'd left Jamie's rooster and six rabbits with Honey to care for while they were gone. Her daughter's plump pet rabbit, Grendel, surprised them by being pregnant when they first brought it home, and Meredith looked forward to giving away the five baby rabbits upon their return. "Two pets are plenty."

"Dogs aren't pets. They're best friends," her daughter countered. "She can sleep with me at night."

"Speaking of your new house." Curtis broke in with the topic of another one of her dilemmas. "I was thinking a playroom would make sense, and it could transition to a den down the road."

He grabbed a napkin and started sketching on the back, and Jamie leaned in close to watch. The two of them brainstormed together, Jamie requesting turrets above and tunnels below and he obligingly drew them in. This crazy project arose with the rapid disintegration of Meredith's house, its roof partially collapsing just as winter set in. Curtis, who designed and built his own home, offered to build her a new house as well. Out of friendship. Even as she protested his generosity, he delivered a trailer for them to live safely in until spring, and Honey set up a community event to demolish the old house and raise funds for the new one. Her opinion on the matter was ignored, something which irked her to no end. She didn't want to be Hay City's charity case.

"And a moat," her five-year-old suggested.

"Don't you think a moat could be dangerous for your little brother?" Curtis chided, raising his pen from the napkin.

"I'll teach him to swim."

"In that case…" He sketched out a waterway surrounding the castle they'd created. "Any alligators?"

"No alligators," Meredith said, her automatic reply to any more creatures roaming about her home, make-believe or not.

"No alligators," her daughter agreed. "They might

eat the dolphins."

He sketched in a pod of dolphins and then raised his eyebrows at Jamie. "Maybe we should ask your mom what she'd like in the house."

Both sets of eyes peered at her. This new house was going to happen whether she liked it or not, this unbelievable generosity of his. Never in her wildest dreams did she imagine having a house of her own design. Brand new and built by someone she was, well…she was in love with him, wasn't she? The whole thing was like a dream.

"Three bedrooms, one for each of us." Her voice was hesitant, unsure if this was asking too much. "A kitchen…"

He chuckled, breaking in. "Are you sure? A kitchen in your house?" His eyes twinkled at her, his smile teasing and gentle. "Tell me if you want a big dining room, to host dinners, or a walk-in shower in your master bath."

"Simple," she decided, then and there. "With lots of light coming in. Build it just like yours."

With this declaration, had she committed herself once and for all to accept the goodness of her neighbors and friends? She never expected to throw herself on the mercy of others, accept their generosity, just when she learned to stand on her own two feet. She took a shaky breath. Nothing in her life made sense, so why not a free house? Dolphins and turrets too. What the heck.

"No moat, then?" His expression was mock disappointment, but she recognized the hopefulness in his eyes. She couldn't bear to hurt him.

"We'll learn to live without one."

They exchanged a mutual look of amusement…and

something else, something deeper, more intimate. It was this moment when she knew, absolutely and without any doubts at all, she'd waded in too deep with him. She dropped her eyes to hide the dangerous emotion surging through her.

****

The sun was high in a cloudless sky by the time they emerged from breakfast, with all signs of the earlier rain vanished. There were hours to go before visiting Sarah Givens-McHenry. It made no sense, then, to be so near the beach on a perfect day and not enjoy it. Only when Jamie and Curtis were deep into barbecue chicken sandwiches and fried onions, settled on the beach, she stood and announced she was going for a stroll with Atticus. They barely glanced at her as she hefted her toddler onto her hip and strode away, heading down the boardwalk to get her mind off the upcoming meeting with her newly discovered aunt. The boards were bright, not aged wood, and so wouldn't have been around when her mother lived here. The beach would have been pristine and nothing but smooth sand and low dunes, all the way to the murky swamplands. Now, this was a tourist destination lined with small shops.

T-shirts and baseball caps, key chains and handbags—all were imprinted with palm trees, neon-pink flamingos and beach scenes. She window-shopped distractedly and let Atticus pet stuffed animals at store-front stands and toddle alongside. She tipped a boardwalk clown for making a balloon hat for her son, and consoled her toddler after the balloon popped. She turned into town where boardwalk ended, a warning sign declaring the swamplands ahead were unsafe. It was only when she passed a jewelry shop that she stopped, and without thinking twice about what she was doing, went inside.

If there was one thing out of place in the box left to her, it was the ring. Tanzanite had always been her mother's favorite stone. Why then, had she left it behind when she ran away? It also was an unusual piece of jewelry for a teenager to own—big, gaudy and old-fashioned. And if it was a family heirloom, her grandmother would certainly have commandeered it from the box before sealing it up. A child's toy, she decided, and probably not even tanzanite at all. Something from a gumball machine.

The store was empty and quiet except for one man, who worked on a watch at the far counter. Glass jewelry cases lined the walls, with gemstones of all kinds displayed inside. She stopped before the tanzanite counter and gazed down at the varied shades of violet in the rings and necklaces. There was nothing similar to the ring she'd tucked away in her handbag.

"Can I help you find something?" The jeweler didn't glance up or budge from his perch. He probably was used to tourists looking and not buying.

She dug out the black cloth-wrapped ring from her handbag and set it on the counter. She unwrapped it to display the ring. "I'm hoping you can tell me what this is—the stone, I mean. My mother left it to me. I was thinking maybe it's tanzanite."

The jeweler gave another twist of his tiny screwdriver and snapped the back of the watch on before hopping off his bench. He approached and picked up the ring. He extended a loupe that hung from a chain around his neck, and leaned over the stone, nearly touching it with the glass. After a moment, he straightened up. "You have a big stone here. Not tanzanite though," he announced to her disappointment.

"What is it then?"

"Unusual," he muttered. "Hold on a moment." He opened a drawer and withdrew a different loupe. He resumed his examination with the more powerful loupe, turning the ring this way and that. "Would you mind if I popped out the stone?"

She was startled at the suggestion and shook her head firmly. "Oh, no. I'd rather you didn't."

"I won't hurt anything. I can clean the stone for you and make sure the setting is secure. If this is old, the stone could be loose."

She hesitated and then agreed, worried he would damage her mother's ring. He was a jeweler, however, and if the piece was a toy, what was the harm? In fact, it most likely *was* a toy, something her mother got out of a candy machine. This would explain how the ring ended up in the box, along with other childhood mementos. He disappeared with her ring into his back room where she could see him through a window, hunched over a worktable under a strong light. After several minutes, he returned and set the ring back on the counter.

"Where did you say you got this?" His gaze raked over her faded T-shirt and the flip flops she'd purchased that morning at a dollar store. Atticus roamed the store, flattening his nose against the glass display cases.

"My mother. From her estate."

His lips compressed together as if he doubted her story. "Spinel, could be," he announced. "Pretty unusual gemstone, if that's what this is. I've only seen it once before. You have a pretty fine ring here, though there are some inclusions."

She stared at him. "Spinel?"

He took in her blank expression. "Think of it as something like a ruby. And there's nearly two carats here, well cut, nice setting. I'd buy it from you for four hundred dollars."

Four hundred dollars could buy spring clothing for her growing children. The money would buy a month's worth of groceries, gas for her car, heat for the trailer they lived in. She could stretch four hundred dollars so far you'd hear it scream for mercy. But no. She snatched up the ring, and quickly wrapped it back in the black cloth and tucked the ring into her handbag. "It's a family heirloom; I don't want to sell."

The jeweler appeared disappointed, but he shrugged. "I gave you a fair price. I'm not guaranteeing it's spinel, you know. You won't get a better price. If you change your mind, I'm here."

"No. Thank you. I won't change my mind." She backed out of the store as she spoke, grabbing Atticus on her way.

She was grateful to be back on the sidewalk. It wasn't her intent to sell the ring at all. She was glad the ring had value although she'd never heard of a gemstone called spinel before. It didn't have the same appeal as tanzanite. Regardless, the jeweler believed the ring had some value if he offered to buy it outright. The piece would still be something to pass along to Jamie someday. This had belonged to her mother and that alone made the ring something to cherish.

****

She found Jamie and Curtis down at the water's edge building a castle with a moat. Her daughter floated shreds of seaweed in the moat while he focused on the castle's thick walls.

"These are the sea monsters," her five-year-old explained. "They protect the castle since the princess isn't allowed to have a dog."

She dropped to her knees while Atticus squatted beside his sister. "Sounds like a dangerous kingdom."

Curtis planted a twig atop one turret and hung seaweed from it to serve as a flag. "How was the sightseeing?"

"Can you research spinel on your phone? There was a jewelry store and the man there believes my mom's ring is a semi-precious stone. He likened it to a ruby and even offered to buy it."

"I've never heard of spinel," he said with a frown, and slipped his phone from a pocket.

He tapped on the screen and she scooted close, her shoulder touching his, and peered into the tiny display. A quick search revealed a stone varying in color from a bright red to violet to green and described as a valuable precious gem. The website also confirmed what the jeweler disclosed about spinel being difficult to find. This would be the most valuable piece of jewelry she ever owned. She and Brian married so quickly, there was no point in getting an engagement ring—or so he explained. He promised he'd buy her a diamond ring, someday but that day never arrived. She touched the hard lump in her pocket. Her husband would have sold her mother's ring without a second thought, along with the silver teardrop earrings if they were worth anything.

Curtis sat back and stretched his legs out on the

sand. "I've been wondering, ever since you showed it to me. Is a ring like this something a teenager would own? And now...even if you're wealthy, would you really give a young girl a two-carat ruby for instance?"

It did seem odd her mother would have such a large stone, especially in an oversized clunky setting.

"It is a little, well, showy. More my grandmother's style, I'd guess." While the idea the jewelry could have belonged to her grandmother reduced the value in Meredith's eyes, it also added to the mystery of why the ring was included in the box. Therald Holt might know the history of the ring, but if the piece had any value, he was also cunning enough to steal it away from her.

"Something to tuck away in a safe place. Good thing you have your own personal law enforcement officer standing guard." He stood and stretched, dusting the sand off his legs and bathing suit. He propped the cell phone across the moat, creating a drawbridge into the sandcastle. "Think I have time for a quick swim before we go?"

Without waiting for an answer, he stripped off his shirt, dropped it to the sand, and headed into the light surf. His long legs pumped through the low breakers and he dove into an oncoming wave. Within seconds, his muscular arms powered him through the water. Farther out, a trio of brown pelicans skimmed the water on a hunt for schools of herring or other prey. Above, the sky was an undefinable blue—so deep and pure and dark, it was nearly purple.

She turned her attention to the sandcastle before her. Who would live inside? A princess and her two children, of course. That wasn't how the story ended though, not in fairy tales. There was always a prince.

Her eyes focused once again on Curtis' arms cutting above the water. Her life was anything but a fairytale. No one needed to tell her there'd be no simple happily-ever-after.

Life is messy, her mother always said. Wasn't that the undeniable truth.

Curtis emerged from the water farther down the shoreline, tall and handsome, and appearing invincible, as though he could slay all the dragons in her life. A smile lit his face as he sought, and then found, her returning gaze. She recalled the last part of her mother's saying: *It's all about how you handle it*. In other words, stay strong.

She lifted a hand in a wave. "Over here," she called. "We're over here."

Chapter Six

Sarah Givens-McHenry lived in a large white mansion guarded by two stately marble lions. The place was nothing compared to Leila Brittan's sprawling estate, but grand nonetheless, especially to someone who lived in a borrowed trailer. The home bespoke a comfortable bank account, elegant vacations, and a summer getaway cottage somewhere in the pines. Far from her own leaking Hay City with ice crusting along the edges of the window sills, a hole in the roof big enough to crawl through, and black mold creeping up the walls.

Curtis gave her shoulder an encouraging squeeze as she climbed out of his truck, and he promised to be back in forty-five minutes. He would take her kids to a book store and then to find snow cones, enough activity to fill the time and keep them entertained. Food, in any case, always kept Jamie amused and out of trouble.

The door, painted sunflower yellow and trimmed in white, chimed a symphonic melody that went on for nearly twenty seconds. She waited and just as she lifted her hand to ring again, the door opened. A tall, slender, perfectly coiffed woman of an age difficult to discern stood before her. The woman could have been thirty-five or fifty-five. The resemblance to her father jarred her—same golden hair, blue eyes and fine features—and words stuck in her throat.

The woman's welcoming smile didn't crack a wrinkle on her face or touch her eyes. "Meredith? Come in. I'm Sarah. What a surprise this is, hearing from you. But I suppose you're in town for your grandmother's estate."

She stepped into the foyer. "No. Well, yes. I mean, sort of."

The woman's heels clicked on the entry's marble floors as she led the way to a room next to the foyer. The room, though small, was furnished with large, heavy furniture in shades of white and yellow. Plush cream carpet sank under her shoes, so soft she could have slept on it. Large landscape paintings dominated the wall, making the room appear smaller and a tad claustrophobic. Meredith perched on the edge of a white sofa overflowing with embroidered throw pillows. Her blue sundress was too wrinkled for one more outing, so instead she wore dark blue shorts and a striped tan and white blouse. The casual outfit was clean and neat, but she was conscious of her sunburned knees, nose, and forehead, and wished she'd packed nicer clothes.

"I remember your mother," the woman said once they'd settled. "Everyone from those times would remember her. She stood out in a crowd, she was that pretty. Did she keep her looks?"

She blinked as she recalled her mother's tired face, puffy and bloodshot eyes, and the premature gray hair snaking through the short, darkened blonde. Already petite, Laura was chronically malnourished from drinking her meals. Toward the end, she couldn't keep food down.

"She was beautiful." Meredith didn't feel a twinge

of guilt for this statement. Her mother was interesting, funny and kind, and everything that mattered. She glanced at the alabaster-framed clock on a marble-topped table at her side and realized there wasn't time to spare. "I'm actually here to ask about your brother, David. I'd like to talk to him, about my mother."

Sarah waved a well-manicured hand in dismissal. "David? Finding him would be a bit difficult. He went down a different path in life." The woman drew a deep breath and let the air out slowly, as though the very mention of her brother was too much to take. She paused and poured coffee from a pot sitting on a table.

Meredith went still, frozen at what she was going to hear. A gang. Drugs. Prison. Her heart raced. *A terrible person.*

"He lives in Sustainable Farms in California," the other woman continued. "One of those ridiculous commune places. No phone, no email, no way to contact him except by old-fashioned mail. He calls their kind of living 'off-the-grid.' I call it out-of-their-minds." She tittered at her own joke. "They live on a barter economy, I hear, for the most part. Someone's bound to be making money, if you ask me. Those communes are a big scam."

Relief flooded Meredith. If he was alive, she could track him down. A commune. The lifestyle sounded different, but not so terrible on the face of it. Not dangerous, surely, and not criminal.

"I haven't heard from him in years," Sarah went on. "I was hoping maybe you were stopping by with some news. Did your mother stay in contact over the years? They were such good friends in high school."

It was on the tip of her tongue to blurt out

everything. Didn't the woman have eyes? There must be some type of family resemblance somewhere in her. Although she couldn't see the similarities herself—not in the color of her eyes or hair, not in the shape of her nose or chin—a likeness had to be there. The other woman, now warmed to the subject of former days, didn't wait for an answer.

"David was pretty devastated when Laura took off, you know. He was the only person I know who ever confronted your grandmother, and he was just a teenager at the time. None of it was really any of his business, but we laughed over his nerve at insisting on signs around town after your mother ran off. I mean *no one* was brave enough to take on Leila Brittan. Your grandmother was a bit of a wolverine; nasty tempered and with claws, too. I hope you don't mind my saying so, bless her heart. A tough, tough lady."

She gave a polite laugh. "I suppose David was worried about my mother. Her safety, you know."

"Well, I'm glad everything worked out in the end." Sarah studied her over the rim of her coffee cup. Her glance darted down at Meredith's scuffed shoes and then up again. "What are your plans with the estate? All the artwork and antiques? Your grandmother was quite a collector."

Meredith was struck all of a sudden why this woman, her aunt, was so willing to invite her over and make polite chit-chat about the old days. Sarah believed she was the heir to her grandmother's fortune. Rich and, therefore, someone to know.

"No plans at all." She decided she didn't much like her aunt. "My grandmother didn't search for my mother when she left. Any idea why?"

Sarah raised her eyebrows and was silent for a moment. "I was away at college at the time. David said Leila hounded your mother into leaving, to avoid the embarrassment." She lowered her voice even though there was no one else in the room. "Did you know your mother drank in high school? I mean everyone drank some, but your mother showed up to school drunk in the mornings. Lots of gossip about her. Pretty awful, I understand. We all figured Leila heard the gossip and kicked her out. She was under a lot of stress at the time, with her husband leaving, you know. Terrible timing."

Meredith studied her aunt. Had the pregnancy been a well-kept secret? Or was she keeping up a decades-old pretense of ignorance? "I suppose my grandmother could have helped her instead," she said, trying to keep the bitterness from her voice. "Sent her to rehab, got her some counseling. There wasn't a lack of money."

The other woman's gaze had slipped away and she stared out the front window where a trellis labored to hold a bougainvillea vine bursting with pink blooms. "Older men take younger wives all the time, but let a woman do it and everyone judges her. I say, brava for Leila. Nothing wrong with an older woman and a younger man." She focused a glare on Meredith as if expecting disagreement. Was the woman even thinking about Leila or rather something more personal?

Meredith didn't care about her grandmother taking up with a younger man. She should have been taking care of her daughter. In a flash, she thought about her own situation—recently widowed, traveling with two young children and a handsome sheriff. Her eyes widened. My situation's not the same, she insisted to herself. I'm not old or rich, and my kids come first in my life. Still, a residue of disquiet lingered.

The other woman glanced at the platinum and diamond watch encircling her bony wrist and set her coffee down. What promised to be a few minutes of gossip along with a promising connection clearly had gone in the wrong direction. Her voice resumed its normal pitch.

"Well, this has been nice, hasn't it?" The woman stood and Meredith realized the visit was at an end. "It's too bad you didn't get Laura's hair color. Yours is more...what would you call it...not really blonde..."

"Brown," she filled in, rising from her chair. "I have brown hair."

"Oh no, not as bad as that. You're more an ash, maybe even a café au lait, if you ask me. You could try a little highlighting, to perk things up."

"The place in California," she interrupted, "where your brother lives...do you have an address?"

Her aunt stared at her and, for a moment, appeared as though she might refuse. Apparently lacking any good reason, she agreed.

"Be prepared he might not remember his high school days or your mother. He probably won't answer at all. Those communes brainwash people." She stalked out of the salon into the depths of the mansion, the echo of her heels tapping on the marble floor faded, then disappeared.

A light scent of gardenia and vanilla, with undertones of furniture polish, wafted around the room. The combination of sweetness was cloying. Someone whistled a tune somewhere in the house and there was no way the happy song was coming from Sarah's lips. Five minutes passed and she twisted her hands together.

It occurred to her in a rush her father wouldn't be overjoyed at hearing from a long-lost daughter, if he even was aware she existed at all. If he was anything like his sister, he might resent any intrusion from his past life. She would be an imposition on his tranquil commune life. She knew his name and where he lived. Maybe that was enough. It could be a disaster to reveal herself twenty-five years after the fact. What was the etiquette for contacting a father you'd never met?

Five more minutes crept by and the house was still, with whoever had been whistling finished. Could Sarah have slipped out the back door and dashed off to her hair appointment? She slung her handbag over one shoulder and headed to the broad foyer, trying to peek down the hallway. Grit under her shoes made her realize she'd tracked beach sand inside.

"If you write to him, say hello for me." Sarah startled her as she strode into the foyer from the other side, carrying a crumpled plastic grocery bag and a note card. "I would write but I never seem to get anything in return. Let him know I have boxes of his stuff here. I can't store it forever."

The woman thrust the bag at her. "Here. Letters from your mother, from back in the day, before email was so popular. David saved them all. He's never going to want them, so you may as well take them. I peeked at a couple of them once. Kid stuff. School's boring, too much homework, teenage angst. You know."

She took the note card with her father's address on it and accepted the bag with a trembling hand. Letters from her mother from long ago was a bonus, when she was the beautiful teenager with a golden future. If only she'd achieved it.

Meredith glanced down at the card: Sustainable Farms, 101 Sheep Alley, Bodega Bay, California.

Her father was on the other side of the country, living in a commune, but he was alive. If only she'd known, they would have spent this winter holiday on a different beach, by a different ocean. There wasn't time or money left to track down her father in person now. She'd have to write a letter. And wait weeks to see if he would answer. It was frustrating beyond belief to come this close to finding him, yet be unable to meet and talk to him. At least she had his name and address. In the meantime, she possessed her mother's letters.

Sarah cleared her throat delicately. She held out a small business card, edged in sunflower yellow. The woman's eyes flickered from her toes to the top of her head, making one last assessment. "Let me know if you need an agent, for the estate. I dabble in real estate here and there. You know, if you decide to sell."

She took it automatically, not bothering to correct the other woman. "Sure. No problem."

When the door closed behind her, Meredith crumpled the card and stuffed it in her handbag.

****

"Bodega Bay, California," Curtis repeated with a frown, as she related the conversation. "We headed in the wrong direction all right."

She clutched the plastic bag, unable to let loose of the collection of letters. Regardless of not finding her father on this visit, she'd found insight into her mother's broken past. The letters, mementos, and personal accounts, no matter how dismal, were invaluable. She had a name and an address. The trip to Fifteen Palms wasn't wasted at all.

They sat on the same elephant-shaped bench as before at the city park and watched her kids at play. Curtis had promised her daughter hot dogs on the beach for dinner so they were marking time until the sun lowered farther in the sky. In the morning, they'd rise early and start the long drive home.

She bit her lip. "I'll write a letter, I guess. I don't know." What if her father never wrote back? She would never know for sure if he received her letter, didn't care, or just didn't want to answer.

He glanced at her and then down at her hands, still clenched around the plastic bag. "Did you ask about the stepfather? He may have some information."

"He didn't come up in the course of the conversation. Anyway, Mr. Holt said he's long gone."

Curtis raised his eyebrows and gave her a sidelong look. "And whatever the lawyer says is true."

She twisted on the bench to face him, worried she missed something important. "Why would he lie about Leila's ex-husband?"

"In my experience, people don't disappear. Usually, they're hanging around somewhere."

In her mind, Anthony Noble was just another disposable person in her grandmother's life. If her grandmother dismissed her own daughter without a second thought, a second husband would be less than nothing. "You think he knows something the lawyer doesn't want me to learn?"

"He's a loose end and I don't like loose ends." His gaze settled on her. "In general, there are three kinds of missing persons. The ones who don't want to be found, those whom no one's searching for, and the dead."

"Dead," she decided. "My relatives tend to die."

Jamie ran up and patted at her arm. "What time is it?" she asked urgently. "Is it dinner time yet?"

Curtis scooted over so the girl could hop up on the bench between them. "Another hour at least, and then we'll head to the hot dog stand."

The five-year-old blew out a long breath. "I can't wait a whole hour. I'll starve to death. How long is an hour anyway?"

Curtis unclasped the large watch at his wrist and handed it to the restless child. "Look here," he explained. "This line is on the four. When it moves to the five down here, we'll go. Put this in your pocket and take good care of it for me."

The girl's eyes lit up and she tucked the watch in her pocket and ran back to where her little brother sat in the sand.

"She adores you," Meredith said, her gaze following her daughter.

"Is she the only one?"

She shifted to sit closer to him, until her thigh touched his. His arm drew around and rested on the bench behind her shoulders. "I think you have a team of admirers."

"Like who, exactly?"

A light smile danced at her lips. "Jamie, of course."

"Right, you said that. Who else?"

"Atticus, too."

He caught up a lock of her hair and twined it around a finger before letting it loose. "They're my team, huh?"

She tilted her chin up and gazed into his face. Her breath quickened at what was in his return gaze. "Me. I was your first fan. Your biggest fan."

The plastic bag in her hands crinkled as he leaned down to kiss her. The crinkle was like static disturbing one's favorite song on the radio, and for a split second she wished the bag and all it might contain would simply vanish. But it was there, filled with memories of her mother, and this made her break away from him. She stared down at her hands. His chest rose and fell, and his breath released audibly.

"You've had a lot to take in this week," he said, his voice tender. His gaze, too, lingered on the bag in her hands. "If I've learned anything about you, though, it's you're strong enough to take anything on."

She wasn't sure of that, but appreciated the words. The odd thumping in her chest that had started when Sarah handed over the bag hadn't lessened. She felt a growing unease about what the letters contained. "I'll open these later; maybe when the kids are settled in bed tonight."

****

The letters were rubber-banded together with tiny dates scribbled in the corner of each envelope. A quick glance told her they'd been organized by date, with the earliest on top. Once her kids were bathed and tucked in bed, she took the top letter and sequestered herself in the tiny motel bathroom. These were letters to read alone, without the distractions of her kids. There, with the door shut so the glare of light wouldn't wake her children, she pulled the first letter out of its envelope.

"*Dear David,*" the letter began, in her mother's tiny jagged handwriting. "*Why does planting a tree remind me of digging a grave? Both require shovels, dirt excavated from a hole, and then a still, quiet creature tucked down inside and covered with earth. In one instance, life grows. In the other, it rots."*

Meredith slid to the floor with her back against the cool, porcelain bathtub. The letter was dated in May, a year before her mother left home. Why would she write to her boyfriend about death? A teenage girl should write overwrought love notes with hearts and flowers in the margins.

"Mother dearest locked me in my room last night. She thinks I hate it, but I love my prison. A locked door goes both ways. I got my science homework done for once and even started the dreaded English essay. I may pass all my classes this year. Yay mom."

The rest of the letter spoke of friends they had in common, with no more bewildering comments about death or locked doors. She replaced the letter in its envelope, peeked in on her sleeping children, and then returned to the bathroom floor to continue reading.

"Kings and presidents, who cares about history? Not this girl. Summer is too close to think of anything but vacation. More family comes to stay in August. I don't know where Anthony finds them all. I don't think he likes being alone with Mother. But first, some summer fun."

This second letter, dated a month later, was a relief after the first. Just the idle chatter of a bored teen seeking to express herself and glad for a break from studies. She smiled at her mother's youthful self. She could almost believe her mother was a normal girl with few problems and a faithful boyfriend who listened to her problems. There were a handful of letters yet to go. The words inside would be with her forever, the last dreams and complaints her mother would ever express. She tucked the letters back into the bag. Reading the letters was like having her mother alive again. Best to parcel them out one at a time.

They were going to leave early in the morning for the long drive home. As much as she dreaded the lengthy trek cooped up in the truck, even worse would be one more day in this dismal motel room. After three days, the room reeked of dirty clothes, her toddler's nighttime pants, and damp bathing suits. Dirty clothes were heaped in a corner of the closet next to sandy shoes. She wanted her washing machine and dryer and, surprising to her, the fresh smell of new-fallen snow. Getting away in the depth of winter had high points, but she missed her trailer home with all its familiar odors and cozy comforts.

With a sigh, she rose to her feet, stripped off her clothes and stepped into the shower. Five minutes of warm water sprayed down before the shower ran cold. Hurriedly, she twisted off the tap and toweled off, hoping the brisk water wouldn't keep her awake. Dressed in a long sleep shirt, she brushed her teeth and pondered what had been accomplished in the past week. Lots of question answered, but the answers prompted even more questions. Perhaps this is how it was with all families. Some mysteries never solved and relationships tangled and muddled.

She stared into the foggy mirror and then swiped the mirror with a hand to get a better view of herself. Plain brown hair, a narrow face and only those flecks of green in her eyes to remind her of her mother. In a long ago high school class, her biology teacher lectured about genetics. There was something about dominant and recessive genes, but she couldn't quite remember how the chart worked. The chart explained how two brown-haired people could have a blonde child, but was the reverse true as well? Her parents were blonde, light-eyed, beautiful swans who'd given birth to a plain, beige duckling. She lifted her hair up off her neck and turned from one side to the other, examining her profile. Nothing of her parents' young beauty had passed down to her. Life wasn't fair.

She leaned in and blew on the mirror, fogging the surface over. Her image faded away into a shadow.

Chapter Seven

Up through Alabama, into Jackson, Mississippi, then Shreveport. The high spirits they all carried on the journey to Florida flipped upside down on the return trip. All four suffered searing red sunburns and a series of mosquito bites. Atticus' usual happy disposition turned bad-tempered. Meredith covered him in a soothing aloe lotion and suffered guilt at not protecting his tender baby skin better. Still, he cried and whined and wiggled in his car seat as he tried to get comfortable. Jamie, too, was crabby and wouldn't allow the green aloe anywhere near her.

"It's slime," she protested. "It'll eat me up."

"The slime will make you feel better."

Arms flailing, her daughter continued to refuse. Finally, Meredith gave up. From her seat, she coated her own arms and legs. Hesitating only a moment, she then smoothed it on the back of Curtis' neck and arms while he drove, enjoying the feel of his warm skin glide under her fingers. When she finished, he twined her fingers in his and they held hands between the seats for most of Alabama.

The second day, they crossed into Dallas, and cruised through Amarillo. They dug sweaters out as the high desert grew wintry and snow coated the ground. They stopped at a cheap motel in Albuquerque, their last stop before the last long haul to Hay City. As night fell, she stepped gingerly across the icy parking lot and sat in the truck facing the motel room door. The window shades were open so she could see Jamie and Atticus laying together on one of the beds, watching a cartoon. She clutched her mother's letters and drew out the next one in the pile.

The third letter was similar to the first two, with references to friends they had in common, and then:

"Someday, I'll break out of this jail. I'll leave and go so far away no one will ever find me again (except you). It's only then I'll finally be free."

It was painful to read, knowing how unhappy her mother had been. Her wild spirit was so unsuited to the world she'd been born into, and the strict expectations of a domineering mother. Running away catapulted her into an unstructured life where there were no rules, living from day to day and never planning more than an hour ahead. The letter marked a moment in time when Meredith was certain her mother still could have been saved from the calamitous future rushing toward her.

She sat with the letter on her lap for a while before folding it gently along the same folds and sliding it back into the stack. Her gaze traveled to the motel door next to theirs, where Curtis was staying. His curtains were drawn closed and light showed around the edges. A shadow shifted inside, crossing from one side the room to the other, and then all was still. She sat with her musings another few minutes and then returned to her room to prepare her children for bed.

She traded off driving with Curtis the next day, and each of them napped in-between stints. Sleet in Albuquerque softened into a steady snow and the landscape transformed to a blinding white as they headed due north. Jamie's bright pink skin blistered and peeled, and she grudgingly allowed Meredith to dab her here and there with green slime without further dramatics. They hit Salt Lake City late the next afternoon and all of them cheered when they crossed into Idaho's lower eastern border.

It was amazing to her how thankful she was to return to this far northern state. She had lived here less than a year but this place felt more like home than any other place she ever lived. She had a home, a job, and friends. Jamie was in school, making friends there as well, and Atticus...well, her toddler had a chance to grow up knowing one stable home in his life, a luxury she couldn't imagine.

Curtis' voice interrupted her reflections. "You haven't spoken a word in two hours."

She gazed at his strong profile. He'd stopped shaving during their trip, deciding it was a good time to test out a beard. The rough stubble was struggling to become much more than a scraggly mess. There was one bare patch about the size of a quarter under his jaw. The sad excuse for a beard was ridiculous and entirely lovable. He was the best part about moving to Idaho. She couldn't imagine never knowing him.

She laid one hand atop one of his, and squeezed lightly. "I was thinking how lucky I am."

His chest rose and fell as he took a deep breath. "I'm the lucky one." His voice lowered. "I never believed you'd let me go all this way with you to Florida and back. But you did. Spending time with you this week...it's been one of the best weeks of my life."

"Are you going to kiss my mom again?" Jamie's voice piped up from the back seat.

Meredith had been unsure how much her daughter understood about her relationship with him, wary the five-year-old would be confused by a new man in their lives. So much had happened in the past year and she didn't want her children to suffer from it all. Apparently, her daughter understood plenty.

He grinned at Meredith. "If she'll let me. Just as soon as we stop for dinner."

She kept her eyes on his face, color rising high in her cheeks, her stomach aflutter. "Why wait that long?"

He glanced over at her and appeared struck by something he noted in her expression. The truck slowed and he swerved to the side of the road and hopped out into the snow. She laughed as he ran around the front of the truck to her door and swung it open.

"In the snow?" She made it sound like a protest, but her fingers found her seat belt and unlatched it. She climbed out, her feet landing in icy slush, and then his warm arms were around her, lifting her up.

"Anywhere," he said before his lips met hers.

****

The last few hours of driving were endless, as the anticipation of arriving home again grew. Jamie and Atticus fell asleep soon after their dinner stop in Pocatello, and she kept one hand tucked into Curtis'. Headlights broke the darkness along with an occasional lighted billboard advertising farm equipment, but otherwise there was little to see. From time to time, she caught him glancing sideways at her with an expression on his face she couldn't define.

She fell into a broken doze, with random images flickering through her mind. Her mother as a teenager, golden hair long and loose, running across a well-kept lawn. As she approached a set of tall iron gates, her hair grew shorter and her body withered. Tinier and tinier, her size contracted, until she ran out the gates and then her mother winked out and disappeared.

The scene shifted and now the ocean rose and fell before her. She perched on the sandy beach, shaded by a massive sand castle at her side, the turrets so high they blocked the sun. A small crab scuttled past and a green tendril snaked out of the moat. Meredith darted a hand out to save the crab from its fate, but the sea monster was too quick and the crab disappeared into the castle's murky water.

She listed to one side and jolted awake. In the back seat her children slept the deep sleep of babes, and Curtis stared out the darkened windshield at her side. "Want me to drive a while?"

"Almost there now. Just a bit longer."

She rubbed his shoulders and then settled back in her seat. Their progress slowed as they turned toward Hay City onto snowy roads not as well traveled, and not as well plowed. Antsy at being cooped up so long and now nearly home, she opened her satchel and grabbed her mother's letters. She reread the first few again, using a penlight on her keyring, and lapsed into memories about her mother. Wanting more, she unfolded the next letter and started reading.

Almost immediately, she noticed the tone had changed. The letter, dated in December, meant they were back in school and in the midst of studies. Her mother's script was more erratic and topics zigzagged from school and friends to Laura's life at home.

"Do you ever feel like you're a ghost and your real life already happened somewhere else? My life can't be

here and now. I'm being punished. You are the only one I can say this to."

Meredith shivered. In just a few months from this writing, her mother would run away and never return. Some final rupture in the family would occur. She ran a finger over the words, wishing she could erase them along with her mother's pain.

"Are you getting cold?" Curtis snapped the heater up a notch without waiting for an answer.

Her fingers fumbled as she unfolded the next letter, the second to the last one. She'd meant to stretch out her reading of them so she could savor her mother's words. It would be as though her mother was alive again, in the same room, talking to her. But the teenaged Laura was nothing like the mother Meredith knew. Her mother had been cheerful and fun, even though she was wildly irresponsible as a parent. There'd been the drinking, sure, but nothing like the despair emanating from this last letter. Reading them was supposed to give her more time with her mother. Instead, they painted a journey toward breakdown.

She had to know everything her mother wrote to David all those years ago. There was no point in prolonging it now. Her eyes raced over the words on the next page. The handwriting was erratic as though written in a rush and, probably, she realized with a sinking heart, when her mother was drunk.

"It's all coming to an end for me. The ring proves it. It's a trap. A noose that squeezes so tight I can't breathe. I have to breathe. Your solution is so simple, but I've told you so many times why it won't work. I tell you again, I have to do it my own way."

The ring. Her mother had to be talking about the

one wrapped in black cloth, the one left behind and sealed away in the cardboard box. It held some sort of evil sway over her mother, a symbolism of something bad and not a treasured memento at all. *It's a trap.* What had she meant? Did her mother steal it? Did she fear she would go to jail, and so she ran away?

Ahead, one light shone in the darkness, far in the distance. A year ago, traveling here for the first time with Brian, she feared the solitary beam marked her home. Of course, she soon discovered nothing at all lit their house. The lamp glowed from the back of Honey's farmhouse just a few miles from away. Her friend kept the light shining to illuminate the yard, and give her a line of sight to the barn where chickens, goats and now Jamie's family of rabbits were housed.

The truck's headlights beamed over a landscape piled high with snow and they made the final turn onto the narrow road to her home. Curtis slowed even more as he followed the curvy plow lines scraped into the snow. Deli-boy, an awful teenager who worked at the local grocery store, ran the plow service and deliberately created the snaky pattern on her road out of plain meanness. From the first time they met, they'd hated each other. The annoying kid barely registered with her now, although Curtis grumbled next to her that he would have to talk to the teen about his driving. Her mind was on her mother.

There was one last letter. She had to know how the story ended, even though it was already finished. Her mother ran away. She became a dedicated drunk. She dragged her only child from one homeless situation to the next. Her mother's story was like a book with the final pages torn out, leaving the reader hanging and empty. It was unreasonable, but Meredith wished this last letter would foretell a different ending—one in which her anguish was simply teenage dramatics. Her mother deserved a different, happy future.

This couldn't be so, but she gasped anyway when she opened the final sheet of paper. She expected a farewell or regrets or, at best, some clearer explanation of why her mother left. Still unexplained was what David did to make her mother hate him so much that she never would speak of him again. She stared at the letter in shock. Anything was more likely than the words printed on the page before her.

The same three words filled the page over and over, filling the margins and squeezed into the corners. The paper dropped from her hands and fluttered to her feet, face up on the floorboard.

"Meredith? What is it? What's wrong?" Curtis steered the truck into her driveway, parked in front of the trailer, and turned off the engine. "You're home."

She snapped off her penlight and the truck cab fell into darkness. The letter at her feet disappeared in the shadows but it didn't matter. The words were burned into her brain. Three terrible, terrible words:

"I'm a murderer. I'm a murderer. I'm a murderer."

Part 2—The Middle

The high-heeled shoe hit the wall behind Laura's head, denting the Italianate plastered wall. The cost of the custom gold-flecked finish would've purchased a moderately priced new car.

"I told you to stay away from him." Leila's mouth twisted downward in a scowl. "Always playing cat and mouse. What did you think would happen? You'll have to leave."

Her body ached still, three sleepless days after the night of the spring dance. Laura had run home and confessed it all. Everything. There was no sympathy. Her mother raged and created her own story. There was the ring, after all. Why else would a grown man give a young girl such an expensive gift? Why else would she accept it?

Her mother didn't want the truth; she wanted an acceptable story where none existed. Her mother was furious over the ring, and how it ended up in her possession. Once, it was her mother's and then Anthony's, and now she had it. A plus B equals C.

There was nowhere in the massive house or its gardens where she could flee that he didn't eventually find. Laura's life had become a series of escapes and captures, escapes and captures.

"Where is he? Where are you meeting him?"

"Mom," she moaned.

"What a mess. Look at you. Just look at you."

Laura sank to the floor, now carpeted in her shorn hair, and dropped the scissors from her hand.

"He can go to hell. But you're going nowhere."

Leila slammed the bedroom door as she left. Down the hall, her mother's voice raised to a screech. "Anthony!"

Laura wrapped a long strand of hair absently around one finger. Her mother was wrong; she was the one in hell. There'd been a couple years' reprieve when he went away, but now he was back. The days since the dance were a blur and she was grateful for the moments of oblivion. She wondered which bothered her mother the most—her rotten marriage or the ring. Surely, not her daughter.

Grabbing the bottle of gin from under her pillow, she crawled under the covers and tilted the bottle to her lips. There was an archaic term she'd learned in class. Wild (verb): To abuse an animal...or person...in such a way so they become agitated. She took another deep swallow. Used in a sentence, the word could be used thusly: Don't comfort or cheer or nurture the girl, in order that we wild her.

Nothing wrong with reverting to a natural state, where freedom beckoned. The problem with wild things is they don't like cages. Gin was her only escape, for now. A long, drawn out swallow emptied the bottle. She crawled on all fours to the floor and curled in a ball. Bottle empty, Laura passed out on the floor.

Chapter Eight

After they carried the children inside and she tucked them straight into bed, Meredith's mind went numb. She added extra blankets to their beds until the temperature inside the tiny trailer rose. Curtis waded through a foot of snow from his truck to the trailer with suitcases and refastened Atticus' child seat in her car's back seat.

Tasks completed, he hesitated inside the doorway with hands jammed in his pockets. She avoided his questioning gaze.

"I guess…I'll go on home now. It's late." He didn't budge as though giving her an opportunity to share what she discovered.

The clock on the kitchen counter showed just after eleven-thirty p.m. and her children had barely stirred through the transfer to their beds. Already, Jamie snored softly, while Atticus lay curled into a ball. There was a new job to start in the morning and Curtis needed to be back at work too, just hours from now. She needed to let him go home and get some rest. But she couldn't say goodbye. Not yet. Not after the last letter, with those words resonating in her mind.

She couldn't meet his eyes as she murmured, "My mother may have done something unforgivable. I think it's the reason she left and couldn't go home again."

He edged closer. They spoke in hushed voices,

aware of her children sleeping a few feet away in the cozy space. The entire trailer was just twenty-two feet long and three long strides could carry her from the door to her sleeping compartment in the back.

"Those letters you read, whatever she wrote, she was young. She couldn't have done anything so bad that she couldn't go home again. Teenagers make mistakes."

I'm a murderer.

It wasn't possible. She lifted her eyes to meet his. "I want you to read them. Tomorrow, if you'd like."

She retrieved the letters. He accepted them, holding them with both hands. He raised his eyebrows, questioning. "I can read them here. Now."

She glanced at the children's beds, a set of bunk beds against one wall. An arm's length away was a compact dining table. The only separate room in the trailer was a small compartment in the back where she slept. Her shoulders slumped in fatigue as she led the way to the compartment and then slid the door closed behind them. A double bed filled the cramped space, leaving only a narrow gap between the door and bed. She climbed onto the bed, and leaned back against the headboard. With a stony expression, she patted the space beside her. "Come put your feet up."

Obediently, he kicked off his shoes and sank onto the bed next to her, his hip coming to rest next to hers. The old mattress squeaked and sagged under his weight and, with a frown, she realized she'd invited him into bed with her. This was far from a tender moment. She darted a nervous glance at him, hoping he realized this wasn't the time nor place for a romantic interlude. His worried expression assured her that he understood this wasn't an amorous gesture on her part, and his gaze focused on the letters on his lap. Already, he was opening the first envelope and soon a small smile crept to his lips as he read her mother's adolescent complaints.

His eyes swept the pages one by one and by the time he reached the fourth letter, his countenance had grown somber. Like her, he concluded something unusual had transpired in her mother's life. These weren't the typical complaints of a spoiled teen. Halfway through the fifth letter, he opened the first one again and checked the date just as she had. All the letters were written over an eight-month period. In her last year at home, something major had changed, and for the worse. Her gaze fell away as he opened the last page. She couldn't bear to see those three words again. Why would anyone write such a thing, let alone send it to someone else? If there was any doubt at all that she should seek out her father, this eliminated it. She *had* to talk to him.

"Meredith."

His warm breath was at her ear and the impulse to lean against him was overpowering. She yearned for the comfort of his arms and the forgetfulness she could find there. Circumstances had kept them at arm's length for too long. How much longer would his patience last? Hers was at the breaking point. But it was too difficult to forget her kids were just a few feet away on the other side of a flimsy panel. Not only that, but these letters could change his feelings toward her. She leaned forward and placed her arms around her knees to create distance between them, and then inhaled deeply.

"She was mentally ill, wasn't she?" The words

emerged in a hoarse whisper.

"I believe she was confused and afraid." He spoke in a gentle tone, selecting his words carefully. "This is beyond teenage angst, or whatever they call it. Her mother locked her in her room? Her home life wasn't normal. Sarah didn't give you any clue about what was going on?"

"She didn't say much of anything. My aunt was away at college that last year, when my mother ran away. She said my grandmother must have been embarrassed to have a daughter who was an alcoholic." The words were sour in her mouth. No one seemed to care what happened to her mother back then, or what happened since.

The three words written over and over again on the last letter weren't true, of course. Her gentle, free-spirited mother never hurt anyone, never even spanked Meredith as a child. The truth of the matter sank in— her mother must have been mentally ill. The realization was a shock. How would a child know their parent's behavior was odd when there was nothing to compare their behavior with? This note, though. The words jolted her into understanding the wonderful woman who raised her, moving them to places barely habitable and drinking herself into a coma, was unstable. How foolish she'd been to believe any of her early life could have been anything but abnormal.

"I have to go to California, to talk to my father. As soon as possible." The words popped out before she was aware she'd made a decision. "Sustainable Farms commune in Bodega Bay."

She sagged back against the headboard, suddenly exhausted beyond belief. Curtis lifted a hand toward her shoulder and then shifted away as though he changed his mind. He didn't move for a moment and then swung his legs off the bed. She was disappointed and grateful. He couldn't stay, not with her children right on the other side of a flimsy panel door. Not when they were both dead tired. The only thing she wanted more than him was sleep.

"Get some rest and we'll talk tomorrow. This isn't something to discuss when you're exhausted." He laced up his shoes and set the letters on a side table. He stood at the doorway of her bedroom and stared at the floor, indecision evident in his posture.

Stay.

He stepped to her side of the bed and touched her arm. His chest rose and fell. *Stay.* Her eyelids drooped, despite her fervent wish for his embrace. He leaned over and warm lips touched her forehead. She closed her eyes, held her breath, and waited for his arms to encircle her.

The compartment door slid open and then closed. A moment later, the trailer door latched with a soft click as he left. She scooted under the covers fully dressed, too bone weary to brush her teeth or change into pajamas. She didn't want to think anymore. A few minutes later the sound of chopping drew her eyes open. She stared at the ceiling and listened to the crunch of boots over snow and the scrape of a snow shovel, and understood he was clearing a path from her door to the driveway. As exhausted as he must be, his thoughts were for her. The steady rhythm of the crunch-scrape, crunch-scrape lulled her into a doze. Soon echoed the sound of his truck door slamming shut and the engine coming to life.

Sleep took her as the rumble of his truck faded.

****

Stout, dependable, opinionated Honey Stohler threw open the front door to her cozy farmhouse. "Happy New Year, little chickens. Come in, out of the cold, hurry now before you freeze up like icicles."

Jamie ran in and launched herself into the older woman's outstretched arms. Meredith set her toddler down inside the door and tugged off his boots and coat. He wrapped his chubby arms around one of Honey's legs and the older woman chortled in triumph.

"Honey, Honey, Honey," Atticus chanted and then her daughter joined in with enthusiasm. "Honey, Honey, Honey."

The three of them began to dance around the room while Meredith remained at her spot at the entryway. The edges of her mouth twitched upward at the scene before her. "I guess they missed you."

A morning fire burned in the living room fireplace and the aroma of fresh baked scones drifted from the kitchen. The dining table was set for five, with coffee cups on three of the place mats and sippy cups filled with orange juice on the other two. Her friend clearly expected her to stay for breakfast and share the details of the trip. Sharing information with Honey often meant sharing with the entire community. The woman lived for fresh gossip, and more than once had taken it upon herself to inform most of Hay City about Meredith's latest news. Still, in a town this small, you couldn't be too choosy about your friends or you wouldn't have friends at all. And, despite her faults, the older woman had taken them in as family.

From down the hall, a deep voice hummed a tune,

occasionally singing a random word or two before returning to a basso hum. The fifth setting at the table now made sense.

Honey noticed her attention trained down the hallway toward the bedrooms, and gave her an innocent smile. "Crusty stopped by for some of my famous scones. We can all have some breakfast together and you can tell me everything about your trip."

Crusty Connery, the pony-tailed, eccentric owner of the local hardware store and bar, had given her a part-time job through the summer and fall—a job where she did scarcely anything, and a paycheck that didn't cover her bills. Her new position as assistant city clerk was more than she could have hoped for. It was a real job with a more meaningful paycheck, one which would allow her to support her children, and Honey and Crusty pulled some strings to get her hired. This older couple were the best friends she ever had, even if they tried her patience time and again. The gossipy woman, especially, had no boundaries and often her meddling went much too far. It had, in fact, led to Brian's murder nearly a year ago.

"I only can stay a moment. I can't be late on my first day." Meredith hung their coats on the rack by the door and kicked off her heavy snow boots.

"First day of work. You need something in your stomach. You've been looking a bit peaked lately." Honey bustled past, into the kitchen, her generous hips swaying. Atticus and Jamie followed, indeed like little chicks scuttling after their mother.

"Can I go see my bunnies and Laf?" Jamie's rabbit had birthed five babies, now living in Honey's heated barn. The five-year-old's pet rooster, Laf, also thankfully received an invitation to spend the winter there and not in their tiny closed-in trailer. With no space to house them, the animals were just one more problem to sort out come springtime.

"After a good breakfast. And I want to hear everything about your trip." Honey darted an avid peek at Meredith. "You and I will catch up more when you have time. I'm sure there's *lots* you want to tell me."

Meredith helped her son into his chair at the table and tucked a napkin into the neck of his shirt as a bib. Jamie hopped onto the chair next to her brother, her attention riveted on the kitchen where Honey lifted scones out of the oven.

"Look who's here." Crusty appeared in the dining room, slapping aftershave on his neck under a heavy mountain-man beard. His long silver hair, as usual, was slicked back into a ponytail. It was obvious to Meredith he'd slept over and didn't simply "stop by" for breakfast. His lusty affair with Honey was well-known, mostly because he exulted about his good fortune all over town. He'd been chasing the widow for more than a year. "This woman's been sulking all week."

Honey placed a heaping plate of scones on the table and then tightened the apron strings around her well-padded middle. "I never sulk."

He caught hold of Honey around her waist and, drawing her close, patted her hefty bottom. She swatted his hand away, but a smile danced at her eyes and lips.

"Um, hello." Meredith was embarrassed at their libidinous play. They were old enough to be her parents, or even grandparents, for heaven's sake. Whatever they got up to in their private time, she didn't want to hear or see any of it. Truth be told, she didn't even want to think about what a couple their age got up to in the bedroom.

"I'd like some coffee," her daughter piped up, her voice authoritative.

"Not a chance," Honey shot back as she poured steaming mugs full for the three adults. "Coffee makes you wrinkled and old."

The five-year-old studied Honey's face, her own face stern and serious. "You aren't old."

"Bless you, child. Did I tell you how much I missed you?" The woman slipped a scone onto the plate in front of the girl.

"Crusty's old, but I don't mind." Jamie turned an assessing gaze on the pony-tailed man. "He's funny."

He blustered out a reply, his tone offended. "Not so old I can't..."

"I can't thank you enough for watching the kids," Meredith broke in quickly, knowing he was likely to brag about his nighttime prowess no matter how young his audience. "Jamie goes back to school next week and Atticus can come to work with me once I settle in. "

Honey tsked, whisking off her apron, and sat at the head of the table like a roosting hen fluffing her feathers. "They're welcome to stay anytime," she said. "Their energy is what keeps me young these days."

Crusty took a seat at her side and stretched out his long legs underneath. There was no question of who was in charge in this relationship.

Meredith sipped at her coffee and munched the soft, warm scone, finding plump huckleberries inside. There was always warmth, laughter, and delicious home-cooked food to be found in her friend's cozy house. She helped Atticus take a sip of orange juice, while her daughter's eager voice told of the beach and eating monsters. The older couple gave enthusiastic cries of astonishment. The last thing she wanted was to step back into the frigid air, but her new job awaited.

Heedless of protests to stay longer and how the job could wait, she rose and tugged on her boots. "I need to make a good first impression."

Crusty gave a guffaw. "Not like the old clerk, Stacey Pringle. They threw her out on her ear when she didn't bother showing up for work at all." He helped Meredith on with her coat and patted her on the shoulder. "You'll do a much better job."

"I'll be back a few minutes after five," she promised Honey. City Hall and the few buildings serving as Hay City's town center were just five minutes down the road. "Thank you again for watching the kids."

Honey raised her eyebrows and gave Meredith a meaningful look. "We'll have tea then? After work?"

The underlying meaning was they would discuss the outcome of the trip, any private and juicy details about her relationship with Curtis, and whether she was successful in discovering the identity of her father. Her friend was always a great sounding board to her troubles, with advice and encouragement. It took someone with troubles in her own past to understand the dysfunction of Meredith's family—and Honey had known plenty of heartache. What would the older woman say about those three awful words in the letter?

"After work," she agreed. She zipped her coat up to her chin and headed into the wintery outdoors.

Chapter Nine

Hay City's former city clerk, Stacey Pringle, waved her hand in the air in a trivializing manner. "A monkey could do this job."

The woman, in her early thirties, sported a bowl-cut hair style, nails bitten to the quick, baggy jeans and pink fuzzy sweater. A paste-on beauty mark sat on one side of her lips. She bustled around the office importantly, opening and slamming file drawers as she gave Meredith an official tour of the city's compact two-room office.

"Be sure to take lots of breaks. It'll make the day go by faster. Honestly, a monkey could do this job."

She made the monkey remark twice more over the next few minutes, and once her eyes misted over. Meredith knew the woman hadn't enjoyed the job as city clerk, but was saving money to realize her life's dream. Sunny California, a place where she believed her natural talents would shine, beckoned but was farther away than ever.

Now, patting her auburn hairdo, Stacey glanced around the office, her gaze wistful. "I should have shown up to work on time," she confessed. "I shouldn't have sent my brother to work in my place. I should have tried harder. Now I'll never get to California."

"Something else will come up," Meredith said in an attempt at consolation, though there were few jobs to be found in this rural town.

She hadn't taken offense at the monkey remark, but instead felt sorry for her new found friend, who'd been fired for routinely not showing up to work. It didn't help she'd also sent her snooping brother, Jonathan, to serve as substitute city clerk when she had a hair appointment, slept in late, or just didn't want to work. The woman's cavalier attitude toward the job was something everyone in town was willing to overlook in this remote outpost, where good employees were difficult to find, but Stacey and Jonathan finally stretched their unsanctioned job-sharing too far. Meredith couldn't help but like the ditzy woman. There was something innocent and pure about her dream.

She surveyed the disorganized office. "It's nice of you to show me around, and explain what a city clerk actually does."

At first glance, it appeared a city clerk didn't do much at all. Papers were strewn across the desk, and a stack of files lay haphazardly on top of the nearby cabinet. Decades-old newspapers were stacked on the floor and a chair with a broken leg slumped in one corner. As far as she could see, a monkey would be bored stiff for lack of things to do, unless he had a penchant for tidying up. Her heart slowed to a more normal rate as she realized the job might be manageable after all.

"You're the only full-time city employee, okay? So, no offense, but you may want to get an appointment over at Sue's." Stacey gave her a critical head-to-toe examination. "She's a whiz at hair. People'll expect you to make an effort."

Meredith self-consciously lifted a hand to her neat

ponytail, her go-to style. There was already enough to do in the morning, with getting the kids up, fed and motivated to get out the door. In any case, she didn't need to spend money on a haircut when her toddler was on a growth spurt. He'd already outgrown the clothes she bought just a month ago. Yet one more expense to add to the growing list tacked on the refrigerator.

"Not many people come in, to be honest," Stacey continued. "But when they do, they expect top-notch service. The mayor may wander in, but he doesn't do any work here. His office hours are at Crusty's bar."

The woman lowered her head and dug through a file drawer. "Dog licenses, new business licenses...they're here somewhere. No one bothers licensing their dogs out here. I mean, if someone asked for one, I'd tell them not to bother. What would they be licensing them to do exactly? And last time a new business opened was years ago. I was probably, like, twelve."

Meredith glanced over at the only other desk in the office. The city shared its office with the only full-time county employee, Sheriff Curtis Barnaby. Any other work required by either the city or county was doled out piecemeal to independent contractors. She and Curtis would be alone in the office, their desks no more than fifteen feet apart. They hadn't talked about what it would be like to work so close together and she was nervous about how it might affect their relationship.

Stacey straightened, then hitched at her pants, a file in her hands. She dropped it on the desk and papers scattered. "The most important part of your job is keeping everything in order and handling the elections every four years. By the way, this is an election year."

Meredith eyed the file, worried, and listened carefully. It would be imperative she got this right. An election was too important to blunder on.

"There are thirty-five official residents of Hay City and many of those are too young to vote." Stacey rattled off the facts of the rural town. "Only twenty people are registered to vote and we're lucky to get eight people to the polls. Most show up right before the polls close. I buy a good trashy novel to read on Election Day."

Still, the responsibility of something as important as an election filled Meredith with anxiety. Eight votes were eight votes. She went over the requirements for the election over and over, certain she would forget a key detail such as setting up the city's sole voting booth. Fortunately, the election wasn't until the fall and there was plenty of time to settle into her job first.

The other woman plopped into her old chair behind the desk and leaned back far enough to make it it creak like an old crone. "Now tell me about our hunky sheriff and your trip to the beach. Right now."

She colored, and hoped her blush wasn't too obvious as she settled into Curtis' desk chair. "We had a…good time. He was overdue for a vacation, I think."

"And…" Stacey prompted, eyebrows raised. The woman wanted another type of information, details of a sizzling love affair.

"I suppose things have progressed."

Her friend's high cheery laugh filled the room. "I'd say so, running off to Florida with a man like that. How'd you work it, with the kids in the room and all? Did you put them in the bathroom, while…you know?"

"No!" The protest burst out. "We didn't…I

wouldn't….no."

A drawn-out sigh escaped Stacey's lips as she leaned back in the chair. "You are so lucky. I did my best but he wouldn't give me a second glance. He must not like city girls."

Meredith smiled to herself. As far as she knew, her friend had lived in Hay City her entire life. To the other woman, being a city girl involved high heels, long nails and heavy makeup. Whatever Stacey dreamed of as being a "city girl" was far from reality. As for her, she'd lived in cities up until a year ago and was glad to be out of them. Crime, traffic, and crowds were things of the past. She hadn't heard the blare of a car horn once since moving to Idaho. The only sounds at night were the occasional howl of a coyote and the soft collapse of snow sliding from the roof.

"I'm okay with taking it slow," she said. "After everything. I don't need another mistake right now."

Stacey nodded her head vigorously. "I understand, but don't wait too long to seal the deal. Men are hunters and eventually they need to make the catch or they seek fresh prey."

She gave a wry smile. "I'll remember that."

"You'll need to clean up all that dead skin, too. You're peeling like a snake in molting season."

She brushed at her sore nose and skin flaked away in a shower like dandruff. The office door slammed and they both jumped in their chairs. Curtis strode in, clad in blue jeans, work boots and a heavy tan jacket. He yanked a ski cap off his head and rubbed at his hair, then halted abruptly when he noticed them. Meredith scooted out of his chair, her cheeks coloring at being caught at his desk, especially this very first day. Stacey sat up straighter, shoulders thrown back, her eyes locked on the sheriff.

"Hey, stranger," Stacey greeted in an outrageously flirtatious tone.

"Hi, Stacey," he said evenly, then his tone warmed as he gazed at Meredith. "Hey there."

His eyes were affectionate and questioning. The night before leaped back to mind. His thigh unyielding against hers on the bed. The gentle kiss on her forehead. The effort he made to clear her a pathway in the snow despite his exhaustion. But then...the letter. She frowned at the memory. Lurking under everything. *I'm a murderer.* The words hid in a corner of her mind all morning and she wanted to keep them there for the moment. She wasn't yet ready to deal with what they could mean.

Stacey's eyes darted between the two of them, a smirk on her lips. "I hear you've been keeping busy."

He ignored her as he shucked off his jacket and hung it up on a hook near the door. "Domestic dispute call last night at two am." His eyes darkened and his countenance went grim. "Third time I've been out there this month. I was there until four talking to them and the wife doesn't want to file charges."

Stacey leaned forward eagerly, her mouth slightly open. "The Lees?" She swiveled to Meredith. "He's always beating on his wife. I bet it's the Lees. Or the Evers fellow. He gave me a mean stare the other day. I bet it's him. Am I right?"

Ignoring her her comments, he kept his eyes steady on Meredith. "Your road straightened out okay? I put in a call at four-thirty this morning. Had myself a little chat with Jeffrey."

Jeffrey, aka Deli-boy, earned extra money plowing roads during the winter. The teenager took every opportunity to lob insults her way. These days, he found an outlet for his animosity by clearing the road to her house in a zigzag manner. The idea of the kid wakened from his slumbers by the county sheriff satisfied her need for revenge.

"Straight as an arrow," she answered, recalling the early morning rumble of the plow. "Thank you."

Stacey glanced back and forth between the two of them, and then stood with an audible sigh and hitched at her pants. "I guess I'd better get going so you two can get to, uh, work. Oh," she added, digging into a coat pocket, "you'll want these." She tossed a pair of fingerless gloves to Meredith. "This office is freezing in winter and hot in summer."

She gave Stacey a little wave and smiled her thanks. Curtis nodded once at her in dismissal. Once the woman was out the door, he was across the room in three long strides. He drew her into his arms and held her against his warm, broad chest. His heartbeat drummed against her ear. "You okay this morning?"

She accepted his embrace gratefully, breathing in his clean, soapy scent. His chin was freshly shaven and smooth, with no trace of the scraggly beard he'd attempted to grow over the previous week. Aware someone could walk through the door, she broke away. Canoodling with the sheriff would be a bad first impression for the city's new assistant clerk. Working so close together was going to be a challenge.

"I'm fine. Trying not to think about it. But you," she said, studying his face and now seeing the weariness there, "you must not have slept at all."

He shrugged off the comment. "Goes with the job. My longest stretch was fifty-two hours. Ask Crusty sometime about when the raccoons got into his bar and tipped over half his stock. He had to close the bar for two days to clean up. I stood guard at the door to keep World War Three from breaking out. Almost called in the state police for backup." He stepped back and leaned against his desk.

A smile twitched at her lips. She was never sure all the stories she heard about life in Hay City were true. His eyes softened and crinkled at the corners, and then she was certain he was joking. At least about part of it.

"Meredith," he said. "Those letters were from a long time ago and your mother was very young. Kids say a lot of things they don't mean."

"This is too horrible. She wrote those words and then ran away from home. I need to talk to David…my father," she insisted. "I can't just let this go."

"I thought you said his sister told you he's in a commune, somewhere in California. No phone, living off the grid."

Her gaze lifted to the window and she stared unseeing through the pane, past the parking lot and across the empty two-lane highway to the snow-covered field beyond. The journey to find her father had gone in the wrong direction, east not west. This man she'd never met held the key to her complicated past.

She blinked as a memory struck her. "My mother always said my father was a terrible person. What if David was the one who killed someone? No wonder my mother never wanted me to meet him." The idea was encouraging and appalling at the same time. Her mind raced forward. "My father could be a murderer and hiding from justice in a secret enclave. This makes perfect sense. He left the scene of the crime for some far off location. Maybe he changed his name."

"Even more reason not to meet him. Your mother was protecting you from him for some reason."

She shook her head vehemently. "I can't leave it at that," she protested, her voice rising. "You don't know what this is like. You had a perfect childhood—a farmhouse in the country, a tire swing in the front yard, never worried about where you were going to sleep each night or whether you'd have enough to eat."

He studied the floor and rubbed his smooth jaw. "Maybe there's something we can do from here," he said. "If there was a murder back then, when your parents were teens—and I'm not saying there was— there would be some record of it, right?"

Of course there'd be a record of suspicious deaths. Why hadn't she considered researching murders from her mother's era? She regarded him with hopefulness. "We could explore old murders in the area. My mother was a teenager so she couldn't have traveled too far from home then. David too. If one of them did something...killed someone...it must have been someone they knew, close to home."

"Something unsolved, I would think," he mused. "A case left open, without the perpetrator apprehended, would narrow it down even more. And there would have to be some link to your mother, or father, a reason they would kill someone." He paused. "Meredith. Young girls, or boys, don't go around killing people. It's very rare."

Behind her, the door swung open. She turned to see Deli-boy slouching to the counter. His skinny body was shrouded in a long leather coat at least two sizes too big for his frame, and a Russian-style fur cap sat atop his sandy hair. He appeared like a boy playing dress-up in his father's clothes. If there was ever a suspicious-looking character…

His eyes darted to Curtis and then cut over to her. "I have my time-sheet here, for the plowing." The teen slapped a piece of paper on the counter. "Big snow year, more hours. It's cutting into my time at the store, you know."

She stared at him, unsure why he was in the office telling her this. Deli-boy glared at her when she didn't budge. "You," he said to her, his tone sharp. "You need to pay me."

"Me?" She glanced at Curtis. Stacey hadn't said anything about paying for plow service.

Deli-boy rolled his eyes and leaned over the counter so his torso lay across it and his head hung down the other side. He grabbed at something on a shelf under the counter and then straightened himself again. "Here's the city checkbook. You've written checks before, right?"

"Jeffrey," Curtis broke in, "beard's shaping up."

The teen stroked the few stray whiskers on his chin and a proud grin lit up his face. "You noticed."

"Sure. Makes you look older."

She coughed and strode forward, irritated both by Deli-boy's snarky attitude and the fact she was unprepared for this event. Under her irritation skulked a rising urgency to search for murders in Fifteen Palms, Florida. Despite wanting to get rid of the teen quickly, she couldn't resist holding his time-card up and perusing it thoroughly.

"It didn't snow on Wednesday," she pointed out, nodding at the card where he'd noted two extra hours.

He scowled. "Mrs. Jacobs complained her driveway got plowed in. I had to go back out there and clear it for her. Costs gas, you know. Made me late for work at the store, too."

She scribbled out a check for Deli-boy, signed her name with a flourish, and flipped the check back across the counter. "We'll pay this time, but the city expects good service for its tax dollars."

He snatched up the check and whirled toward the door. "My family has the only road plow in ten miles so don't get all uppity with me. Your nose is peeling something awful. Put something on it, fer crickey sake. See ya, Sheriff." The door slammed behind him.

Her hands clenched the counter for several seconds before she turned to face Curtis, expecting backup to her indignation.

"It's true," he said evenly. "If the kid quits, you'd have to find someone else to come in and plow our roads. It'd probably cost double."

She took a breath and then another. The teenager had a way of getting under her skin. Deli-boy wasn't important; her mother was. "Do you have a way to search a database for murders in Florida?" she asked, changing the subject.

He jutted his chin toward his computer and she followed him there as he settled in his chair and logged on. She scooted around behind his shoulder, peering at the screen as he tapped at the keyboard.

Her heart thudded, and she could barely concentrate on the task. If there hadn't been a murder, her mother was unbalanced. If there was a murder, her mother was a killer. Curtis believed she'd simply been an overly-emotional teenager, but what teen writes "I'm a murderer" over and over, and then flees from home? It wasn't simply the one letter; it was one of several detailing serious anxieties.

Her mother spiraled toward an event that culminated in her running away and being cut off from the family forever. There was also her father, who'd hidden himself away in a commune, virtually unreachable. If there was a murder at all, let my father be the killer, she thought, and then was appalled at herself. What kind of person hoped a parent was a murderer? With another shiver, she stared at the computer screen.

"There were about a thousand murders in Florida the year your mother left," Curtis informed her, his fingers still clicking at the keyboard. "Two of them were in Fifteen Palms. Both were listed as solved."

"What about the adjacent towns?" she asked, her eyes glued to the screen.

He tapped some more and a map of Florida appeared. He jotted down the names of four nearby towns on a scratch pad. He resumed his search of the database and scrolled down the page, identifying crimes in those cities. Nine more murders popped up; two unsolved. Her heart beat faster, and she peered more closely at the computer. But he was shaking his head.

"One appears to be linked to a drug gang," he said. "The other was a seven-year-old child who was abducted and found dead." He glanced over his shoulder at her. "Neither fits."

She bit her lip as she stared at the database. A child. Her mother would never have killed a child.

Certainly, she couldn't have been part of a drug gang. David either. Not then, at least. The clean-cut teenager built houses for the homeless and planted trees in parks. "No," she said. "What about farther away?"

"We're talking sixty miles," Curtis said, shaking his head. "I can keep searching, but she was a sheltered teenager. Where would she have gone? How would she have gotten there? The same with your father."

Relief flooded her. This ruled out murder, surely. Still…the words were there…*I'm a murderer*. What did they mean and why did her mother write them? Once again, she'd come full circle to the same answer. Now with her grandmother dead, one living person had the answers. "My father would know," she asserted. "He knows what happened. He knows why she wrote those letters—and what happened. He knows why she ran."

She chewed her lip until she tasted blood. David Givens was two states away, hidden in a commune where there was no phone and sparse mail service. Convenient for him. Bitterness filled her mouth. Just when her mother needed him most, he'd abandoned her—both of them.

There was only one thing to do: Seek him out. Confront him. Make him tell her what had happened to a teenage girl twenty-five years ago in Fifteen Palms. It was imperative now to find out why her mother wrote those three words on a page, and why she ran away. The more she discovered, the more there was hidden from her.

She backed away from the desk in a daze and went to stand before the window. An occasional fleck of snow drifted down, something locals called frozen air and not really snow at all. The landscape was stark, colored in shades of white and gray. In the distance, above the high peaks of the mountains, the sky was charcoal. A fresh storm was on the move.

"You were going to write a letter to him," Curtis prompted. "To your father."

She needed her job. No one just picked up and took a vacation their first week at work. In any case, there was no money in her bank account to travel to California. Jamie's holiday vacation would be over in a few days and school would be back in session. As much as it drove her crazy, she'd have to wait a little longer to find her father. At least now she'd discovered his name and where he was. She swallowed thickly.

"I'll write the letter," she conceded, though she fretted David Givens would ignore it or throw it away, just as he apparently did with letters from his sister. "It's all I can do for now."

****

There wasn't much more damage a storm could do to her decaying house. Still, she felt some responsibility toward the place. It figured, the only house she ever owned, and it was falling down. The ceiling literally caved in right before Christmas, nearly collapsing upon her sleeping daughter. Since then, rivulets of water found their way into every nook and cranny, soaking the walls into mush and forming icicles from her kitchen ceiling.

"Watch your brother," she ordered Jamie that evening, as she grabbed a flashlight and left the trailer.

The house was no more than thirty yards away, but she started shivering two steps from the door of the trailer. To travel to her house, she'd put on an extra sweater, her coat, hat and gloves, and still her breath was taken away. It was hard getting used to how cold the winter was here, biting past skin and bone to the very marrow.

The front door was unlocked. Wouldn't it be great if someone simply jacked the place up and hauled it away, complete with their secondhand furnishings, worn-out clothing and chipped dishes? There is something frigid about an empty house and the still air inside. She'd left the heat on to about forty-five degrees after Honey explained her pipes would burst if the heat was turned off altogether. As it was, the cabinets stuck as she opened them and two wicked icicle shards loomed over the kitchen stove, ready to impale any meal dared cooked below. A thin layer of ice crusted in the toilet bowl and, was she imagining it, or were the wooden boards slightly spongy under her feet? A slow drip-drip-drip sounded somewhere in the house, water seeping in from one of a dozen leaks she'd already identified. The low heat had accomplished nothing but to allow repeated melting and freezing of incoming water, and prolong an impending catastrophe.

Jamie's bedroom door had been kept closed. The room was the site of the first collapse. Ground zero for the final ruin of her home. A chill seeped under the door and when she opened it, her heart sank. The tarp above had caved in under the weight of fresh snow and, once more, there was a view to the gray and indifferent winter sky. The floor was a mix of soppy carpet and ice. Hopeless.

She hadn't wanted to move here from their Oakland apartment last spring. Brian surprised her one morning, with a truck and two men who dragged their meager worldly belongings downstairs. In one day, everything familiar and nearly everyone she knew had been left behind. By midnight, they were in Hay City, Idaho, and her life veered down an alien course. The abasement she'd put up with for years erupted into overt abuse, secrets uncovered, and a murdered husband. Soon after unfolded a real job, friends, a place where she belonged. What started as disaster turned out to be good fortune.

She'd worked hard to make the house habitable for her children—even nice—by scrubbing away years of grime and scraping black mold from the bathroom walls. New green eyelet curtains framed the front room window, and the old stained carpet ripped out and the wood floor polished. Over the summer, she dug a vegetable garden at the side of the house, and Curtis hung a swing from the large tree out back. Once the rains started, however, the tide turned. The mold emerged once more, and the burn marks on the wood floor darkened under the polish, reminding her of the home's history of violence. Then, the leaks began. Nothing she did slowed the damage.

Meredith leaned back against one wall and closed her eyes. She could almost imagine she could hear the sound of rushing water moving through her house, inside the walls and under the floor. Waves and whitecaps were building toward the day when they'd overtake the solid structure and wash it away in a cataclysmic spring flood.

The past was part of her, but she needed to figure out a way to find her future. So many promising things in her life and she clung to this house as though it were a life raft. A leaking life raft with the shore in sight. She needed to let go and swim.

Chapter Ten

Jamie wriggled under the hairbrush. "Mom!" she protested. "You're hurting me."

Meredith untangled the brush from the snarl of curls. Her five-year-old's head was as dark and wild as her personality, with shake-like ringlets shooting in all directions like an angry Medusa. Smoothing her unruly hair into any semblance of normality was more unlikely with each passing day. After she let loose, the girl darted to the trailer door and snatched up her backpack.

"Hold on," she called, noting her daughter's hand on the door handle. "I have to get Atticus ready."

Jamie huffed impatiently and slouched against the door. "You two are so slow."

"Turtles," she agreed, as she tugged high-water pants and then a sweater on her toddler. In a week, Atticus had shot up at least an inch. Maybe more, she thought. Brian had been a shade over six feet and her son was sure to match his height someday. Both kids, in fact, underwent sudden growth spurts where, practically overnight, wrists stretched beyond sleeves and toes rubbed in their shoes.

Her five-year-old giggled, irritation gone in a flash. "Slower than turtles."

"Ice cream melting in January," Meredith said, playing along as she strapped on Atticus' shoes, zipped up their coats, and then hefted her son onto one hip with a grunt. His solid little body, weighed down by winter gear, was getting too heavy to lift. Her babies weren't babies anymore. She exhaled a wistful sigh.

"Slower!" Jamie exclaimed.

"Waiting another year for Christmas." She grabbed her bag and glanced around the messy trailer. Empty cereal bowls remained on the dining table and toys were strewn across the floor. There just wasn't enough time to be a working mom and a housekeeper.

She threw open the door to the blinding white of their snowy yard and stepped down into the three inches of new snow that had arrived overnight. A routine day at work was ahead, which meant there would be plenty of time to draft a letter to her father.

****

"*Dear Mr. Givens*," she started, and then crossed out the words, Mr. Givens.

"*Dear Father*," came next, but she quickly scratched out the too-familiar word and crumpled the paper. She grabbed a fresh sheet of paper and stared at the blank page. He was nothing to her. Just a name, a guy her mother knew in high school. A long ago former boyfriend who got a girl pregnant and then sauntered on into a new life without a backward glance.

"*You don't know me*," she wrote in careful, legible script, "*but I'm your daughter. Yours and Laura's.*"

Her hand paused over those words, wondering what to write next. You couldn't just send a letter about murder to a complete stranger. Neither could introduce yourself as someone's daughter through the mail. This was silly.

She rose from her desk and paced the empty office. The only unsolved murders from the area surrounding

Fifteen Palms back in the day involved a child and a member of a drug gang. Neither seemed related to her mother and this consoled Meredith. Still, something had happened that year. Just an overly-emotional teenager, Curtis had suggested. She strode back to the desk and crumpled the note, then grabbed a fresh sheet of paper.

"Dear David. I'm a relative of Laura Brittan's and have some important information to share with you. Could you please contact me as soon as possible? My address and phone number are below. Regards, Meredith Lowe."

The note wasn't great but it would have to do for now. Contact would have been made, when the letter finally found him. If he didn't reply, at least she'd tried. Next vacation, she vowed, she'd go to California and hunt down the elusive man. She folded the paper, tucked it in an addressed envelope. Patrick, the mailman, wouldn't show up until late afternoon and there was plenty of time to decide whether to send it, rewrite it once more, or try anew another day. She pasted a stamp in the corner and laid the envelope in the middle of her desk.

With that, she turned her attention to organizing messy files and cleaning up the dusty stack of newspapers leaning against one wall. The work wasn't difficult and staying in motion kept her mind busy. Although her gaze lifted again and again to the office door, Curtis didn't appear. She knew sometimes he started his day out in the field, either on patrol or responding to a call for assistance. Eventually he would check in, but mostly he was a one-man show and only called when something unusual occurred. With no business calls to interrupt her filing duties, the morning drifted by, quiet and still. She realized she was more than qualified to handle an assistant city clerk's duties, certainly in a town as small as Hay City where there was little business to transact.

When lunchtime approached, she decided to stretch her legs and get some fresh air. Crusty owed her a last paycheck and bills were due at home. The "Not a Bar" hardware store he owned, and where she'd worked part-time through the summer and fall, was a quarter mile down the road. Her final paycheck would be an unimpressive four digits long, including the decimal place in the middle. A paltry sum, but the money would fill her car's gas tank and pay the utilities for the small trailer. Every little bit helped.

She locked the door to the office and taped a note near the doorknob which said: Back after lunch. It only occurred to her a couple minutes later no one would have any idea how long "after lunch" would be. Her break could be an hour, it could be three. There was no one around to supervise her. But she craved stability and self-worth. She would supervise herself and not go down the road Stacey Pringle had taken, a path ending in dismissal.

As her boots stomped through the fresh layer of snow, she pondered her mother's blithe, disinterested attitude toward money. As a child, she believed anyone with the good fortune to live in a house was rich.

"Those people are the poorest people of all," her mother would respond. "They owe their lives to a bank. Hundreds of thousands of dollars of debt. They're stuck paying the money back, month after month, for a large chunk of their lives. They're the opposite of wealthy. We own everything we have. So, who's rich?"

"But we pay, too, Mama," Meredith protested. "For our motel rooms."

Her mother's eyes went steely and her jaw tightened. "No one owns us. We're free. We go where we want."

The bohemian lifestyle worked for her mother, but Meredith wanted something different for Jamie and Atticus. For the moment, her old falling-down house was paid off and Curtis refused to take payment for the loan of his trailer over the winter. In the spring, she would figure out how to repair her moldering house or have it torn down as he advised, and start over. For now, she was house rich but cash poor. They had enough to survive and her kids were safe and healthy.

These thoughts encouraged her as she approached the hardware store, located in an old log building shared with the Hay City bar. Neither place had an official name. Crusty merely posted a small sign atop the bar door which read "Not the Hardware Store". Similarly, above the hardware store door another sign read, "Not the Bar".

There was something comforting about being back in the hardware store, with its musty odor of car tires, paint, birdseed, and cardboard boxes. At the front of the store sat a large wooden crate, which she knew contained a jetted bathtub, and suspected was stolen from a shipment somewhere. The crate arrived along with a collection of tattered boxes several weeks earlier, and she'd discovered they were filled with construction materials for her new house.

"No payment necessary," Crusty had told her. He would say nothing more than someone owed him a favor, and the bathtub and most other items were free.

There were already enough battles in her life to fight and she decided not to think too much about where or how the boxes had been 'acquired.'

She peeked through the adjoining door in the hardware store, which led into the bar, and found Crusty alone in the room, on a step stool busy at work restocking the top shelves with full bottles.

"Someone was in here asking about you, late yesterday afternoon," he greeted her, glancing at her in the reflection of the large mirror behind the bar. His gray-blue eyes matched the long-sleeved shirt he wore, rolled up to the elbows. As usual, his gray hair was drawn back into a long tidy ponytail. Half mountain man and half surfer dude.

She surveyed the dark bar room as she waited for him to fill her in on details. Hay City was home to a few dozen residents and she'd met about half of them at one time or another. Most, she knew by sight. There was a handful of recluses who rarely emerged from their ranches or hideaways in the hills. It was easy to disappear in a place as remote in the world as this, and some people did. She couldn't think of anyone who would be seeking her out in the local bar. Everyone was aware of where she lived and worked.

"Who was it?" she finally asked when he didn't volunteer a name.

"Hell if I know. Told the guy I never heard of you. He didn't like that."

Her mouth dropped open. "Why would you say you didn't know me? Why didn't you send him to the city office? You know I'm right down the road. All day, eight to five."

His eyebrows lowered as he growled, "Didn't like

the way he asked."

Getting details from her former boss was like pulling teeth. He was going to make her drag the information out of him, piece by piece. "Crusty, what was the problem with him?"

He stepped off the stool with a snort and faced her. "Ugly, for one thing. Disrespectful to the bar, for another. Everyone knows you need an invitation to sit right there in the middle. New people at the end. Those're the rules. Over time, you work your way to the middle."

She gritted her teeth. Her former boss would tell a story in his own sweet time. Her mind clicked through the possibilities of who could be searching for her at the Hay City bar, and drew a blank. She didn't know anyone outside of Hay City, and there was no reason anyone would search her out. When she added in the fact Crusty didn't like the man, she grew nervous.

"Why would someone be trying to find me?" she asked, puzzled. "Pretty much everyone I know lives right here."

"Outsider," Crusty confirmed with a nod. "No one told him anything."

"He could have been here about Brian," she protested. Everyone in the state seemed to know about her murdered husband, although half the time they got the details wrong. Many people still believed she killed him. "Something about him being dead."

"Exactly," he shot back. "Murder's a bad business. You don't need someone bothering you about him anymore. You've moved on."

While his brisk dismissal of her dead husband might have seemed rude to someone else, she understood he meant well. She heaved a sigh, realizing there was no point in arguing. "All right already. I don't why you mentioned anything to me in the first place."

He rummaged under the counter, brought up her paycheck and slapped it on the counter between them. "He had two beers, the imported kind, and said you stole something from his family."

Her eyes grew wide and her mouth dropped open again. "I've never stolen anything," she said, which wasn't entirely true. There'd been a candy bar from a store when she was eight, and a very close call with a dine-and-dash situation with her mother when she was eleven. That last situation cured her of ever wanting to steal anything again. "He mentioned me by name?"

"Meredith Lowe," he confirmed with a nod. "Said your name right out loud, clear as could be. Had Florida plates on his car."

A chill went through her at the mention of Florida. "Someone drove all the way out here, from Florida, because they thought I stole something?"

Her mind tracked back through the people she met on her trip there, and the stores she visited. There were cheap restaurants and motels, with nothing of value to steal even if she were so inclined. The only place she visited was her aunt's house, filled with beautiful objects. Did the woman really believe she stole something, and then sent someone all the way across the country to retrieve it? No wonder people found dealing with relatives so stressful.

"I don't need to hide from anyone," she said firmly. "If someone has something to say to me, let them say it." Giving Crusty a steely glance, she picked up her check and tucked it in her pocket.

****

She peered under the office bookshelf, on her hands and knees. Two folders were in sight, laying in the dust in the shallow space underneath. There was no telling how long they'd been there or what they contained, and the folders lay just beyond her fingertips. She stretched her arm just a little farther and wiggled her fingers, but her shoulder stopped her reach. A cold draft alerted her the door had opened and then closed, and she realized whoever entered had a comprehensive view of her raised backside.

"You're Meredith Lowe?"

She scrambled to her feet, her arm and hand full of what must have been the accumulation of decades-old dust. Crusty had lied. The stranger wasn't anything close to ugly. He was as close to beautiful as a man well past his best years can be—slender, tanned and toned, his skin smooth and shiny, like one who had weekly facial treatments. The effect was ruined by his lush curly hair dyed an unnatural jet black, with not a single strand of gray, framing a face clearly pushing sixty. There was something oddly familiar about him. His eyes raked over her, taking in every detail of her features and shape in one uncomfortable moment.

"You're Leila Brittan's granddaughter? You're a tough lady to find, way out here in nowhere's land. I've never seen so much snow in my life." He took a deep breath, then played a little drum roll on the counter with his fingers. "Let me introduce myself. I'm Raymond, your long-lost cousin."

He gave a little laugh and stretched out a slender-fingered hand over the counter. She stared at him and strode forward automatically to shake his hand. He held the grip a moment too long and she tugged, almost yanking her hand to get it loose. They both wiped their hands on their pant legs after noting the grime she'd transferred over in the handshake.

She eyed him. "My cousin?" The man was much too old to be a cousin. "I don't have any cousins."

"We're both in Leila's thorny family tree," he said in an abrupt tone, not explaining further. "I like to think of myself as one of the roses, though. I traveled all the way out here—my, what a long drive—to pick up the ring."

She froze and kept her tone flat, hoping her expression gave nothing away. "Ring?"

He couldn't possibly be referring to her mother's ring, the gaudy golden piece of jewelry hidden away in a box for years. Absolutely no one in Florida, not even the lawyer, was aware of the ring. Her mind flew back to her trip and whether she'd mentioned the ring to anyone there. The jeweler in the store, of course, but the man had no idea who she was. Anyway, the ring was willed to her. It belonged to her and not some…long-lost cousin. Unless he was talking about some other piece of jewelry entirely. Anyway, this guy could be anyone, some stranger pretending to be kin.

He grinned, displaying professionally bleached teeth far too white and far too large, tipping their appeal from attractive to creepy. Crusty had been right; family or not, this was a man to avoid. "There was a mistake, I believe. The item in question was meant for me."

Meredith shook her head and took a step back from the counter. "You've been misled by someone. Leila didn't leave me anything. I never met her and she disowned my mother a long time ago."

It was very unnerving that he knew she'd been in Fifteen Palms and then traced her back to Hay City. He smiled obligingly as if they were in on a joke together. "It's silly, I know, but there's some sentimental value attached. You know how these things go. Not about the value—just about the memory. You see, I actually *knew* your grandmother and she promised it would come to me someday."

He leaned forward, partially across the counter, and she edged backward, repelled by his false smile and overly doctored appearance. His spicy overdone cologne sent her back an additional step.

Giving this supposed 'cousin' the ring would solve a dilemma. It didn't fit her finger and was too gaudy to wear. She was also certain the ring never belonged to her mother at all. Why it ended up in the box left to her was a mystery. Still, the man was unpleasant and bizarre, showing up out of the blue and demanding something given to her. And although there was some strange familiarity about his features, he offered no proof he was a relative at all. There was no way she would hand over a piece of jewelry to a stranger just because he asked for it.

She decided to call his bluff. "Really, I wasn't given anything aside from some old pictures of my mother. Did you know her? Laura, I mean?"

His gaze traveled around the room, but she was certain there was a flicker of recognition at her mother's name. His face was a studied blankness and then his eyes widened in an innocent way. "Laura. No, we never met, unfortunately."

Meredith waited, hoping he would say more. He scrutinized the room, his gaze traversing the desks, the file cabinet, and the bookshelf, as though the ring he sought would be sitting on display in the city office.

"My grandmother probably left the ring you're seeking to the hospital, to sell, along with her house and everything else, for the new wing she endowed."

He shrank back and his tone was harsh. "She wouldn't have. We would have heard."

A tingling went through her. The Fifteen Palms jeweler offered to pay four hundred dollars for the ring. It was a lot of money to her, but not for the world at large. Not enough someone would drive across the country; not enough that anyone would notice it missing. "I don't understand. You said it's not worth much. I'm sure no one would mention it at all."

He raised his smooth, hairless chin in a haughty manner, and his gaze continued to shift about the room. "People would talk about the ring because *everyone* knows Leila meant it for me. She talked about it every time we spoke. It was a thing between us, you know. A family *thing*."

Her eyes narrowed then. This man was, without a doubt, a phony in both words and appearance. "I don't understand exactly how you're related. You're a cousin? My mother didn't have any siblings." Again, she was cut adrift from family matters, not even knowing who her relatives were. There could be a dozen cousins out there in the world, or none at all. Her mind raced, trying to figure out what branch of the family tree he could be from.

A buzzing captured his attention and he slid a phone from his jacket pocket and studied the screen before shaking his head and returning the phone unanswered. "I'm sure I show up in those family pictures you mention, the ones your mother left you. Leila was always hosting family get-togethers."

This rang false as well. The little she understood about her grandmother indicated the woman wouldn't host anything resembling annual family gatherings. In her imaginings, her grandmother was an evil witch, avoided by everyone, near and far. Still, if there had been one or two reunions, there would be stories to relate. She was torn between wanting to hear more regarding the relatives she never had a chance to meet, and wanting him to leave. There was something about this man she couldn't put her finger on…something repellent, yet familiar.

"You weren't in any of the pictures I have," she said bluntly. She was being rude, but couldn't help it. The man annoyed her in some instinctive way.

"Too bad. It would have been nice to revisit myself as a younger man." His fingers stroked through his hair with a flourish. He grinned and oversized white teeth flashed in his orange-tan face. "What else were you left, in the will?"

None of your business, she wanted to say. "Just mementos. You should have called. I would have saved you a very long trip."

This concept appeared to stump him, because his mouth opened once and then closed with a snap before he unearthed a response. "I wanted to meet Leila's one and only grandchild, but you scooted out of town before I had a chance. Anyway, I have friends in Seattle and this is more or less on the way. Detouring here gave me a chance to kill a few birds with one stone, so to speak."

"Sorry. I mean, you really should have called. I never met my grandmother and she didn't leave me anything of value." She stared straight at him, as unpleasant as that was, daring him to challenge her more. Her nose twitched against the powerful odor of his cologne.

His eyes hardened. "I do remember Laura," he said suddenly. "Seeing you helps me recollect those days. She had an independent way about her. She'd square her shoulders and stare you down when she set her mind to something. Exactly like you."

Her breath went shallow and she waited for more.

"Didn't she have long blonde hair though?" he continued. "Not like you at all."

His gaze raked over her again in an assessing manner and then he spun away and strode to the exit. "Strange," he said as he opened the door and an icy gust blew in. "Your bartender down the road said he'd never heard of you. I thought everyone knew everybody in these small towns."

The door closed behind him and her shoulders sagged in relief. Raymond and Sarah were the only relatives she ever met, and a little of each went a long way. Maybe being rude was an inherited trait. He hadn't asked anything about her or her life, and nothing about her mother. All he wanted was to collect a piece of Leila's estate. Perhaps having family was over-rated.

From the office window, she saw his small sporty sedan slip and slide out of the parking lot and turn north. That direction would lead him on a long, winding route to Seattle, through steep and dangerous avalanche territory. The quickest way would have been to go south to Boise where a wide freeway would carry him on a more direct path into Oregon and along the famed Columbia River and then across to Washington.

Her own experience taught her to expect the unexpected on narrow snowy roads—take your mind off driving for a few seconds and you could end up staring down a steep ravine.

The rest of the afternoon, the strange visit lingered in her mind as she tried to puzzle out the relationship and how he could be a cousin. Nothing made sense, except...perhaps her grandfather had a previous marriage. Even that didn't add up, because her grandmother hadn't been the type of woman to accept step-children or promise step-grandchildren anything. There was her second marriage, of course, but her aunt said he was much younger—too young to have a child as old as Raymond. Still, something was familiar in him she couldn't put her finger on.

****

Her full-time job left her just a couple hours with her kids before bedtime. Any concerns about Raymond's stopover receded as she focused on making dinner and chatting with Jamie and Atticus. Showers for both children in the trailer's narrow bathroom were always an adventure and filled with thrilled shrieks as the water hit their heads. Afterward, she mopped up the water that sprayed the floor, the mirror, the toilet, and halfway up the walls. At least the bathroom got a thorough cleaning at the same time. They'd mostly gotten used to the lack of a bathtub, just as they had adjusted to all the other recent changes in their lives. Games, story time, then bed. That was all the time there was on weekdays.

As she tucked her daughter in bed, Jamie's dark curls spiraled on the pillow behind her. It struck her then. Raymond and Jamie. They had the same hair, the same wide cheekbones, and the same flare at the end of their nostrils. The resemblance tugged at her heart in an unexpected way. She and her children had kin and connections out in the world, even if someone as distasteful as Raymond was that family member. You didn't get to choose your relatives and sometimes they weren't nice people. Sometimes they abandoned you, sometimes they lied. The physical link to others, though, fostered a feeling of belonging, which was something she'd always craved.

Her five-year-old closed her eyes; soon her chest rose up and down in steady, rhythmic movements. Meredith wished she had asked Raymond more questions about their kinship. He must have been related to her grandmother's first husband, after all, passing along the dark-haired, dark-eyed genes. Those genes skipped over her fair-haired mother and cropped up a generation or two later. This wasn't unusual. Even some siblings looked worlds apart, each grabbing a unique set of genes from the bloodline. One tall, one short. One fair, one dark.

Okay, she conceded. The man is a relative. But Raymond didn't detour to Hay City to establish a familial relationship. The man wanted to seize a piece of her grandmother's estate and, thwarted, now headed to Seattle. She'd likely not run into him again.

Relative or not, there was something fishy about the guy. And whatever he said, he'd probably never met her mother.

Chapter Eleven

Wiry, energetic Patrick McCarty, the county postman, thudded the day's packet of mail on the office counter. The stack would consist mostly of junk mail, at least one letter of complaint about city roads—most of which were potholed—and, if Meredith was lucky, a bill to pay. A 'real' bill meant something interesting to do—beyond filing and sweeping. Any complaints would be copied and distributed to the city council who, as a rule, ignored them. The quiet town of Hay City conducted little business and seldom changed.

"Another love note from Captain Harry," Patrick announced, tossing a blue envelope on top of the pile.

She rose to greet him, thankful for someone to talk to. Curtis started his morning in the town of Misery, visiting a store owner whose windows were soaped overnight, so he wouldn't be back until lunchtime. She smiled at Patrick's small joke about the Captain, a crotchety old man who voiced opinions, all of which were strident, and about everything. "I wonder what he's complaining about this time."

Laced with profanities, Captain Harry's tirades were well-known in the community. His letters rambled about everything from Chinese tariffs to claims that pollution drifting from Los Angeles to Hay City affected his lungs. He lived in his own mountain compound, surrounded by barbed wire, where he'd dug his own pond. In the summer, he could be found cruising about the pond each day in a home-built canoe, thus the tongue-in-cheek nickname, "Captain."

"Probably another one about seceding from the U.S. of A. He gave me an earful about taxes and federal lands and privatizing the postal service."

She eyed the thick blue envelope, envisioned the rant it might contain and grinned. "Great. Can't wait to read it."

The letter to her father sat on her desk and she glanced back once in indecision. Was the wording right? Should she hand it over to the U.S. mail?

He leaned against the counter as she ducked her head and thumbed through the rest of the mail. "You have a pretty stone there. May I see it?" Patrick gestured toward her hand and leaned forward.

She extended her hand and the mailman bent over the ring, holding her fingers lightly.

Upon rising that morning, prompted by Raymond's interest, she'd taken a perverse pleasure in wearing her mother's gaudy ring, aware if her cousin showed up again she'd need to slip it off and pocket it. Promised to her cousin or not, and most likely *not*, her grandmother decided to pass the ring down to her. Finders, keepers. She was both flattered and surprised the mailman noticed the ring, but it was probably because it was a bit garish. At almost two carats, the stone was a size that screamed "look at me."

"Very nice. Very, *very* nice," he muttered, and then eyed her with an assessing gaze. "Where'd you come across this?"

"It was my mother's. Not quite my style though."

He held on to her hand, and turned an intense eye

to the ring. "Unusual," he murmured, then released her hand. "I know a thing or two about stones. I used to have a jewelry store, before I moved out here."

Surprised, she raised both brows. "You gave up a jewelry business to come here?" She wanted to add, "and to become a mere mailman," but there was no way to say that without sounding discourteous.

His lips tightened into a thin line. "Family fight," he said, the words coming out tense and short. "My brothers and sister owned a part share and we disagreed on a few things. I sold my share to them and got out. I'll never go back."

She nodded as if she understood, but the inner workings of families were a complete mystery. She grew up without siblings or cousins or uncles and aunts. There'd been no relatives around to launch a feud. What a luxury it would be to have people who knew you from the beginning, who were familiar with your story and loved you through thick and thin. Or to fall out with, as in the case with Patrick.

"Family," she added in sympathy, not knowing what else to say.

"You know what kind of stone you've got there?" he asked, returning to her ring.

She shrugged and rolled the ring around her finger. "A jeweler told me maybe something called spinel. I hoped it was tanzanite, my mother's favorite gemstone, but I guess not."

Patrick gestured at the ring. "Spinel, huh? May I?"

She slipped it off her finger and at once felt relief. The large stone and setting weighed too heavy on her hand and irritated the skin between her fingers. By the end of the day, she wouldn't be surprised if it left a green mark around her finger, a sign of cheap metals.

He rubbed the stone and turned the ring in several directions, studying it from all angles. "Maybe spinel," the jeweler turned postman muttered. "Interesting...interesting." He peered at her with a frown. "This was your mother's, you say?"

There was doubt in his tone and she recognized its meaning. Where would someone like *her* get an "interesting" piece of jewelry? She held out her hand for the ring.

"I could get this identified for you," he said, clutching the ring and leaving her hand stranded in mid-air. "Get a value on it."

She shook her head and let her empty hand settle on the counter. "I don't really care. The value doesn't matter to me."

"Your daughter might want to know when she grows up, if this is something you'll pass down someday. Unless," his eyebrows raised on the next words, "you decide to sell."

The word "sell" hung in the air. She hesitated and Patrick hastily went on. "I can make you an offer."

She gave a short laugh, but couldn't help being curious. "You don't even know what it is, and you're willing to buy it?"

"I still have friends in the business who might be interested. There's always a market for unusual stones, especially one as nice as this. I know one guy with a pretty exclusive clientele. He could reset this, modernize the style, and charge quite a premium."

She rubbed her finger where the ring had been. It was an ugly, clunky piece. Despite this, two people had offered to buy it in short order. Not just this, but

Raymond drove all the way from Florida to claim ownership. There was something special about the ring she didn't appreciate. Perhaps the stone, whatever it was, should go to someone who would enjoy wearing it. Not to her new-found cousin, though. She'd taken an instant dislike to the man, even if he was a long-lost family connection. In contrast, her mother wanted her to have the ring. *There's not much I have left of her.* Indecision nibbled at her mind.

Patrick let out a long breath. "I can see you might be interested. What if I gave you a thousand dollars? If it values at less, you keep the money. If it values at more than double the price, we do a seventy-thirty split of anything over a thousand dollars. I get the seventy percent," he clarified before she could say a word. "For doing the work."

She choked back a gasp. A thousand dollars was a huge amount of money, far more than the Florida jeweler offered. A possibility occurred to her. A thousand dollars would get her to California and back. She would lose an ugly ring, and gain a father. Her children would have a grandfather. A relative to feud with, and answers to long-held secrets surrounding her mother. A resolute smile crept to her lips. She would sell the clunky ring and, with the money, go to California and confront David Givens. Her plan was falling into place.

"You can trust me to negotiate the best price," he added, when she didn't respond. "Maybe you can get another hundred dollars. Or more."

There were spring clothes for her kids to buy, a new windshield to replace the cracked one on her car, and a dozen other things they needed. The ring was unlikely to ever be in style again, if it ever was in the first place. Better to put the piece to use than to lock it away for another twenty years in a box.

She lifted her chin and straightened her shoulders. "Make it an even eleven hundred dollars now and I'll do it. And I'll do your seventy-thirty split on the rest."

They shook on it. He reluctantly dropped the ring in her hand and she slipped it back onto her finger, worried she made the wrong decision.

"Give me a couple of days to get the cash," he said. "But we have a deal."

****

Curtis wrapped a sheet around his taut, bare waist and threw one end over his shoulder like a toga. She leaned against the headboard in his one-bedroom house and ran fingers through her mussed hair. With a choice between spending the lunch hour at her desk or between the sheets with this handsome sheriff, there was no competition. Jamie was back in school and Honey had Atticus during the day. A quick lunchtime rendezvous was one of the few times they could arrange to be alone. Working in such close proximity had its benefits.

"I don't like you going on this trip by yourself," he objected, after hearing about her scheme to sell her mother's ring and use the money to find her father. "What kind of person is he? Remember what your mother said."

"Bodega Bay is fifteen hours away. I can get there in a day, talk to him, and get back quick. It'll be a long weekend, no more."

The clock at his bedside indicated just minutes remained to dress, wrangle her hair into order, and get back to the office. Oh, to stay in bed with Curtis all afternoon, though. She eyed his muscular bare legs and broad chest, peppered with soft auburn hair. Desire twisted low in her abdomen, followed by dejection. This was a man who'd never play hooky even if she suggested it.

"I wish I could go with you this time." A troubled frown flickered on his face. "The county doesn't provide much of a backup for me. The coroner and I are each other's backups, and neither one of us has much experience in the other's job. One vacation a winter is about all we get."

He didn't need to add he was the youngest sheriff ever elected in the state, and strove to live up to his grandfather's reputation as dedicated, fair, and someone to rely upon. Being sheriff was his dream job and he wore his silver badge with pride. The people of High County trusted their sheriff to never let them down when they called, no matter if the call was about a lost heifer or a dispute with a neighbor. They didn't elect someone who'd go running off coast-to-coast the minute his girlfriend crooked a finger.

"I'll be fine," she assured him. "My father lives on a commune. There'll be other people around."

He wrinkled his nose. "What kind of people?"

"I'll be fine," she repeated, getting annoyed. "I've dealt with difficult people all my life."

Of course, she hadn't dealt with them well. Her own husband belittled her, berated her, even raped her. Her husband was so "difficult" that she fantasized ways to murder him. She hated recalling those days, especially when she was with Curtis. She scooted out of bed and tugged on her jeans. She wasn't that timid, brainless person anymore. In the past year, she'd toughened up and grown resilient. No one would ever mistreat her again.

Curtis pulled her into his arms as she snapped on her bra. "You can do anything," he said. "But you don't have to do it alone. Wait until spring break. Jamie will be out of school and I can take more time off then. And, Meredith, maybe you and I…"

She interrupted, laser-focused on her own plans. "I've been waiting my entire life and I can't wait anymore. Honey will watch the kids and if they won't give me a day off at work, well, I'll just quit." She wriggled out of his arms and slid into on a long-sleeved shirt, followed by a chunky cable sweater. "You don't understand how important this is to me."

Hurt showed in his eyes. "I just think you could wait a couple of months, and not rush into anything. I'd like to be there for you. I don't like the idea of you driving so far by yourself."

"Stop," she interrupted as she finished lacing up her boots and stood at the end of the bed to face him. "I'm going. This is important to me, and someday to my kids, too. We need to know where we came from, who our family is. I need to know what happened to my mother. Once I know…"

What then? What if her mother had killed someone, what if her father was some type of criminal, what if there was something in the past so terrible she couldn't even fathom? She shook her head. Not knowing was worse. "Once I know, I'll be able to put the past into perspective. As soon as I get the money, I'm going."

He studied her and then heaved a sigh. "Okay then. Tell me what you need and I'll help however I can."

Tears sprung to her eyes. He'd already taken his vacation to drive her to Fifteen Palms, tended to her children while they were there, loaned her the trailer she lived in, and planned to build her a house. Would any other man do half as much? The support meant everything to her. With Curtis behind her, she'd be brave enough to tackle anything. David Givens, watch out, she thought. I'm coming to find you.

She stepped back into his arms where his warmth enveloped her. "This works fine."

Chapter Twelve

Now that she'd made the decision to go to California, there were a few details to iron out. Nothing but the biggies, money and time. The money would be solved as soon as Patrick made good on his offer to buy her ring. She hoped he showed up with the cash quickly though she worried he may have raised her hopes for nothing. Just in case, she tucked the ring in her pocket.

It was hard to imagine, but as events of the past weeks swirled in her mind, life went on. She went to work, made dinner, washed clothes—and somewhere out there beyond the western mountains, her father breathed and held the secret to her mother's life, banishment and possibly a murder. There had to be a way to get there.

Her first couple days on the job, Stacey stopped in each day to check on her, offer more advice and chat. The former city clerk seemed chagrined to see the stack of old newspapers had disappeared and files straightened and organized, as though the improvement was a reflection on her old work habits.

"I'm here more now than when I had the job." Stacey gave a wry smile as she leaned on the front counter. "The place is more fun with you around to talk to. I'll have to find another job soon, though. Dad's driving me crazy at home. If I don't get out of Hay City soon, I just know I'll end up working at the mine for the next thirty years like he did."

They had something in common. For both of them, California was the goal, though for vastly different reasons. To Stacey, the golden state represented the beginning of something. For Meredith, the end.

"As long as you don't give up, you'll get there," she encouraged her friend.

By week's end, the office cleaned and organized, the floors swept and mopped, and no business to conduct, she started reading the files. One file, two inches thick, held all the business licenses taken out in the city for the past eighty years. Another smaller file contained marriage licenses and two more held a variety of forms. She scanned through a book on ancient Idaho laws and laughed as she learned it was against the law to live in a doghouse, sell a rotten potato, or frown in public.

She'd just started sweeping the floor again, when Patrick arrived, mailbag slung over one shoulder. "Did you remember the ring today?" he called out before she even had a chance to greet him. "I wanted to catch you before the weekend."

Deep in the pocket of her jeans, she twisted the ring around her finger with her thumb, worried she was making a mistake. The items in the box were saved all these years for her and now she was cashing out. Silly, she told herself. The jewelry's mine to do with whatever I decide, she reminded herself. There's no one who would judge me—and even if there were, this is none of their business.

Patrick dug in a pocket and laid a handful of bills between them. One after another, he counted out eleven crisp one-hundred dollar bills. "No reason we can't make this a cash deal."

Her throat tight, she slipped the ring off her finger. She clutched it for a moment, worried she was making the wrong decision. *Sorry, Mom*, she whispered to herself before dropping the ring in the mailman's waiting hand. A sense of liberation struck her immediately. Her life going forward would be one of self-determination and not driven by what others wished for her.

He wrapped the ring carefully in a velvet cloth and set it in a jeweler's box before tucking it away in his coat's deep pockets. "I'll overnight it to my connection this afternoon. I called him and he's eager to see it."

Meredith scooped up the cash, each bill smooth and cold in her hand, and glad Curtis wasn't in the office to witness the transaction. Selling her mother's legacy wasn't something that made her feel proud. The mailman swung around to leave and opened the door. An icy blast whistled in, the remnants of an overnight storm layering another inch of snow on the ground.

"Oh," he gasped, and stopped with a jolt to shoulder the door closed. "I almost forgot your mail." He strode back to the counter and handed over the day's packet. "Your personal mail is in there. Might as well bring everything over here from now on. Save you steps and me a trip out to your place. Sometimes Jeffrey plows your road crazy, as I'm sure you've noticed."

She smiled her thanks and thumbed through the stack as he headed out the door. The usual real estate solicitation card, credit card pre-approvals and a pet magazine. She dropped them one by one into the recycling bin now kept at the counter for this very purpose. A blue envelope from Captain Harry she set to one side to address later. The man expected a reply and she'd drafted a form letter to let him know his concerns were being taken seriously.

Her fingers paused over a letter addressed to her, with the return address of Holt, Holt and Bailey Law Offices. She never expected—or desired—to hear from the lawyer again. What could the man possibly want now? More praise for her grandmother, perhaps. She slipped a finger under the flap and, with a sense of trepidation, pried it open. The thick-woven stationary felt weighty in her hand, and she knew this was the impression the lawyer wanted to give.

"Dear Mrs. Lowe," the letter read. *"It's come to our attention a grave error was made regarding your grandmother's will. When we last spoke, I assured you there was nothing of value in the box left to you. In fact, this was specifically conveyed to me by the esteemed woman herself.*

Since then, I've learned you are in possession of an item of jewelry requiring appraisal. You may send it via overnight mail, insured and receipt required. I will take care of further details. The item will be returned to you if appropriate.

It is crucial you act without delay to avoid further action.

Regards,

Therald Holt, Attorney at Law

Her breath went shallow the more she read. The ring was gone, sold for a stack of brand-new hundred dollar bills. She took three steps toward the door, but no, let Patrick take it. The ring would continue on its journey to another place, the stone pried out and reset to modern standards, and then sold again. She paced back to the counter and reread the letter.

It is crucial you act without delay to avoid further action, it said.

A warmth grew inside, starting in her stomach and rising to flush her neck and cheeks. Her grandmother willed a box and all its contents to her. Perhaps the woman told Therald Holt the contents were valueless, but was such a statement legally binding? It wasn't right that he could demand the ring, have it appraised and taken from her. In any event, he was too late.

She took a shaky breath. The eleven bills, folded in a thick wad and tucked in her pocket, weighed heavier than before. She dropped the lawyer's letter in the recycling bin, watching as the paper fluttered on top of the pet magazine. She would ignore the demand. If he sought further action, what could he do? He had no proof the ring was in the box, and anyway, it was gone. The last remnants of indecision dropped away. She squared her shoulders. She was glad she sold the ring. The last person she wanted to have it was Therald Holt.

I'm living a life of self-determination, she thought, and stiffened her back. But she couldn't help glancing at the lawyer's letter in the recycling box. She chewed her bottom lip bloody the rest of the day.

****

Stacey lived behind the coroner's house in a converted red barn. Meredith rapped on the door, clutching her friend's favorite chocolate chip cookies in a bag. When her friend opened the door, the words popped out of her mouth before she even said hello. "Want to take a road trip?" she said. "To California."

Her friend's eyes widened into saucers. "No way. You and me? Road-tripping to California?"

The idea struck Meredith late in the afternoon. Inviting the other woman along would solve two problems: Curtis' concern about her confronting her father alone, and the cost of the trip. Stacey never stopped talking about her desire to visit, and soon bask forever in, the Golden State. Plus…a little companionship would be nice, if only to keep her nerves from overwhelming her.

"Can we rent a convertible? Put the top down?" Stacey needed no convincing. "Wind blowing through our hair? I need to get some sunglasses. A hat. Not a bathing suit, though. My thighs are a Swiss cheese nightmare." She whirled and marched from the entry way down a dark hallway.

Meredith stepped inside, noting the usual disaster of clothing, old shopping bags, knick-knacks, and magazines covering every surface. The place was well on its way toward being a hoarder's den, where belongings would accumulate year after year, piling up and eventually tumbling over and crushing the occupant. The best thing her friend could do was leave her current situation and get a fresh start. Hopefully, she would leave the mountain of miscellany behind.

The sound of raised voices rose from a back room and she understood Stacey was talking to her father. She winced. She hadn't meant to trigger a family argument. A moment later, her friend stomped into the room and hitched at her pants. "Dad wants to know who's cooking for him while I'm gone. He can eat corn chips and sardines for all I care. Lazy bastard."

Meredith had never set eyes on the man. Every time she visited, he stayed in his room. "He can get around, can't he?"

"He can run laps around both of us. Trust me." Stacey tilted her head toward the back room and raised her voice. "But he won't get *out of bed*." She continued in a chipper tone. "When do we leave? I just need fifteen minutes to pack."

This was moving much faster than expected. Bodega Bay was more than six hundred miles away and a giant step closer now she'd made the decision to go. There were still two major details to factor in: her children and her job. Honey would without doubt require something in trade for watching Jamie and Atticus. It was easy to know what such a trade would involve. Beyond family, the older woman loved three things most of all: her chickens, food, and gossip. The hunt for a long-lost father would satisfy Honey's thirst for information. And her job...well, they could do without her for one work day. She and Stacey could pack sandwiches, catnap at roadside rest stops and keep moving. The quicker the trip, the more of those eleven hundred dollar bills could go for other necessities.

She lifted her chin. "Tomorrow's Saturday," she decided. "Let's go first thing."

"I'll get some snacks for the ride. Oh, and the convertible's on me. I have some money saved for California, and hey, that's where we're going. We'll have a good old-fashioned girl's weekend."

A deep voice rose from a back room. "Stacey. Stacey Abigail. You get back here."

Her friend dug into the bag and fished out a cookie, acting as though she heard nothing at all. "Probably need a flashlight. And pepper spray—all I have is some old bear spray—I hear big cities are dangerous. Think we can swing through San Francisco? I wouldn't mind seeing San Diego too, while we're at it."

"Bodega Bay," Meredith said in a firm voice. "We are going straight there and straight back. I can only take three days. My job, remember?"

Stacey stared at her and her shoulders sagged a little. "Three," she repeated. "We can't see much in three days."

"Stacey Abigail Pringle," the voice in the back bellowed, and then ended in a hacking cough.

"You sure your dad's okay back there?"

"Right as rain. Just putting on a pout. Stick around long enough and he'll really get going." She lowered her voice. "Understand why I need to cut loose? I'm thirty-one, fer heaven's sake. I'd get him married off if I could, but he doesn't offer much to the ladies. He wants someone who'll cater to him hand and foot. Sent my mom into the grave before her time."

Meredith glanced down the dark hallway, unsure if the old man would survive, but decided to trust her friend's assessment. "Let's get on the road when the sun comes up. We have a long drive ahead of us."

With a beaming grin, Stacey hitched once more at her pants.

****

Honey waved one of her plump hands in the air, dispelling her last hurdle. "Don't you know Monday's a holiday? Human Rights Day in this state. No city business goes on, dear. Guess no one told you."

Somewhere in the paperwork for her new job was a note about paid holidays, but she hadn't paid much attention in the excitement of starting work. The stars were aligning, finally, with everything in favor of her finding her father. The money from the ring, the holiday, Stacey's willingness to pay for the car—all this made her believe the time was right.

"Anyhow, I'll watch the kiddos if you're sure this is the right thing for you to do," her friend continued. "Hate to mention this, but last time you drove too far in the snow, you almost skidded off the side of a mountain. And, my goodness, you just drove across the country. You must be a glutton for punishment."

"We'll be fine. Once we're over Donner Pass."

"Tsk. Isn't that where people turned into cannibals to survive?"

She wrinkled her nose at Honey. "I doubt we'll get stuck for the winter."

The other woman shrugged, her mouth in a thin line as though this very well could be a possibility, and poured steaming peppermint tea into their waiting mugs. "There was a whole group of them who didn't think so either. Cannibals."

The first sip of the peppermint tea burned her lips and traveled a warm path down her throat and into her stomach. It didn't always make sense to argue with the other woman. She had one little slide-off in the snow the month before which required Curtis' help, but her mishap occurred on a narrow mountain road in deep snow. The highway to California was broad and well-traveled. Her friend's reference to the ill-fated Donner Party, stuck on the high pass near Lake Tahoe in the mid-1800s, was silly.

Honey bustled around the small kitchen and carried two plates to the table. She lifted a cake stand over to the table and served up a hefty slice of an iced lemon loaf in front of Meredith.

"Oh, I can't right now. I'm sure your cake is

delicious but I just…just had lunch," she lied. The truth was her stomach was in knots, adrenaline-fueled from her travel plans.

"You eat up. I won't take no for an answer. You're much too thin. A man doesn't want to grab hipbones or get poked by sharp ribs. He wants something soft underneath him."

Warmth surged to her face. "Honey…"

"Or above him. Whichever way, you know. I know Crusty enjoys tussling around with a full-figured woman. He was just saying the other day…"

"I think I'm hungry after all, thank you," Meredith broke in, speaking quickly to stop her friend from saying more. The last thing she wanted was a mental picture of two gray-haired and wrinkled bodies "tussling." She forked a piece into her mouth and spoke through the cake. "You'll have to give me the recipe."

A satisfied smile stretched across Honey's face as she sipped at her own mug. In the living room, Jamie and Atticus watched a nature program where lions chased gazelles. The ending on these programs was always the same—the slowest prey became a bloody feast. Her daughter's attention was riveted on the show.

"Anne McGill says a strange fellow's staying over at the motel this week," Honey continued. "City guy with an orange tan and needing a haircut. Anne says he asked for a second ice bucket. Tell me, what does a man do with two ice buckets?"

Meredith's stomach clenched, the knots inside giving the lemon cake an overly sweet and cloying taste. "I may know him," she said. "Black hair? Bleached teeth?"

Ever the magnet for gossip, Honey leaned forward,

eyes glittering. "A friend of yours. You didn't say you were expecting an out-of-town guest."

"I wasn't. And he's not a friend." She swallowed. "Apparently, we're related. He's a cousin. But I didn't invite him here." The words emerged stilted, and she took another bite of cake that now tasted like sawdust.

Honey's gaze was assessing. "Anne says he's a bit uppity, if not downright rude. Hope you don't mind my passing her remarks along to you. She goes out of her way to get coffee going first thing in the office, and this fellow—your cousin—asked if she had dark roast. I mean coffee is coffee, and Anne doesn't have to provide anything at all."

Meredith played along, sipping her tea as she let her friend prattle. What was Raymond doing back in town? His trip to visit friends in Seattle was short, if he'd traveled there at all. She didn't like the idea he'd be in Hay City while she was gone. Could it be he was aware she lied about the ring?

"We might not be related at all," she said. "My mother never mentioned anyone named Raymond."

"Hmm." Honey paused, clearly hoping for more dirt. "Well, you did polish off your cake. Let me wrap up a few pieces for you and the little ones before you go. You never know when you might get hungry for a midnight snack."

She took another sip of tea, and eyed her friend. Surely, Crusty already told her about the stranger who stopped by the bar. Just as well. If Raymond decided to stay in town while she was gone, Honey would keep a close watch on the man. The woman was a crack shot and would do anything to take care of family.

Meredith—and her murdered husband—learned

that well enough. Without her friend's interference, Brian would probably still be alive. Her friend's sweet grandmotherly face hid a determined and interfering nature with few boundaries. Raymond had better stay clear.

Chapter Thirteen

Tired kids or not, the cupboards were bare. She wouldn't have the time or energy to shop for the coming week after her whirlwind trip to California. Her pocket bulged with bills, so there was no excuse for a refrigerator filled with nothing but milk, string cheese and broccoli.

Jamie groaned as they swung into the grocery store parking lot. "I don't want to shop."

She twisted in the driver's seat to face her daughter. "Let's have a treat tonight,"

"Choco Puffs?" Jamie asked about her favorite cereal, her eyes wide. "They're my favorite."

"Sure. Let's get two boxes."

"Can we get turkey? And ice cream?"

She made a show of considering it and then agreed. They all deserved a few indulgences. She strolled around the store and her daughter skipped alongside. Atticus sat in the cart and counted the items inside, although the number he arrived at always added up to three. A jar of pickled beets and a container of dried apricots were for Honey, as partial thanks for taking her kids for the coming long weekend.

"Half pound of turkey today," she ordered at the deli counter.

For once, Jeffrey the deli-boy wore an apron that was clean, white, and even appeared ironed. His sandy hair was trimmed and combed off his forehead. A couple wiry strands, in no way resembling a beard, erupted from his chin and darted in different directions. He stood straight with shoulders thrown back. Despite these attempted improvements, the sneer on his face hadn't changed.

"Always happens," he said. "One of you outsiders shows up and then more come running. Pretty soon, we'll have freeways crisscrossing Hay City."

She had no idea what he was grousing about. "Just the turkey, hold the gridlock."

"You don't believe me, but New York City used to have more mosquitoes than people. That's in the history books." He flicked on the meat slicer and her gaze drifted away.

Down the cereal aisle, she spied Curtis hefting a basket bulging with oranges, potato chips and what appeared to be frozen food meals. He frowned at the selection before him, his eyes scanning the shelves.

Her package slapped on the top of the deli counter. "Half-pound, exactly. I'd like to see anyone else handle a slicer like me."

She grabbed the package and spun away without a word. Thanking the kid would only prompt some other complaint. Anyone who'd regret the loss of mosquitoes had to be dimwitted. People were a big improvement over blood-sucking insects. A teenage girl, gangly and feet anchored in army boots, clomped up to the counter. A glance over her shoulder confirmed her suspicion. No wonder the kid had cleaned up his attire. Deli-boy wore a silly grin at the girl's approach.

"Hey cutie," she whispered at Curtis' shoulder. He whirled around and his eyes lit up at seeing her. In his hand was a box of Choco Puffs. She raised her eyebrows in mock despair. "Not you, too."

"This stuff's not bad."

"It's my favorite," Jamie said, grabbing two more boxes from the shelf. "Mom said we're 'plurging today so I get two boxes *and* turkey."

He chuckled and ruffled Atticus' hair. "Boy, your mom really knows how to throw a party." His eyes scanned her cart and then met hers with a twinkle. "Need some help out to the car with all this?"

"Sure, I may have a big tip for you. Later."

Color rose to tinge the tips of his ears and she smiled to herself at how easily he blushed. The first time they met was right here in the grocery store. He'd blushed then, too.

They finished their shopping together and, as promised, he helped her to the car. Five full bags of groceries were to her the same as holding bags of gold. Would she ever get over not having enough food as a child, or enough money to buy one bag of groceries? Even though those days were years in the past, she still reveled in the luxury of buying non-essentials like Choco Puffs and deli turkey.

Lurking below this satisfaction, though, was the news she needed to deliver to Curtis. He wouldn't be thrilled with her impromptu plans. Even worse was the way she planned to ignore the lawyer's demand for the ring, and keep the money from the sale.

The parking lot was nearly empty as he loaded her bags into the car and she helped Jamie and Atticus into the backseat. She bit her lip and winced. She'd chewed her lips so much lately, they were tender and nearly raw. As Curtis closed the trunk, she cozied up beside him. Hands in his pockets, he seemed to be in no hurry to get to his truck, despite the bitter cold.

A sporty ice-blue car skidded into the slick parking lot, resumed traction, and rolled up to the gas pump. "Damn fools drive too fast," he grumbled. "I spent my day driving from one end of the county to the other towing cars back onto the road. Don't they understand snow compresses to ice?"

"Curtis," she interrupted, now wanting to get the conversation over with as soon as possible. She'd seen this car before and knew who was behind the wheel. "I'm going to California this weekend. Tomorrow."

He blinked, his gaze returning to her.

"I can't stop now," she said. "I have his name and last known location. I'll just find him, meet him, and then I'm done. Honey will keep the kids. I have everything planned out."

"So soon? I don't like you going alone."

"I won't be alone. Stacey's going with me."

One brow raised nearly to his hairline. "Stacey Pringle?"

"She'll be company on the road, and help share the driving. She offered to rent a car, too. Her dream is to ride into California in a convertible." She gave a short laugh. "Doesn't matter that it's January."

She explained how Stacey refused to share costs for the car, taking on the full burden. "Let's face it," her friend had said. "This may be the first and last time I ever get to do this." Meredith couldn't protest as her own car wasn't up to the task. The offer was a godsend.

Curtis wrinkled his nose. "I can't imagine she'll be much help if you run into trouble."

"There won't be trouble." Of course, she had no

way of knowing this. She was dredging up a decades-old relationship, springing paternity on a man, and then asking him about a possible murder. What could possibly go wrong, she asked herself wryly. But she didn't want Curtis to convince her to delay the trip, or fill her mind with doubts.

The car at the gas pump idled. A tall man wearing a blue wool coat emerged, his black hair shiny and glistening against the backdrop of unsullied snow in the field beyond. He took his time unscrewing the gas cap, then leaned against his car for a moment before inserting the nozzle in the opening. Meredith met his glance once, and gave him a polite smile she instantly regretted. He didn't need any encouragement.

"Will Jamie and Atticus stay with Honey?"

"Hmmm."

He glanced over his shoulder to see what captured her attention, then half-turned to meet the man's frank stare. "Strange-looking fellow for these parts. Fish out of water."

"He wants the ring," she said out of the corner of her mouth. "My mother's ring."

Curtis frowned as Raymond offered a small wave. "You know him?"

"That's the guy I told you about. The cousin who stopped by the office the other day saying my grandmother made a promise to him. He's pushy and a little creepy."

He narrowed his eyes and glared toward the figure. "He wants more than a ring. I don't like how he's hanging about."

"I told him I didn't have it, I didn't know what he was talking about." She was somewhat embarrassed to admit her lie. "That's half true since I really don't have it anymore. There's more I didn't tell you, though."

She had his full attention again. "What?"

Guilt rolled up with a vengeance. She'd sold something possibly not truly belonging to her. She was as good as a thief, fencing stolen goods. "My grandmother's attorney, Mr. Holt, sent a letter. Somehow, he knows about the ring too. At least, I think he does. The letter said if there was anything valuable in the box, I need to return it."

Curtis shook his head. "I don't see why. Unless the ring was specifically willed to someone else, the contents of the box are yours. That's how I understand it. Was it willed to this cousin of yours?"

"He says my grandmother promised it to him. Mr. Holt's letter didn't actually specify the ring. No one knows about the ring except you and me." And Patrick the postman, but she wasn't ready to tell Curtis about this. "Apparently, my grandmother told him the contents of the box were worthless."

"I suppose a woman can lie to her attorney," Curtis mused. "My uncle's a probate attorney up in Coeur d'Alene. I'll give him a call and see what he thinks."

Raymond gave another small wave and got into his car. A fish out of water for sure. She never felt like such a small-town local before, passing judgment on a big-city outsider and wishing he'd go back to where he came from. He doesn't belong here, she thought; not in Hay City and not in my life. The car pulled out of the lot and crept down the road. Could be he was on his way to Seattle or back to where he'd come from. The idea he'd remain in town even while she was gone unsettled her. Hopefully, Honey would have sense enough to keep the kids away from this man.

Curtis slipped an arm around her and tucked a loose strand of hair behind her ear. "I'm going to miss you while you're gone. Call me every day so I know you're safe."

Warmth surged through her, lessening the uneasy feeling her cousin's presence evoked. Curtis would keep a wary eye on her cousin. "It's only three days."

"You could hit a storm and get delayed a day."

"Three days," she said in a firm tone. "No sightseeing this time. I have his address. We'll go straight there and straight back."

"If anyone starts talking about you joining the commune, run for it."

She smiled. "I will. I promise."

A rapping on the window drew her attention to her kids waiting in the backseat. The windows were fogged with their warm breath.

"You'd better go," he said. "But I expect my tip."

"As soon as I get back." She leaned in for a kiss. When she maneuvered out of the parking lot, his truck went one way while her car went another. His taillights grew smaller and smaller until she veered off onto Road 41 and aimed toward home.

Three days—she couldn't spare more time—a day and a half there, a day and a half back, and an hour or two with her father. In twelve hours, she'd be on the road to Bodega Bay. A tingle rippled through her. In thirty-six hours, she'd be face to face with her father.

****

With the decision made and plans laid out, sleeping was hopeless. Midnight passed and the clock ticked toward one a.m. Twenty-five years of waiting. She couldn't imagine what her life would be like a week from now, after David Givens shared his version of events. Would she be relieved or shattered? She wavered between being certain of herself and terrified she'd discover too much.

One a.m. and still her eyelids refused to close. Frustrated her body wouldn't cooperate and go to sleep, she tiptoed past her children into the kitchen and opened the refrigerator. Yogurt or a slice of the lemon cake Honey sent home? She reached for the cake.

A clank and a metal-on-metal noise sounded from outside, toward the shed. She froze. There was nothing, no one, out here. Not for miles. Just her and her kids in a thin-walled trailer anyone could break into. She strode to the door and twisted the lock in place.

Closer, there came a light crunch, like a stealthy footstep on snow. They definitely weren't alone. Her breath shortened as she peeked out the window, but the shed was just out of sight. Another crunch, even closer. Someone was prowling about. They could have taken whatever they wanted during the day when she was at work and the kids were at Honey's. Instead, the prowler waited until dark and they were at their most vulnerable. Her children slept, unaware of the danger on the other side of the wall.

There were two choices. Call Curtis and hope the person didn't break in before he arrived, or... She darted to her bedroom and slid open the closet door. At the top was a lock-box Honey gave her.

"For critter control," the woman had said. "The two-footed kind too. A woman alone has to take care of her own business. And let me tell you, there's nothing scarier than a woman holding a gun."

Meredith unlocked the case with trembling fingers and drew out a handgun. This cold piece of metal was heavy in her palm as she loaded the bullets.

Target practice hadn't gone well at Honey's place. Over and over, she aimed at cans and never hit a single one. The snowfall interrupted any more practice, but she planned to refine her aim in the spring.

"In the meantime, hang onto this," Honey said, insisting she take the gun, bullets and lock-box. "Just the sound of a gun going off is usually enough to scare anyone or anything away. Just make sure you aim away from your house."

Her hand shook as she returned to the trailer door and laid her ear against it. Anyone who knew her also knew she didn't have anything worth stealing. A light bump against the back wall of the trailer startled her and she almost brought the gun around to shoot.

I have to go outside.

Her heart raced, but she jammed on her boots and grabbed her coat. Taking a deep breath, she unlocked the door and cracked it open.

No sign of movement. No car in the driveway or footprints in the snowy yard. Keeping the gun pointed downward, she crept along the trailer wall and peered around the side. Now she heard him. The man gave a low moan, clearly in an attempt to scare her, and succeeded. She shrank against the trailer, her heart thudding wildly.

Raymond, she thought. The man drove across country and detoured to get a piece of inheritance. What if he decided to take what he wanted?

There was no turning back now. She took a deep breath and clutched the gun more tightly. She rounded the corner and approached the back wall where a trail led from the shed. Just around the corner, she heard his breath, heavy and labored.

"I have a gun," she called out in a hoarse voice.

There was a scuffling sound and she brought up the gun with both hands, just like she'd seen on TV. The trailer trembled at her side as a huge animal emerged, its hindquarters bumping against the wall, and its massive antlered head looming above her. She bit back a scream. Ignoring her, the animal trotted across the snow toward the shed, on the trail it had created. Tall ungainly legs, heavy body, and a long nose. A moose, she realized, and lowered the gun. The animal must be seeking shelter.

Behind her, Jamie spoke in a sleepy voice. "Mom, why are you outside?"

She whirled, heart pounding. Her daughter stood behind her in pajamas and slippers. "Oh Jamie! Let's get back inside." She slid the gun in her coat pocket and hurried the child back into the warm trailer.

Her daughter tucked back into bed and the door locked, Meredith climbed under her own warm covers. With a start, she leaped out of bed and removed the loaded gun from the pocket of her coat. The bullets removed, she returned the gun to the lock-box. I could have shot a hole in my trailer as well as a moose, she realized with alarm. *Or my daughter.* She swallowed and decided a few more practice sessions were necessary before she took the gun out of its case again.

Adrenaline rush over, exhaustion swept over her. They were safe. There was no one who wanted to hurt her and her children. Her limbs grew heavy and, finally, she slept.

Chapter Fourteen

Stacey folded her arms atop the car rental counter and spoke in a firm voice. "Red. White interior."

"And I'm telling you," the rental clerk repeated in an annoyed tone, frowning down his nose at both of them, "no one wants a convertible in the dead of winter. Not red, not white, not any color in the rainbow."

Meredith read his mind like the face on a watch. *Idiots. Driving a convertible in the snow.*

"Well, where can I get one?" her friend countered. "Between here and Reno."

His fingers tapped on the computer keyboard, and Stacey's tapped their own impatient rhythm on the counter. Meredith strolled to the glass double doors. Two-foot long icicles dripped from the eaves like daggers, and white lumps against the building hinted at a row of snow-covered shrubbery. Only two crazy ladies would insist on a convertible in January. She wondered for the twentieth time if her friend would be more hindrance than help. For the other woman, the next three days were an exciting adventure of a lifetime. For herself, the prospect of this trip to Bodega Bay had left her sleepless and terrified. Curtis was right; so much could go wrong.

"Reno," the rental car clerk finally said. "Nothing in between. We have a nice minivan on the lot here, brand new, safer for you gals. I can let you have it for a great price. Much more sensible."

Stacey sneered at him and shrank away from the counter. "We're not driving a *minivan* to California. We'll take the one in Reno." She whipped out a credit card. "Reserve it for me."

They hit the road, and the trip lurched forward in short segments. They stopped in Boise for sodas, in Ore-vada so Stacey could say she stood in two states at one time, in Winnemucca for gas and lunch, in Lovelock for a break and snacks. Each time they stopped, her friend gasped at the sights around her—the mountains, the cattle, the sagebrush—and ordered food. It was difficult to imagine never having traveled more than a hundred miles from home and she tried to be patient at all the delays.

Her friend laughed over her midnight adventure. "A moose? Good thing you didn't shoot. It'd take more than a few bullets to stop an angry moose."

Ten hours into the trip they finally hit Reno. Stacey was starving again and wide-eyed as she gazed at the tall casino buildings and neon lights flashing against the dark sky. "Let's play roulette. Maybe I'll win enough to buy us dinner, and maybe the rental too."

There was no way Meredith would throw money on a table for someone to take away. She had a firm budget for the trip and it didn't include gambling. "I packed sandwiches for tonight. I thought we could rent the car, then catch a few hours of sleep at a rest stop up the road—you know, save a little money."

Stacey's mouth opened and closed twice. Her eyes widened in disbelief before words emerged. "We can't eat *sandwiches*. We're on a road trip. Please, please, *please*. I have to go in a real, live casino." Her eyes were wide and pleading, signaling that not giving in would be just plain mean.

They picked up the car—a red convertible, white interior—and drove down they city's famed Virginia Street under the arched sign *The Littlest Big City in the World*. She didn't say anything when her friend insisted they don their coats and caps, and put the car's top down while they cruised, even though the temperature couldn't have been higher than twenty degrees. Stacey's toothy grin filled her face and her head swiveled from one casino to the next. "I can't believe I'm really here," her friend repeated over and over, and this made the freezing breeze endurable.

Cheeks and lips numb from cold, Meredith started to giggle at how absurd the whole thing was, and this made her friend giggle too. *We must appear insane*, and this notion made her laugh even more. Despite her anxiety about what awaited her at Sustainable Farms in Bodega Bay, she couldn't help but enjoy the moment.

At the far southern stretch of Virginia Street, they put the top back up and cranked up the heat inside. Stacey aimed the convertible toward one of the casinos, which glittered and glowed all the way up to its rooftops. "Twenty minutes or twenty dollars," she promised. "Whichever comes first. Then, dinner."

Inside, slot machines lined up like sentries. They chimed, chirped and rang. The clang of electronic coins dispensing echoed around the vast space and gamblers milled from slot machine to slot machine, like a random game of musical chairs. Smoke drifted from gaming tables where players smoked while they threw dice or flipped over cards, hoping for a lucky break. A crowd huddled around the roulette wheel and a few people expertly placed bets. The checkerboard table displayed squares that outlined a variety of betting options beyond red or black, and different colored chips dotted the squares. Her friend bee-lined to the table while Meredith hovered a step behind, determined to keep all her money secure in her handbag.

Stacey waved a twenty-dollar bill in the air. "I want to bet on red."

The croupier gave her a weak smile as though recognizing a newbie in need of guidance. "Put the money on the table."

"He can't take it from your hand," another gambler advised.

"Seems rude," she muttered, but dropped the bill and watched it traded away for two ten-dollar chips. The gambler standing at her shoulder coached her on where to set her chips on the table, and the croupier set the wheel in motion.

The wheel circled round and round, and Meredith's stomach tightened, anxious her friend would lose. Twenty dollars was a lot to throw away in a game lasting a few seconds. At least, this would be a moment for her to remember and talk about for years.

"Red! You win!" the man next to them exclaimed. "Lucky lady here."

Stacey's eyes grew huge as she scooped up the extra chips. "It was so easy, so quick." Her gaze stayed riveted on the wheel.

"No," Meredith said, edging forward to her friend's shoulder. "One bet. You had a plan, remember? Let's leave while you're a winner."

Her friend didn't budge. "Just one more. I promise, and then we'll leave."

With a sinking heart, she watched Stacey set her chips once more on red. The wheel began its circuit. Forty dollars would be gone in a flash. It would be sandwiches and tears, for sure.

Stacy gave a whoop. "I'm a genius!" In front of her, in a twinkling, there was eighty dollars in chips.

Meredith crept closer, intrigued by the simplicity of the wheel. Pick right and your money was doubled. She bit her lip, considering the money Patrick paid her for the ring. Two hundred dollars in her wallet. No, she cautioned herself, don't do it. She clutched her handbag tight against her body, as though one of her hands would disobey and remove the wallet against her will.

"One more time and I'll have a hundred and sixty dollars," Stacey marveled. "Five minutes. Why haven't I done this before?"

Meredith touched her arm. "We should go now. You promised."

Her friend was riveted on the chips, still sitting in the square. "It wasn't really a promise. I didn't swear." The wheel spun and they both traced the circular motion of the metal ball as it raced around and around.

The gambler at her side shouted, "Yes! I won."

Stacey's shoulders slumped. "It's black. I lost."

Eighty dollars in chips were swept away and gamblers immediately tossed more chips on the table for the next spin. Stacey turned away and they backed from the table. Others surged forward to take their spot.

"You won twice in a row," Meredith said, trying to be encouraging. "That's something."

"I'm busted. You said you made sandwiches?"

They headed to the exit and made their way to the parking garage and the convertible. Stacey's spirits perked up again once she was back behind the wheel. "If I'd won a hundred and sixty dollars, my next spin could have been three hundred twenty, and the next would be six forty. We'd be in a suite eating chocolate covered strawberries and guzzling champagne."

She calculated her fictional winnings and spending as the lights of Reno disappeared behind them. For thirty miles, they enjoyed imagining fantasy luxuries a six-hundred-dollar windfall could provide. "A room with a hot tub," Stacey said.

"A city view," Meredith countered.

"Strappy sandals with four-inch heels."

More practical as well as reasonable, Meredith said, "Snow boots with fur inside."

"I'd keep a hundred dollars back," Stacey sighed wistfully, "and do it all over again."

They wound up into the steep Sierra Nevada mountain range. Stacey honked the horn for a quarter mile when they passed the "Welcome to California" sign and radio signals grew fuzzy and intermittent. She snapped off the radio and they drove in silent darkness up the high pass. The freeway through the seven-thousand-foot high Donner Pass was clear of snow and semi-trucks blasted by the small car, making it sway in their lane. Stacey gripped the steering wheel with both hands and leaned over the wheel.

They agreed to nap in the car once they made it over the mountains and into Roseville, a city at a low enough elevation where they wouldn't freeze to death. Stacey steered into a parking spot at the far edge of a grocery superstore, next to a camper and a van, and they set back their seats as far as they would go and locked the doors. They huddled under coats and blankets and Meredith settled into an uneasy sleep.

In an instant, Curtis was there, too, sleeping among their suitcases in the backseat. She twisted to tell Stacey, but Raymond was now in the driver's seat and the car was barreling down a narrow road. He slung a lasso around her neck and as he tugged it tight, she grabbed at her throat only to find the rope had transformed into a large golden ring with a purple stone. Her cousin's ultra-white teeth sharpened to points and he laughed as she choked. Out the windshield a cliff appeared. Instead of stopping, the car accelerated and her mouth opened to scream, but no sound would come out.

She woke at sunrise, stiff and sore, and with her mouth feeling gummy and tasting of peanut butter. She blinked at the bright sunlight shining in her eyes, the vague edges of the nightmare fading away and only leaving her with a sense of disquiet. The camper parked next to them overnight was gone, but the van was still there. Next to her, Stacey was stirring with a soft groan.

"Three hundred and thirty-five million, five hundred thousand," she mumbled, apparently still counting imaginary roulette wins.

Meredith twisted in her seat and dug an overnight kit out of her suitcase. "I'm going in the store to find a bathroom," she said, nudging her friend awake.

"Six hundred seventy…" Rubbing her nek, Stacey straightened in her seat. "Where am I? Where's Dad?"

"We're in California. Four more hours and we'll be in Bodega Bay."

A slow smile spread over her friend's face and she stared out the window at the vast asphalt parking lot. "I just woke up in California. Jeez."

Meredith opened the car door and stumbled across the parking lot to the superstore. She'd slept in a car before and knew how this worked. Beeline straight to the bathroom and out before store security could catch up to her and tell her to scram.

Today's the day I meet my father. Then I'll know everything.

****

A cool breeze streamed through her hair. Mid-morning, now driving northwest, Stacey insisted on putting the convertible's top down. The temperature was already in the fifties and, compared to an Idaho winter, the weather was like a spring day. Meredith had to admit, driving along a California freeway in a red convertible felt pretty nifty.

"I'm not sure I'm a fan of cities," her friend noted with a frown, as they edged through rush-hour traffic in Sacramento. "I may be more of a beach girl. How close are we?"

"Not far. We should be there by lunch time."

"I'm a bit hungry now. Mind if we stop?"

Just west of Sacramento, the thick traffic lessened for a few miles, and the first orchards appeared. Apple and peach trees, walnut and almonds, and orange and grapefruit, the citrus still laden with fruit. Loons and starlings fed from fallow fields, while long-legged white egrets stalked flooded rice fields. Coastal mountains appeared due west, their slopes varying shades of emerald and olive. Wildflowers in vivid cobalt and saffron thrived along the highway.

They stopped at a roadside fruit stand in Davis, a convenience store in Vallejo and a grocery store in Petaluma. When she wasn't eating, Stacey's jaws chewed through an entire pack of gum. Meredith sat quietly, her nerves heightening the closer they drew to Bodega Bay. The last thing she wanted was to eat.

The scenery morphed from flat urban concrete to rolling rural pastures, and the road narrowed to two lanes. Stacey's head swiveled back and forth as she took in the undulating green hills, dotted with cows and the occasional heavy-horned bull. "I don't remember spotting cattle in any of my magazines. Just celebrities and restaurants."

"Northern California's not as crowded as down south. Anyway, we're out of the snow."

"I like this area," Stacey said. "It feels like home here. I don't mind a few cows." They passed a pasture sprinkled with grazing sheep, heavy and creamy in their winter wool. "Or sheep. I've always had a fondness for sheep. Although I was hoping to see a celebrity or two."

"I don't imagine we'll run across any on this trip."

"No," Stacey said shortly, gazing about at the pastoral scenery. "This is nice too."

The first salty scent of the ocean infused the air when they passed through the tiny burg of Valley Ford, inland of Bodega Bay. They were very close now.

"How do we find this commune?" Stacey asked.

"I have an address. About ten-fifteen minutes more, I think." Her throat worked and, for some reason, tears sprung to her eyes. She took a deep breath and filled her lungs with the clean air blowing onshore from the Pacific Ocean. Time was moving too fast. She didn't know if she could ever be ready for the coming meeting with her father.

"It's been a long time since you've seen your dad, huh? I'll bet he'll be surprised to see you."

She twisted her face away from Stacey. She'd told her friend the bare minimum, not sure how to recap her long, unpalatable story. Questions would lead to questions, and she had few answers. Anyway, if she'd explained she wanted to confront the father she never met about long-ago wrongdoings and perhaps even murder, her friend would never have come along. Now they were here, she realized she should have said more. Somehow, Stacey latched onto the notion they were doing nothing more than making a quick familial visit. She hadn't bothered to correct her.

"I haven't actually met him before," she confessed.

"Wow. Oh, wow."

They fell into silence for a moment.

"So, um, think he'll be glad to see you?"

"Million-dollar question." She paused. "It might be a bit touch-and-go. My mother didn't have good things to say about him."

"I get it. My mom complained about dad all the time, him and his family always visiting, up until the day she died."

Meredith pointed to a sign, light green with dark gray lettering. Sustainable Farms. "We're here."

To the right was a small farmhouse edged by a riot of daffodils in full bloom. The trim little house was surrounded by a series of green pastures separated by white fences. Goats roamed the enclosures and two young children ran across the front lawn as they swung into the farmhouse's gravel driveway. Something in her gut twisted. Silly, but she never considered he would have married and had other children. She stared at the tow-headed kids, and her gaze swept the area searching for an adult. A well-built man appeared around the side of the house, his arms wrapped around a small goat. He set it down on the front lawn and the two children squatted next to it.

Stacey shifted the car into Park. "Is that him?"

Meredith studied the man. Mid to late forties, blond, and with an air of entitlement that could only come from a life of plenty and ease. He raised his head at their approach and an easy smile came to his lips. There was no question. The picture in her handbag showed an earlier version of this man, with his arm around her mother's shoulders. Such a long journey she'd undertaken and here he was, hale and hearty, just waiting to be found.

"Yep." Without looking at her friend, she added, "You don't need to hang around for this."

"You sure? Maybe I'll stay just a minute."

The car engine died, and Meredith gripped the door handle and stepped out. For a moment she wondered if this was a dream, but the scenery was too vivid and the sun too warm on her shoulders.

David Givens strode toward them with raised eyebrows and a welcoming smile. She glanced over his shoulder at the two children on the lawn, still kneeling around the baby goat. They would be her half-brother and half-sister, a generation younger than her, just slightly older than Jamie.

Pain filled her chest, and then anger. Why did he choose them as his family and not her? Behind her, Stacey clambered out of the car and stood uncertainly by her door.

"Hi there." The man stopped short of them, seeming to sense something unusual about his visitors.

She realized she was staring with her mouth open.

173

Words fled her mind.

A look of puzzlement wavered in his eyes as his gaze settled on Meredith. "Do I know you?"

She never expected her first reaction at meeting her father would be to want to rip his throat out. "David Givens." Her voice sounded like a hoarse rasp in her ears. "You're David Givens."

His gaze darted back and forth between Stacey and Meredith, puzzlement changing to caution as he registered their serious mood. "What can I do for you?"

There were so many answers to this question. In some unformed fantasy, her father would recognize her instantly and it was painful this didn't happen. She wanted to relive her childhood, but this time, a father would be there too providing extra support and guidance. A father would never let her mother lapse into despair and drink herself to death. Their lives could have been so different.

Of course, it was too late. The best that would come out of this meeting would be hearing the tenor of his voice, gazing into the eyes of a real person, and knowing he truly existed. Part of her wanted to turn around and flee, but she traveled too far in order to meet him.

There were so many questions to be answered. Underneath everything, one particular question loomed.

She set her jaw.

"I want to know what you did," she said, her voice shaky despite her best efforts. "To my mother."

Part 3—The Beginning of The End

Laura left in the night.

A backpack bulged on her shoulder. Two changes of clothes, extra shoes, toiletries, enough cash to disappear for a while. Possessions slowed you down and trapped you. She wouldn't make that mistake.

Before she left, she gathered a few items in a box and left them on the bed for her mother to find. Silver earrings, a twist of long, golden hair tied with ribbon, a picture of herself as the girl she used to be. Remnants of a broken childhood. The ring. Let her mother contemplate what the cursed ring meant. Only one other person had the combination to the safe.

Once she realized she was pregnant, she stopped drinking. The first days were agony. Her insides twisted and cramped, and a raging thirst tortured her. If the baby shriveled and died, all the better. But even wild animals protect their young.

She fought the craving and sobriety became somewhat easier as time went on. Abortion was another option, but the child would keep her mother from dragging her back. A baby was both an accusation and proof of what happened. A scandal of this magnitude was worse than a runaway daughter. Let the girl run and never return.

One last thing to do. Rubbing her shorn hair, she scribbled a note and set it on top of the box.

Dear Mother,

If you drag me home, I will tell everyone. Think how awful it will be for you.

Seriously, I will tell them everything.

By the way, I'm pregnant.

Laura

Chapter Fifteen

Stacey put a hand on the car door and fumbled for the handle, pulling it as she spoke. "Uh, maybe I should get some things at the store. A few snacks and, you know, supplies. I'll be back in an hour."

Neither Meredith nor David paid any attention as she scooted into the convertible and backed out of the driveway. Meredith didn't mind. There was no physical danger in this bucolic setting, where children played on the lawn and goats chewed contentedly beyond the gate. Only emotional damage lay ahead, and an uncomfortable discussion. Just as well they faced each other alone.

He repeated the question back to her, studying her more closely now. "What did I do to your mother?" A vague recognition developed in his eyes, and he frowned as though trying to place her in his memory.

"I'm Meredith. Laura's daughter. Remember her?" Her voice was bitter. "Laura Brittan?"

His eyes opened wider and several emotions flickered across his face. "Laura. I see a resemblance now. I haven't heard from her in a long time." He shook his head as though at a dim and worrisome memory. "How is she?"

"Dead."

His jaw tightened and he took in a deep breath. The news took him unexpected. She watched him as a cat would a mouse, enjoying his obvious discomfort. Perhaps she hadn't come to meet him; she'd sought him out to make him suffer.

"I'm sorry," he said, and motioned toward his house. "Come sit on the porch with me."

She trailed him to the small white farmhouse, scarcely larger than the detached garage set to one side. Once more, she glanced at the two children—half-brother and half-sister nearly two decades younger than her—and then away, her heart twisting. On the porch were two mismatched wicker chairs and an old couch swing. She perched on the edge of one chair, not in the mood to swing during the coming confrontation. He selected the chair next to her and she had an urge to scoot back so their knees would be farther away from each other.

"How did Laura die? Was it an accident?"

She didn't mince words. This man, in his comfortable home and new family, didn't deserve any sympathy. "Drank herself into a coma."

He flinched and shook his head. "I'm so sorry for your loss."

She took a deep breath and let the words fly. "I'm not here for sympathy. I just want to know what you did to her, back in Fifteen Palms. I want you to tell me what made her drink so much."

Simply staring at her, he said nothing.

Once started, the words rushed out in a flood. "Tell me why she left home, why you abandoned her, why my grandmother hated us. If nothing else, you owe this to me. Tell me these things and I'll leave you and—" she gestured at the children playing, the goats, the fields, "—you'll never never hear from me again."

By the time she finished, she was panting like an old train engine. His countenance was one of amazement and consternation. His blond hair showed some light gray at the temples. "You...said something about what I did to Laura. I don't understand. I haven't seen her in years, since high school."

"More than twenty-five years ago," she said softly.

"Yes, I guess it would have been that long now. The things you are asking about though, I can't tell you. Laura was a mystery to all of us."

"Please. You knew her then."

Didn't he see any reflection of his own features in her? Anger rose up in her that he couldn't recognize his own daughter. Or was it a refusal to acknowledge her? Surely, he knew his old high school sweetheart bore a child. She waited, wanting him to say it first.

David leaned back in his chair, causing the wicker to creak. "Something happened, a couple months before she left. Laura stopped going to school. Her home life was topsy-turvy. I mean, her mother was frantic over Anthony taking off like he did. I always assumed it freaked Laura out, all the stress in the house, people coming and going. Her mother wasn't an easy person to be around."

Meredith grew even more tired of waiting for him to state the obvious. Her mother would have told him they were going to have a baby. And what did he do but reject her, just as her own mother did, leaving her with no support. Or perhaps they'd both ganged up on her mother, encouraging an abortion she didn't want. Well, if he wouldn't say it, she would. He wouldn't get out of this. "She was pregnant. Your baby," she added. "Me."

He froze. His gaze darted to his children—his *other*

179

children, Meredith clarified in her mind—before returning to her. A calculation seemed to be going through his mind, twenty-five years tallied up against the woman sitting next to him.

"I'm sorry," he said. "I'm really sorry. Laura told you…me?"

Her tone hardened, recalling the warning her mother gave her. *You don't want to know him,* she'd said over and over. David Givens was a cruel and devious person. Maybe even a murderer. "Not exactly. She refused to ever talk about you. My grandmother named you, in a letter."

An electric car purred into the driveway, its horn sounding a quick double beep as a woman within traded waves with the children on the lawn. The light blue vehicle hummed into the open garage. Meredith's lips curled at the interruption, but she was curious as well. The woman could only be the children's mother—who he chose to marry instead of her mother. A petite blonde in perhaps her late thirties hefted a box from the car's trunk and approached the porch. Her hips swayed easily as she joined them. She was the picture of a true California girl, easygoing, poured into form-fitting jeans and wearing a trouble-free smile. David had traded in his old broken-down high school girlfriend for an uncomplicated wife.

The woman appeared pleased to see company, her tone genuine. "Hi there! I snagged the last of the oranges from Johnson's farm. We'll have juice for a week. They'll be by for some lamb chops and milk tomorrow." She dropped the box at the side of the door with a thud and faced Meredith. "I'm Ariel."

A wicked impulse grabbed her and before she

could stop herself, she stood and responded, "I'm Meredith. David's daughter."

The woman's smile faded, still hanging half-way as though waiting for the punchline to a joke. She, too, glanced over at their young children in the yard, apparent touchstones in their lives.

David rose and laid a hand on his wife's arm. "There's been a misunderstanding. Why don't we all sit down and work this out."

His wife spoke, her voice unsure. "Your daughter."

"He left my mother pregnant, while they were in high school."

Tears stung Meredith's eyes as she recalled the broken life her mother led. Meanwhile, this man had gone on his carefree way and ended up in this idyllic place while they were homeless. She glared at him. "Did you know my grandmother kicked her out of the house because she was pregnant? Because of you?" She didn't know this for a fact, but it was likely. What else could have sent her mother from home?

His voice was both gentle and pained. "Meredith, Laura and I never, we never…you can't be my daughter."

She gestured toward the farm, the deep green pasture set into rolling hills, dotted with white goats and, farther in the distance, black and white Jersey cows. "I don't want anything from you. I wanted to meet you, to understand what happened, and then I'll be gone from your life again. Like I never existed. Again." She spat out these last words, angry he wouldn't come to grips with the results of his teenage actions.

Ariel's gaze darted back and forth between them, bewilderment on her face. "Laura? The high school friend you told me about? The one who—" She stopped abruptly.

He was shaking his head though, his focus on Meredith. "You can't be. Your mother and I never had...had...sex."

She let out a huff of air. As if she would believe this. "I have pictures," she said. "Of the two of you together."

His wife raised her eyebrows in alarm. "Pictures? You and Laura?"

"Yearbook pictures," Meredith clarified. "They did everything together. They dated, school clubs, dances. I can't believe you're denying this."

"We didn't," he insisted. "We were close, but it wasn't like that. Your mother wasn't ready. She was...fragile." He cleared his throat. "Leila shouldn't have told you I was your father. There was a lot of instability in Laura's house when she was growing up. Her mother should have done more, watched over her more."

He traded glances with his wife. A silent communication passed between them and then Ariel spoke. "David has a letter your mother sent years ago, after she left home. I'll get us some iced tea while he finds it."

They rose as one and went into the house. She remained on the porch and imagined them whispering to each other inside, trying to figure out a way to make her leave. The wife would be hurt and angry; David would be defiant and denying everything. Before her, the boy and girl spoke softly to the baby goat, petting it with gentle strokes. They were closer to her children's ages than her own. The early afternoon sun warmed the porch and a lassitude filled her limbs. She considered introducing herself to her half-siblings as this would likely be the only time she'd have the opportunity. Instead, she sat and watched them. There was only one person she needed to trouble here at Sustainable Farms. In front of the porch, bright yellow daffodils nodded their heads on tall stalks as though in agreement.

David and his wife returned a few minutes later, their faces blank of anger or defiance. Good actors, she thought. Ariel placed a glass of tea at her side and he handed her a letter. It contained only a few lines. She read it fearfully, more words from a restless grave.

"Dear David,

I've weighed the pluses and minuses, and know my leaving is best for everyone. Mother is furious and I can never go home again.

Being free comes at a terrible cost.

I love you always and forever.

Laura

Meredith lifted wet eyes to him, her expression tortured and confused. "What happened? What did you do? She loved you."

He took the letter from her hands, then flipped the paper over and handed it back to her. On the back, written over and over again, filling the page in small tight letters, were those same three words:

"I'm a murderer. I'm a murderer. I'm a murderer."

"No." The word escaped her mouth in a moan. Goosebumps rippled over her arms.

He made a move to touch her shoulder and then lowered his hand again. Ariel tucked her arm in his. They were a united front, a family unit that didn't include her. "Laura had a lot of problems."

No kidding. *I'm a murderer.* Meredith blinked those awful words away for the moment. "You knew she was pregnant. You must have known. Or did you meet her later, after she ran away? She wrote to you."

He gave a helpless shrug, his eyes troubled. "I'm sorry. I know you want an answer, but I can't give you one. All I can tell you for sure is I'm not your father. I'll take a paternity test if it'll settle your mind. I don't know why your mother left home or why she wrote this letter to me. If she was pregnant when she left Fifteen Palms, I didn't know. This letter...I don't know...Laura wasn't making sense about a lot of things. And then, what she wrote on the back. I mean, even in high school, she would drink until she imagined things that weren't there. I'm telling you, I don't know who your father is."

She stood. There was no point in arguing with him anymore. David Givens *was* her father and wanted nothing to do with her. He wanted his perfect life, perfect wife, and perfect kids. An imperfect, angry child from the distant past didn't fit into this picture.

"David." Ariel's tone carried a prompt to say something more. "She traveled all this way."

He gazed at the floorboards, freshly painted white, and his brow furrowed. "Your mother told you she was pregnant when she left home?"

"I was born in early December—my mother left home in June the same year." She watched them do the math, which was easy enough. Her mother became pregnant in the spring, at least a couple of months before leaving home.

His throat worked and indecision crossed his face.

"There were problems at home, with family."

"I know. She didn't get along with my grandmother." An idea struck her and little hairs stood up on her arms. There was another possibility, another person in the house until that spring. She swallowed and her words were thick in her throat. "You mentioned family. Did you ever know my mother's stepfather? Anthony?"

His expression flattened into a mask. "I met him a few times, around the house."

"What was he like? She never mentioned him."

His glance flickered to his wife.

Ariel's hands were still and she appeared to have stopped breathing. Even the breeze through the open window behind them died, leaving the drapes inside go limp against the screen. The three of them froze in place, as though riveted to their chairs.

"You should tell her," Ariel said.

Bile rose in the back of Meredith's throat. She could not, would not stop now. "I took time off work to come out here, with money I don't have to spend," she said, pressuring him further. "I left my kids so I could find you. You have to tell me if there's anything else."

He gazed out at his children, and she waited, a creeping certainty coming over her. "Laura never liked him. He was too young for Leila, more a paid companion than husband. He didn't fit in, always inviting in one less-than-palatable family member or another. The story was a brother or cousin or someone would come visit, and a painting or something valuable would go missing. Leila seemed to turn a blind eye to everything he did. After I got this letter, I wondered if he had anything to do with Laura leaving home."

He took a deep breath. "I reflected a lot on this back then, especially after Anthony took off." His voice dropped lower. "At night...Leila locked Laura in her bedroom. But I don't know if she was locking her in...or someone out."

Meredith's breath went shallow, but she needed him to say the words. "What are you saying?"

One of the children, screaming with laughter, ran up onto the porch. "Save me." His daughter grabbed her father's leg. "He's after me."

David rested a hand on her head and gave a weak smile before shooing her back toward the lawn. The porch was quiet. Peaceful. The only sound a ticking clock coming through the open window.

"Laura hated him," he said in a low voice. "She didn't talk about life at home much, but she told me once she wished her mother never married him."

She studied his face for deception, but Ariel was nodding slightly. Unless they were well-practiced liars, they believed this was the truth. If they were being honest, a disturbing alternative was a possibility. The pieces clicked into place, just waiting for her to make the connection.

Her voice was dead, devoid of emotion as she spoke. "You're telling me Anthony's my father. My mother killed him because of it. Then she ran away."

Chapter Sixteen

The cherry red convertible bumped off the pavement and crunched over the gravel driveway. The Beach Boys lyrics blasted through the open top; Stacey sang "fun, fun, fun" along with the boys in an off-key voice. She remained in the driver's seat for a few more lines, and then the engine stopped and the car went silent. She emerged slowly, peering at the threesome on the porch.

"How's it going?" she called out, with one hand resting on the convertible's hood. "Are we good here?"

Meredith didn't budge from her spot but she waved one hand in a slow beckoning manner. Her friend grabbed a sack from the backseat and approached in a bouncing gait, a wide smile on her face.

"Not much in the way of a town out here," Stacey informed them as she climbed the porch steps. "I did pick up some organic wine though, in case we're celebrating." She hesitated, and studied their grim expressions. Raising her eyebrows, she added, "or, uh, just in need a glass of wine."

David nodded at her and then picked up their discussion as though she hadn't just appeared. "Laura didn't kill anyone. I'd bet my life on it. If her step-father…if…even then, she wouldn't have killed him."

Stacey's eyes grew huge. "Wait a minute. You didn't tell me this part. Holy cow. Your mother murdered someone?"

Meredith stared at the floorboards and Ariel sprang into action. She gently removed the bag from the other woman's arms, set it down on the porch next to the box of oranges, and then steered her down the steps. "I'm Ariel. Let me show you our llamas out back."

Stacey's mouth gaped open as she glanced over her shoulder, but she let the other woman lead her around the side of the house. As soon as they were gone, Meredith lifted her gaze.

"There was a reason she left and why my grandmother never talked to her again," she continued in a dull voice, her complete focus on the man in front of her. "She didn't want me to know anything about him, or ever find him. My grandmother never wanted anything to do with me or my children. This would explain everything." This would even explain why her grandmother named David specifically as her father, to attempt to conceal the awful truth. Her grandmother went to her grave trying to preserve a fiction. Better to be an abandoned wife than have her reputation tarnished with this nightmare.

He gestured back to the wicker chair. "Please. Sit. You've had a shock."

She dropped back into the seat and gazed at him, then offered a mirthless laugh. "I thought I was coming here to meet a monster. I was ready to hate you. I saw your children and thought they were my..." She stopped and stared at her hands twisting in her lap. Oh, the damage she could have done by introducing herself to the two young children as their half-sister.

"I'm so sorry," he said once again. They sat in silence for a moment. "Tell me about your mother. You said she drank herself to death."

She let out a long slow breath and launched into the story about her mother and the nonstop drinking, the homelessness, the hallucinations and eventual death. There was an unburdening in the telling. He nodded in recognition as she related the good parts—her mother's sense of humor and mischievous nature. The sun tilted in the sky, the children ran up the porch and into the house, and the sound of Stacey and Ariel's voices filtered through the open window from somewhere inside—and still she talked. He didn't respond except for murmurs of acknowledgment as the words spilled from her, story after story, as much as she could remember. Then there was the day her mother crawled under the bed stupid with drink and imagining monsters that weren't there. In short order, there followed a coma, the hospital, and death. Exhausted, she stopped. Inside, there was a relief at telling someone her mother's story. All of it, the good and bad.

From within the house was the sound of a refrigerator door opening and closing, and two women's voices chattering. Dishes rattled and soft laughter hinted at a new friendship formed.

Then it was his turn. "I loved her," he said simply.

His stories were brighter and of a much younger Laura who studied hard and dreamed of traveling the world. She listened with her mouth agape at this different perspective of her mother. "There was the drinking, yes. But Laura was more than that. She was very beautiful, but was almost ashamed of the reactions she got. Your mother hated when people mentioned her hair, like spun silk. It shimmered in the sunlight."

Meredith tucked a strand of her own ash brown

hair behind one ear. "Apparently, I didn't get those genes. Did Anthony have brown hair?"

"Black," he said shortly. "And a little curly."

Jamie's unruly mop flashed through her mind and nausea rose again in her throat. Raymond with his too-white teeth and jet-black hair must be Anthony's cousin. No wonder the man didn't clarify what their exact relationship was. The screen door tipped open and Stacey poked her head out. She blinked anxiously at Meredith. "We've been invited to lunch. It's all ready."

She rose unsteadily, still reeling from the revelation about Anthony. My *father*. I wish I'd never come here now, she thought. Why did I insist upon learning the truth? My mother was right—I didn't want to know.

****

A mid-afternoon lunch started off with escarole salad, colored with shaved beets and carrots, and speckled with chunks of artichoke and avocado. Ariel whipped the olive oil and balsamic dressing at the table, and drizzled the mixture over the top before piling a hefty serving atop each plate. At her side, their son tore homemade bread into hand-sized chunks, set the pieces at the side, while their daughter circled the table delivering the full plates. David watched his family at work, a smile on his lips.

"I'm the clean-up crew," he explained. "They feed me first and then I get the dishes."

Despite the news she just received, Meredith found she was starving and polished off her salad so quickly she was embarrassed. Images of Anthony and her mother were tucked aside into a dark recess of her mind for the moment. The possibility of such an obscene beginning was too much to comprehend all at once. She'd have to deconstruct pieces, bit by bit, to examine.

Ariel and her children sprang into action once again to serve up the second course, a crab-stuffed manicotti topped with an Alfredo sauce. "One of our members goes crabbing and this is our week to trade with him. Lucky us."

Stacey poured herself, Ariel, and David a glass of wine, but Meredith shook her head. She wanted a clear head to process all she was learning and she rarely drank anyway. Her mother's disease colored her childhood memories.

"I'll say," her friend announced, "this has to be the best meal I've ever had. When I move here..." She didn't finish her sentence. Instead, she took another bite of manicotti and groaned in delight. The children laughed at her obvious and noisy pleasure.

Meredith lifted her eyes to survey the tidy eat-in kitchen, the large expensive-looking double oven and built-in refrigerator. It was obvious the center of this home was the kitchen. "This isn't what I expected a commune to be like," she said tentatively.

"We don't call ourselves a commune," David said. "We helped set this one up. We're a network of sustainable farms, where we all share part of the work and then trade goods amongst each other. But we each own our individual properties and sell outside of our farm partners too. This way, we know where our food is coming from and who's growing it."

His wife leaned forward. "Our business is growing. We already have two employees and we're getting ready to hire another one. The demand for organic products has really taken off, all across the country, and we can barely keep up with orders."

"Don't you have to wear robes or something?" Stacey asked through a mouthful of food. "I supposed at least you'd have your heads shaved."

The children laughed and teased each other about what they'd look like bald. Their mother smiled at their amusement, and tucked a strand of her golden hair behind an ear. "We're not that kind of commune," David explained.

"Well, I'm willing to shave my head to live here," Stacey announced. She gave a pointed glance at her hosts. "Just saying."

"I've heard good things about Idaho," David said in a polite tone, taking a sip of wine. "Potatoes, right?"

Stacey shook her head firmly. "Oh no. You have everything right here. Sun, beach, beautiful scenery, warm winters, close to big cities. This is exactly where I want to live. Someday, when I move to California."

Ariel rose and started clearing dishes from the table. "We'll clean up today," she said with a gesture to the children and Stacey, then nodded back toward the door. "There's lots of help here. You two have lots to discuss."

There was no point in delaying the rest of this conversation. By tomorrow, she needed to be back in Idaho, with her children, fully engaged in a new job and on with the rest of her life. Whatever this old boyfriend of her mother's knew, needed to be shaken out. Now or never. She'd never see these people again, and this notion made her a little sad.

David toured her around the farm, pointing out different features. He answered what questions he could about Leila and Anthony. Long silences punctuated their discussion as she absorbed each kernel of information, tucking it away for further dissection when she was alone.

"I doubt the marriage was a love match on either side," he said. "I remember my parents talking about them. There was a fifteen or twenty-year difference between the two of them. Leila wanted someone handsome to escort her around and Anthony fit the bill. Her money would have attracted a lot of men of a certain type."

Finally, the reality poured in—the man in front of her wasn't her father, and a twinge of disappointment went through her. She'd shown up hostile and defensive, and he'd been nothing but kind. In exchange, she received a harsher truth. At best, her mother had been taken advantage of. At worst—she'd been the victim of an assault.

"Where is he then?" she asked, a little helplessly.

He darted a sharp glance at her. "You're not going to search for him. Not now, after all I've told you."

She avoided his eyes and gave a small shrug. "I don't know. He may be dead."

"Your mother didn't kill him, Meredith. I'd stake my life on it. What she wrote was probably meant metaphorically. You know, as though she'd killed her old life and was starting anew." He didn't sound convinced by his own words. "Your grandmother was a very exacting woman. Laura never felt she could be herself...she was made to feel everything she did was wrong. I was worried sick about her when she left, but also sort of proud of her for getting out."

A kid goat scampered across the field in front of them, stumbled on wobbly legs and then righted itself.

The scent of verdant green pastures mixed with the salty freshness of the vast ocean just a few miles away and filled her senses. A vague image pricked at her memory, of running to and fro on the beach, her mother lounging nearby. There had been a kite and a picnic, as well as the salty, pungent odor of seaweed rotting on the shore. The remembrance flickered and was gone. She must have been very young.

"Listen, Meredith." He paused. "If Anthony...if he's your father...he may have just disappeared. Or your grandmother kicked him out. Either way, he would be out of the picture. I'm sorry to tell you this, but maybe you should leave it that way."

She'd traveled across most of the country, from Idaho to Florida and now to California. An answer dangled right in front of her, but remained just outside her grasp. She wanted to stare into her father's face and see some type of recognition reflected in his eyes. Even if her father was Anthony...even then. There was no way to explain how important this was to someone else. In any case, if she found Anthony, she could put to rest the suspicion her mother may have killed someone.

She nibbled at her lip and changed the subject. "Did you ever see my mother wear a ring with a big purple stone? She left it to me—or rather my grandmother did, I guess. The ring was in a box with a few of my mother's belongings."

He shook his head and frowned. "I don't know anything about a ring. I never saw her wear jewelry at all. It must have been Leila's."

"I don't know why that old woman would leave me anything. I never met her. She had every reason to disinherit me. Her lawyer said not to expect anything of value, but the ring's worth at least a thousand dollars, maybe more."

David burst out laughing. "A thousand or two wouldn't have been much to someone like your grandmother."

"A man showed up in Hay City, alleging he's a cousin of mine. He claims the ring belongs to him. I don't know, though. Aside from the fact he's pretty old to be a cousin, there's something strange about him."

David's lips twisted to one side. "Some people come out of the woodwork when an estate is settled. Nothing like a death in the family to remind people of long lost kinships. Especially if an estate is large, as your grandmother's was. He may have heard about a ring with a large stone and wants to put in a claim."

She couldn't tell him about the way Raymond's dark hair and eyes matched her own daughter's. The resemblance was too strong to ignore. There was a family connection there, and the creepy cousin with his jet-black hair and too-white teeth was the one who held the answers, right there in Hay City. The image of the man hovered in her mind. She didn't need to see a picture of Anthony to know this is what he'd looked like. Why couldn't this man in front of her, with his organic farm and wholesome family, be her father?

Now she'd met him, she would give anything for this to be true.

****

Stacey's voice trembled with excitement when they returned to the house. "Ariel's invited me to come back! To stay and work! She's going to teach me how to milk the goats and make their cheeses. They have a guest house a half mile down the road and I can rent it cheap. I can't believe it. This is my dream come true. I'm really going to live in California."

Ariel gave a gentle laugh and smiled warmly at both of them. "You're always welcome too, Meredith. Bring your kids next time. And the sheriff Stacey's been telling me about."

"She said my hair would be great in a pixie cut," Stacey chattered on. "Bowl cuts like mine are out of style now, I guess. I'm making an appointment as soon as we get back home. Wait until Dad finds out I'm joining a commune. He'll split a seam."

David and his wife exchanged amused glances. "We certainly could use the help around here," he agreed, and then directed his attention on Meredith. "And definitely come back for a longer visit. Let us know how everything turns out."

She pasted a smile on her face, happy for her friend but terribly disappointed for herself. At least the long journey turned out to be a success for one of them.

"It's getting late—are you sure you don't want to stay tonight?" he added. "Start out fresh in the morning?"

"I have to get back to my kids and my job," she said with a shake of her head. "I've been away from home too much lately. We need to get on the road."

"Well, we can't let you go empty handed," Ariel said, heading to the pantry.

They were loaded with cuts of lamb packed in ice, as well as oranges and sandwiches for the road. The children shouted goodbyes from the front lawn and the couple stood with arms linked. Meredith blinked back tears as she shifted the car into reverse. These were such good, kind people and hadn't deserved her earlier hostility and bitterness.

Stacey waved wildly as they backed out the driveway. "See you soon," she yelled out the open roof before dropping down into her seat with a wide grin. "Pinch me. I feel like I'm dreaming."

Me too, Meredith thought as she veered the car east to Idaho. And the monster lurking in the shadows.

Chapter Seventeen

The scenery flashed by faster than before, this time in reverse as they drove east, away from the late afternoon sun. Stacey polished off both sandwiches as they sat in traffic, while Meredith peeled the oranges and licked at her sticky fingers. They stopped at the same roadside fruit stand in Davis before she remembered to check her phone. While Stacey went inside to load up on road snacks and a dried fruit appeasement gift for her father, she stayed in the car and dug the phone from the bottom of her purse. Eight missed calls and eight messages.

One, two and four were from Honey letting her know the kids were fine and not to worry. The third and sixth were from Curtis, chastising her for not calling as promised and telling her he was going to send out a search party if she didn't check in by noon. The fifth and seventh were from Patrick the mailman insisting she call him back immediately. The eighth was a recording offering her financing for a new car.

"Mommy, Atticus bit me," Jamie said when she got on the phone. "Honey said to bite him back, but I didn't want to."

She grimaced at Honey's child-rearing methods. "Good girl. Don't bite your brother."

"I won't."

The phone crackled and Honey's good-humored

voice was instantly reassuring. "All's fine here. How's the road trip?"

"On our way back. We should get there mid-day tomorrow."

"Take advantage of your time. Do something I wouldn't do."

"Probably not," she said with a smile. There wasn't much Honey wouldn't do. "And don't encourage Jamie to bite her brother, okay?"

"Worked for my kids. But if a more permissive approach is what you want, then fine with me."

Curtis picked up on the first ring, relief in his voice. "Meredith. Are you okay?"

"Mission accomplished. We're on our way back. Call off the search party." She paused, wondering how to sum up all that had transpired in twenty-four hours. "He wasn't what I expected. There's so much to tell you, I should wait until I'm home."

One of the many things she loved about him was his willingness to listen to her and bide his time. He didn't always agree with her, but he recognized she had her own opinions and life. He was as different from Brian as bitter and sweet.

"Is Stacey a good driver? Following the laws?"

Stacey appeared at the fruit stand door, her arms loaded with bags and a big toothy grin on her face. "She's great," Meredith said, smiling as she recalled her friend's forthcoming job at Sustainable Farms. "California exceeded all her grand expectations."

"I spoke to my uncle, the probate attorney, about your situation."

She held her breath.

"He said everything's up for litigation, but you

have the advantage of possession. The contents of the box were left to you and the ring was in the box. So, Holt can sue, but my uncle said he'd bet on you."

She took a deep breath and released it slowly. Some good news at least.

"I miss you." His deep voice rumbled through her.

"Me too. I'm ready to come home." She was more than ready. After all her recent travels and emotional upheaval, quiet Hay City—where little changed from year to year, and decade to decade—sounded like heaven.

"Be safe. Keep your car doors locked even when you're driving. And, ah, I hate saying this over the phone, but," his voice lowered, "I love you."

Stacey opened the trunk and dropped packages inside with a thump. At the door, her friend stretched over to touch her toes and then twisted side to side.

"I love you, too," she said softly. "I'll see you tomorrow."

The messages from Patrick she ignored. With her luck, he likely discovered the stone was a fake, plastic and mass-produced from a mold, and wanted his money back. The eleven hundred dollars he gave her was mostly intact, minus a grocery shopping spree and her share of travel expenses, safe in a box under her bed. With the nearest bank a half hour away, the trailer seemed the best option. No one would believe anything of value was in a camper in the middle of nowhere. Best to wait until she was home until she followed up with Patrick. Bad news could wait.

They flashed through Reno, stopping only to return the convertible, pick up Stacey's car and grab dinner-to-go, both of them eager now to get home again.

Exhaustion crept in close to midnight, with her yawns coming more and more often, and they pulled off the road near Winnemucca to rest, the stars brilliant in the midnight sky. She tilted her seat back and her friend curled up in the back seat. They both piled on blankets against the below freezing night temperatures.

"I have motel money," Stacey grumbled. "I'm sick of being cramped up in this car."

"Save it for your move."

Her friend shifted from one side to the other and then back again with a grunt. All was quiet for a few moments before Stacey spoke in a whisper. "Meredith. You awake?"

"Yes."

"What you were talking about...at David and Ariel's. Did your mother kill someone? I mean, if she did, that doesn't matter to me. About you I mean. We'll still be friends. And if she did, I'm sure she had a good reason. She probably didn't kill anyone, though. But, did she?"

"I don't know. I'm finding out I didn't really know her at all."

"Kids don't know their parents, not as real people anyway, do they?"

"She loved me."

Stacey shifted, yawned loudly, then hiked the blankets higher until only her nose and eyes were visible. "Love's the important thing, I think. The *most* important thing."

"Yes," Meredith agreed, and her friend grew silent. Eventually, soft snores emanated from the back seat. Regardless of what she said, whether a parent committed murder was pretty important, too.

Until she found her father, alive, how would she ever put those words—*I'm a murderer*—to rest? She cocooned herself in her own blankets and curled up as small as possible in the seat.

They woke up at dawn, shivering in the freezing car. A hard frost covered the windshield and windows, so they scraped it off and forayed on.

"I don't know about this saving money by sleeping in a car thing," Stacey griped. "I can smell myself."

Meredith stared out the window, her neck stiff and body sore from the twisted position in which she woke. She was sick of the car too. "Atticus needs new clothes. I live in a borrowed trailer. And I don't get my first paycheck for two more weeks. I'm broke." She didn't mention money likely owed back from the sale of a fake piece of jewelry.

Her friend didn't respond for a couple of miles. Beige sagebrush peeked out above the snow-covered landscape and one row of mountains merged into another. And then, in a hesitant voice, Stacey spoke again, "Someday, I'm gonna have kids. Two's a good number. I just have to figure out the man part first."

Meredith rubbed her neck and glanced sideways at her friend. "California first, though, right?"

"Ah, jeez, tell me this is really happening."

"Yeah," she said, slumping in her seat. "This is all really happening."

****

Home again, she stood under a hot shower for six minutes, the exact time it took for the water to run cold. Her trailer's shower was barely big enough to turn around in, but she didn't need to budge. She just wanted the hot water to go on and on, and wash off two and a half days of grime and nervous perspiration. Through the thin wall, she could hear Jamie talking quietly to Atticus. One of the good things about living in a trailer was the small space meant her kids were never out of hearing distance.

The past forty-eight hours were like one very long day. She'd returned home a different person, and someone she didn't know at all. How do I live with this information, she wondered—knowing, or almost knowing—about my beginnings?

She scrubbed at her skin as though she could wash the facts away. A lot of girls grew up wishing they were secretly a princess or had magic powers, adopted away at birth and raised by mortals. Her own story was much darker. I've fallen into a story where I discover I'm actually the child of...of...she couldn't even think of the words. She fought back tears as the water ran cold.

Skin reddened by the scouring and hair wrapped in a towel, she tugged on fresh jeans and her favorite blue sweater. A touch of makeup covered the dark circles under her eyes and she emerged to find her children making pretend cakes on the floor of the kitchen, pans strewn around them.

A light snow drifted down, adding to the two feet already on the ground. In front of the trailer, a series of snowmen and snow animals marched toward the driveway. At some point over the weekend, Honey brought the kids over to the trailer. They'd created some semblance of frozen dogs and cats too, and even a quasi-moose, although one antler already fell off. A blanket of white coated everything, from rooftops to tree limbs, and was in sharp contrast to sunny California's verdant land of green.

"I want to make a snow lion," Jamie announced.

She finished toweling off her hair and wrinkled her nose at the idea of going out in the freezing air. "Curtis is coming over soon. Let's stay warm and dry."

"He can help me."

"Maybe next time. He won't be here until after dark, and in any case, he wants to talk to me this time."

"I don't think so," her daughter said, one of her favorite lines when she wasn't getting her way.

Meredith opened a cabinet and flourished a stack of puzzles. "Quiet time this afternoon while Atticus naps. You can make a snow lion after school tomorrow at Honey's. She needs something to guard the chickens."

While she tidied the kitchen, her daughter opened her puzzle of the United States, the one with the shape of Idaho missing. The colorful cardboard pieces clattered to the table and she began the process of fitting the fifty—well, forty-nine—shapes into place. It hadn't taken Jamie long to learn the geography of the country, and she wondered if her daughter would be doing calculus by the fourth grade. She sang a lullaby to Atticus until his eyes drooped and shut. An afternoon at home, doing a series of nothings with her children, was just what they all needed.

She sat at the tiny trailer table with Jamie and sipped hot Jasmine mint tea, enjoying the aroma as much as the leaves' clean taste. The tea and one of these rare quiet moments were two of her treasured luxuries. With her feet propped up and her back resting against the wall, she reread *The Wizard of Oz* for the fortieth time. The book was a gift for her daughter, but she'd fallen in love with it herself. For some reason, she could never get enough of this story, where a girl traveled over the rainbow and back.

When Atticus woke, she set him on the floor with some pans and then unwrapped one package of lamb chops, studying the meat with a frown. What do you do with lamb? There was a simple foolproof solution for any kitchen challenge. She diced carrots, onions, garlic and celery and browned small chunks of lamb in olive oil before tossing it all in a pot with vegetable broth. They'd have a warm, filling soup once the flavors merged and the lamb became tender.

She played stacking blocks with her son and then puzzles with her daughter while the trailer filled with the aroma of vegetables, lamb, and broth merging and blurring into one savory, mouthwatering blend.

At five-twenty, headlights swung across the window and a moment later, there was a tap on the door. She sprang up and yanked the door open in a flash. Though she expected him, a lump formed in her throat when she saw Curtis standing there. Had it only been seventy-one-and-a-half hours? Not that she was counting...

He stepped up and quickly closed the door behind him. One arm holding a bag, he drew her close with the other one and kissed her, in a way she once would have protested wasn't appropriate in front of her kids. The bag crinkled as he drew her closer. His musky scent filled her senses and her hands locked behind his neck. Warmth flooded through her to her knees and when they broke apart, her lips stayed open in a round "oh." The bed at the back of the trailer was only fifteen feet away, she thought, and the same idea echoed in his gaze. A giggle from behind returned her to the present.

"Get a room," her five-year-old said.

She whirled around. "Jamie! Where did you hear such a thing as that?"

"Rio says it all the time when his dad kisses someone," Jamie said, referring to one of her school friends.

"Well…it's not nice to say."

"Hi, wild child," Curtis greeted the girl.

Her five-year-old's dark eyes shone with expectation. "What's a wild child?"

He grinned at her. "Like an untamed critter, full of vigor and ferocity."

"Is that good?"

"Depends on whether you're the mother or not," Meredith broke in.

He chuckled and set the bag on the kitchen counter. "Chocolate milk for wild children only." He nodded to Atticus. "And their little brothers." The toddler clambered down from his seat and wrapped his arms around Curtis' legs.

She busied herself in the kitchen by setting out bowls and stirring the pot. "Hungry for soup?"

He swung the toddler up into his arms and edged up next to her. "Well, I'm certainly hungry," he murmured near her ear.

Heat rose in her face and she glanced up at him. "I'm starving," she said, as she handed him a bowl of soup. "This will have to do for now."

They set the bowls around the table and Curtis filled them in on the less glamorous side of being sheriff in a large, rural county. "I'm the roadkill removal service and a one-man animal crisis team. My weekend duty included two freshly dead skunks, one half of a deer, and a very angry wounded bull."

Meredith gulped down her mouthful of soup. "Um, one half of a deer?"

"On the highway. I assume the other half is still on the semi that must have hit it."

"Oh, gross," Jamie cried out.

"Tell me about the bull," Meredith said quickly.

While some lands were fenced, he explained, many ranchers took advantage of Idaho's open range laws, where they could turn their cattle loose to forage more broadly. In the fall, when most ranchers ran their herds to lower range land, one bull remained unaccounted for until it appeared over the weekend standing in the middle of the snowy highway. One leg was clearly broken, a deep gash in the animal's massive neck was crusted with dried blood, and its eyes sought to murder anything or anyone who dared to come close. The owner of the two-thousand-pound Angus bull showed up on the scene the same time as Curtis, and initially refused to put the suffering animal down.

"I had to close the highway for more than an hour while we tried to get the animal to move. Wounded or not, those horns are killers," he said, as he refilled his bowl with a second helping of soup. "It rammed my truck and put a couple fair-sized dents in it before going after some damn fool who got out of his car and decided to get a selfie. The rancher had to shoot it between the eyes—the bull, not the selfie fellow, although we both were tempted. Then we had two thousand pounds of bull laying in the middle of a two-lane highway. Of course, then it started to snow."

"Not like my weekend," she muttered.

He entertained the kids with more stories—

although her toddler was more interested in his building blocks—while Meredith cleaned the kitchen. Curtis thumbed through her book while she gave the children quick sponge baths and got them ready for bed. The trailer offered little space for privacy, so they went back to her bedroom compartment, which consisted of little else except a queen-sized bed. She kept the door open to keep an eye on her kids, then sat on the opposite side of the bed from her handsome sheriff to stay her impulse to close the door and succumb to all temptations.

"Tell me about your trip," he said, his expression bare with concern.

She filled him in, keeping her voice low. He asked an occasional question, but mainly listened while she told her story. When she got to the part about Anthony, her voice broke and she couldn't meet his gaze.

"You believe him?"

She nodded. There'd been nothing about David's behavior to indicate he was lying. His story made perfect sense. "The more I find out, the worse it gets. My mother protected me from all this, but I didn't listen." She glanced out the bedroom door at her children, now fast asleep. Jamie's curly head peeped out from under the covers. "Is you-know-who still in town? My uninvited visitor?"

"I saw him at the store this morning, talking to Jeffrey at the deli counter," he said. "Appeared to be resupplying for another few days."

"Good." She took a deep breath. "Florida, California, and now Hay City. I'll find my answers right here at home."

"Interesting…" he started.

"What?"

"We're assuming Raymond is related to Anthony...some kind of cousin, right? And you suspect Anthony is...well, your father. Then Raymond must know what your father did, all those years ago. Otherwise, how else would he claim to be kin?"

She nodded. "I considered that. There's also the ring. Raymond must have known the family better than he admits, if my grandmother promised it to him. I mean, if what he said is even true." She spoke slowly. "I think Anthony may have told Raymond a lot about what happened in my mother's household. I bet he knows a whole lot more than he's letting on—about Anthony and my mother."

She was close to the truth now. Talking to Raymond would be like ripping a bandage off a raw wound, but she was determined to confront the worst. The man had information to share. The quandary was in how to get him to divulge his secrets.

"He may not want to confess anything that accuses his cousin of a crime," Curtis said.

"I'm the skeleton in the family closet," she mused. "My grandmother tried to lock the closet and swallow the key. She must have been afraid I'd show up some day and discover the truth."

"Maybe. Be careful not to jump to conclusions. After all, she left you the letter and your mother's belongings."

"After she died," Meredith said bitterly.

She peeked out the open bedroom door. Her children were tucked in to their beds and Jamie's silky curls lay across her pillow.

"Meredith."

She raised her eyes to his. There was no doubt he was no longer thinking about Raymond. His thoughts had shifted to another topic, one too dangerous to pursue with her children sleeping so close by. Her breath shortened.

"Dinner tomorrow, at my place? I already checked with Honey. She'll watch the kids for a few hours."

The stretch of bed between them grew smaller. If she extended her arm, she could touch him. Jamie snorted in her sleep and rolled over, and the spell was broken. "Dinner," she agreed.

****

The opportunity to talk to her cousin arose sooner than expected. On her lunch break the next day, she spied him in the Hay City grocery store where she stopped to grab a ready-made sandwich. This time, his black curly hair took on a disturbing significance. Could this man honestly know the unpleasant circumstances of her mother's past?

Raymond spotted her, and he lingered at the cash register, eying her as she approached. Meredith's stomach clenched. This new-found relative, her strange cousin, remained in Hay City waiting for her return. The little she knew about the man told her this was a huge sacrifice. He viewed them as back country hicks. Four days earlier, she couldn't wait for him to leave. Now she was glad he stayed. If anyone knew anything about her parents, it was this man. Her gaze drifted up to his dark curly hair. No one else in her family had that color hair, and it made total sense which side of the family he sprang from. The rotten side.

Every impulse told her to turn around and circle the store again until he was gone. Instead, she steeled herself and stopped behind him at the counter.

"I hear you've been in California," he said, with his too-white smile.

"Have you been asking about me?"

"You're family. The reason I'm here."

This didn't make sense. If Anthony impregnated her mother and her mother killed him, then who would share this information with Raymond? Certainly not her grandmother. Her grandmother would have taken the secret to her grave. Someone else must have known what happened. Her theory about her mother's past started to unravel.

He finished paying for his small sack of groceries and nodded toward her sandwich, fumbling again for his wallet. "Let me treat you for your lunch."

"No, no, please don't. I've got this." She quickly laid a five-dollar bill on the counter and was glad to see Raymond put his wallet away. She didn't want to be beholden to him for anything.

He shrugged. "Perhaps we could start over, at least have a cup of coffee."

Considering her options, she forced her lips to turn up in a welcoming manner. "I work until five. There aren't any cafes in Hay City, but why don't you come out to my friend, Honey's, this afternoon, when I get off work? I'm sure she wouldn't mind."

Her friend would be a good buffer and, anyway, her own trailer was too small. She didn't want to be trapped in a small space with this man, cousin or not.

"I met Honey the other day. Nice woman." He paused. "I guess you have children you'll need to attend to? I met them when I saw your friend." He chuckled. "Your girl, Jamie…she's a handful."

She didn't like him mentioning her children. This was another reason to have Honey nearby, to keep her kids entertained while she talked to this strange man. Honey would see through this man in a flash and ferret out any hidden motivations. Her friend would also protect her children with her life.

"Let's say five-thirty," she responded. "She lives on Ham and Eggs Road, the only house out there. Can't miss it."

He scooped up his groceries and gave her another blinding smile. "It's a date."

Chapter Eighteen

"Your cousin must dye his hair with black ink," Honey said with a disapproving sound in her voice after she arrived. "I wonder why no one's told him it's a little too much at his age. And I'm certain he's had work done. The skin on his face is stretched tighter than a drum. Don't get me started on his beak of a nose. Too narrow to breathe through. Outlandish. Like he's put on a disguise."

Meredith had arrived at Honey's farmhouse just after five, wanting to get there well before her cousin. She'd alerted her friend of their plan as soon as she got back to the office, and the older woman was more than happy to host a coffee get-together. A stranger meant fresh gossip and hosting him meant she'd be front-and-center for any juicy information. Having private family secrets revealed was a tough trade-off to gain the woman's protection, but Meredith was willing to make the sacrifice. Secrets always had a way of creeping out anyway, no matter how hard you tried to suppress them.

"I'm not clear on how he's my cousin either. More like a second or third cousin." Or fourth or fifth, she hoped. The less they were related, the better.

"I have a cousin younger than my oldest daughter," Honey said. "You can't count on cousins knowing their place. Family trees are like overgrown shrubbery."

She agreed with this statement wholeheartedly. Her

entire family was a bewildering mess. If she ever decided to sketch her family tree, it would resemble an abstract painting, where considerable imagination and interpretation were required.

With Jamie and Atticus settled in the living room decorating paper bag puppets, Meredith quietly gave Honey an abbreviated sketch of what she wanted to know from Raymond. She laid out her suspicions, about her mother's pregnancy and a possible murder. Her friend's eyes glittered avidly, but she listened to the end without comment—surprising for the garrulous woman.

"Heavens, what a murky muddle. This cousin, then…he may be the key that unlocks this mystery," Honey summed up with a smack of her lips. "We just need to twist him a bit. Jiggle the truth out of him."

Meredith gave a nervous laugh, despite the grimness of the subject matter. Her friend had a way of cutting straight to the point. "If we need to talk about sensitive subjects, will you take the kids in the back?" she said in a low voice. "Jamie's already asking too many questions."

A rap on the door startled her. He was early. The other woman rose and laid a hand on her shoulder. "Don't you worry about a thing."

She took a deep breath. Impossible not to worry.

Raymond stepped into the room, rubbing his hands together against the cold. "What a charming little house," he cried, gazing to his left toward the kitchen and then right toward the living room. "The fireplace crackling, the fresh aroma of coffee and…oh, tell me you've got apple pie baking. Wait until I tell my city friends about this *charming* country homestead."

Honey preened before his lavish praises and helped

him shuck off his navy wool coat, adorned with shiny gold buttons glittering down the front. He strode toward the fireplace and came to a sudden halt. His gaze fixed on Jamie, who sat cross-legged next to Atticus at the far end of the couch. "Oh my," he muttered.

Meredith stepped quickly over to him. "These are my children. Jamie and Atticus. You said you'd already met them."

His glance passed over Atticus and settled back on Jamie. A troubled expression was in his eyes. "This one here had a cap on before. Her hair...she's the spitting image." His throat worked and he coughed.

An icy chill went through Meredith. He *knew*.

Honey bustled in behind them, wiping her hands on an apron. "Why don't we sit and have a chat in the kitchen. The kids will be busy for a while. Isn't that correct, Jamie?"

The five-year-old glanced up at the three adults and rolled her eyes. "I know. Boring grown-up stuff." Without a second glance at them, the little girl went back to gluing spangles onto her paper bag.

"Back room," Meredith hissed in Honey's ear as they turned to go into the kitchen.

The other woman shot ahead in a determined stride and gathered up three coffee cups. "Cream and sugar?"

Raymond's eyes were distant as he settled at the table. He ran a hand over his face and wiped at his lips. "Plenty of both."

"I always say if God didn't want us to eat sugar, he wouldn't have given sugar beets a higher purpose. Have you ever seen a sugar beet? Ugly as a clod of dirt. Now there's a plant shoulda gone extinct, except for our need to sweeten up our coffee. Otherwise sugar cane would have been enough." Coffee served, Honey arranged a chair at the head of the table and sat her generous frame down with a grunt. "Oh, feels good to rest a bit."

Meredith's hands trembled and she fought to keep her voice calm. *The spitting image.* "Is he still alive?"

Raymond gazed out the window, a strange expression on his face. There was no need to clarify who she meant. He blinked, as though returning to the present, and shook his head. "I'm afraid he died a long time ago."

Pinpricks of electricity rippled up her arms. She was aware of Honey leaning in, breathlessly waiting for more. She tried to make her voice casual, but didn't quite pull it off. "How did he die?"

He gave a short laugh. "This is a grim subject for a family get together. I'd rather hear about you and your children. Tell me about *your* life."

"I grew up without a father," she said, "and a mother who didn't want to talk about him."

He sipped his coffee and flashed a smile at Honey. "Perfect. The right amount of cream and sugar. Just how I take it at home."

"Nothing makes me happier than to treat my guests well," the woman said, patting her hair. "How about some homemade apple pie to go with your coffee?"

"I'm just about in heaven already, but homemade pie would put me all the way there."

Honey rose and went into the kitchen. Meredith leaned toward him and spoke softly. "We're talking about Anthony, right?"

The name changed something in his expression and the corners of his mouth twitched downward. His voice was just as soft. "Trust me, Anthony wasn't that type of man at all. Nothing could ever be proven."

"You said my daughter resembles him. *The spitting image*. You're here, claiming kinship. He was, what to you, a cousin?"

He leaned back, away from her. "I never said any such thing. Nor do I like your tone."

She cocked her head to one side. He certainly *had* said something, the implication clear. Wasn't it? If he wasn't referring to Anthony, then whom? She opened her mouth to ask.

Jamie ran up to the table and tugged at her arm. "I want to go home now."

"In a bit," she said, glancing down. "Honey's going to serve pie first."

"I don't want pie."

Raymond raised an eyebrow and he bent toward the girl, his face close to hers. "Your mommy and I are visiting right now. Run along and play."

The five-year-old stared him in the eye. "I don't like you. Your face looks funny."

He straightened up and his lips curled at one side. "What a little charmer you have here."

Meredith couldn't chastise her daughter. She didn't like him either. The man oozed falseness. "We won't be long," she promised Jamie. "Fifteen minutes."

Honey showed up then, with a tablecloth draped over one arm and two dishes of pie in her hands. "My, but I see the family resemblance. What a nice get together. Jamie, you and your brother can have a picnic in the living room." She led the girl away, leaving them alone again.

"I'm interested in a ring you may have," he said.

She shook her head firmly. "We covered this

before. I don't know what you mean."

Honey practically raced back to the kitchen, talking on the way. "A ring, you say? Diamond? I'm not a big fan of diamonds personally. Give me a plain gold band. Now you're talking about an honest ring." She grabbed the pie dish and three more plates before returning to the table to join them.

Raymond waved his hand, indicating he wasn't interested in pie after all, and continued talking. "I happen to know the ring hasn't surfaced in twenty-five years. So either your mother took it with her when she left, which I find doubtful, or your grandmother left my property to you to pass along. The ring's cursed."

"C-c-cursed?"

"The last two people to have it ended up dead," he said. He stood abruptly and scraped the chair back from the table. "Think it over. Your children need a mother."

For a large woman, Honey moved quick. "Enough," she ordered, pointing at the door. "No threats in this house. Out."

Meredith stayed seated as he grabbed his coat and left, with not even a goodbye. Her reaction telegraphed all. She was lying about the ring and now he was onto her. The door slammed and Honey returned to the table.

"No such thing as a curse, dearie. And he didn't even touch my pie. Tsk. Not as nice a man as I anticipated." She sat down heavily and picked up her fork. "Now, what's all this about a ring? Such a mystery." She took a bite of pie and looked at Meredith expectantly.

She shrugged. "No mystery at all. My grandmother left me an ugly ring and I sold it. Cursed or not, it's gone." She rubbed her finger where she'd worn the ring. Could a curse flake off after only a few days?

"Guess your cousin doesn't believe in curses if he wants it so much. Anyway, if the ring was his property, as he said, why is *he* still alive?"

Meredith glanced up hopefully. The man would apparently say anything to lay claim to a piece of her grandmother's estate. Now he was trying to scare the ring out of her.

Honey patted her hand. "Don't you worry, dear. He'll clear out soon. There's a big storm coming in. Outsiders don't usually stick around for those." The woman gestured to the door. "I understand you have a handsome fellow waiting for you this evening. Better not keep him waiting. I wrapped up some pie to take with you. Figured you'd be in a rush to get going."

Curtis, she thought, and her heart beat faster. "What would I do without you?"

The woman's cheeks flushed pink, a pleased expression on her face. "We're family now," she said. "Family sticks together."

****

"I don't like to complain..." Curtis started. He lay back against the pillows, a light sheen of sweat glistening on his neck and bare chest.

Meredith snuggled closer into his arms, drawing circles on his chest hair. The blankets tumbled in disarray on the floor and the sheets had followed. Snowflakes drifted lazily from the sky outside his bedroom window. "You never do. You should try it some time. It feels great."

"I hardly see you anymore." His stomach growled, reminding her they'd ignored the dinner he prepared, and instead went straight to his bedroom.

She sprinkled tiny kisses on his chin and stubble of his late-in-the-day beard scratched her lips. She ran her lips down to his neck and he sighed with pleasure. "I'm doing my best to make it up to you."

"You're doing a great job. But, still. I'm not kidding. I miss you."

She tilted up her chin to meet his serious gaze. "Everything's going so fast for me. My entire life has changed this year. Moving here, Brian's murder, my house collapsing. And now, all this with my mother...and...Anthony." She couldn't call him her father. She never would.

He sat up and raised her with him. The weight of his arm around her shoulders was comforting. He cleared his throat twice before speaking. "This wouldn't be a bad time to do some work inside your house."

She gave a short laugh and glanced up to see if he was serious. "The roof needs fixing first. Otherwise, the water just keeps coming through." She sighed. "I'm going to have to wait until the snow thaws. I promise we won't live in your trailer forever."

Curtis withdrew his arm and scooted a bit away from her. "I'm not worried about the trailer. And I'm not talking about fixing your house up either." His jaw tightened. "I want to start demolition. We can start clearing out the interior now. Decide which appliances and fixtures we want to save or sell. Of course, all your furniture and belongings will be put in storage. My parents have a shed we can use."

"What are you talking about?" she interrupted. A flash memory came to her of Brian moving them abruptly the year before from California to Idaho. He hadn't asked if she wanted to leave her home, or even consulted her. Her former husband bullied and bossed her into being a person she couldn't recognize. "I never said I'd let you build a new house for me. Not for sure. This is my decision, remember? Not yours. There's no 'we' about it."

For the first time since she met him, Curtis' face darkened in anger. She shrank back, Brian and his rages coming back to her in an instant. Her breath shortened and tears sprang to her eyes. This is how it was with Brian. Everything would be fine as long as she agreed with him. Any opposition raised the possibility of cruelty and violence.

His expression softened immediately and, making slow movements—as though approaching a frightened animal—enfolded her hand in his. "Meredith." He shook his head as though frustrated. "We can disagree and still talk about things. I can be upset, even angry and…" He made a disgusted sound in his throat. "I'm not Brian. I'd never be like him."

She curled her hand inside his, hating the reaction automatically triggered by an irritated response. *Like Pavlov's dog, I'm well trained.* Curtis didn't deserve being treated like the cruel, callous man she'd married.

Curtis let go of her hand and rose from bed. "I want to show you something."

He crossed the room, showing no embarrassment at being unclothed, and there was certainly no reason he would. His body was a solid, taut line, from long muscular legs to well-defined abs and broad chest. He returned with a sketchbook and sat next to her, his bare hip next to hers. She grabbed a sheet and wrapped it around her shoulders, not as comfortable in her own skin, a by-product perhaps of Brian's frequent jibes about her bony shoulders or too-small breasts.

He flipped open the sketchbook. On the paper before her was a schematic for a house. "I'm thinking three bedrooms. The master bedroom will have its own private bath and there will be a second one in the hallway for the kids to share. Big open kitchen, high ceilings like my house, and a roll-up door in the great room that will open up onto a deck. A really big deck where we…you…can sit in the summer and watch the kids play." He stopped and waited for her reaction.

She needed to get her head out of the sand. Her old house was uninhabitable, leaking in nearly every room and rotten at its core. She lived in a borrowed trailer next to it and visited her home nearly every day to check on its condition. The day before, going inside to use the washing machine, she found an icicle dripping down from the middle of the kitchen ceiling like a dagger. The entire community of Hay City was involved with the planning of tearing down and building a modern house for her in the spring. Honey was spearheading the demotion and fund raising, Crusty was accumulating building materials, and Curtis was at the helm of design. As difficult as it was for her to accept this amazing generosity of so many people, she had no idea how to repair her existing house. The place was uninhabitable and beyond repair.

She ran a finger lightly over the plans, tracing the lines he'd drawn. "It's beautiful. I can't believe it could exist someday."

"It can and *will* exist. As soon as you say yes. As soon as the snow melts, we can get started." He flipped a page to another design. "Step two will be to get a decent garage built along with a shed on the side."

"A two-car garage," she exclaimed with a laugh, trying to dispel the earlier mood. "That'll be the day. I barely have one car that works."

His throat worked. "Just in case, you know."

Her gaze lifted to meet his.

"Meredith. This will be your house. Someday, I hope it could be our house, together. What I'm saying is…I…I think about you all the time." His throat worked and his Adam's apple jumped. "I miss you every minute I'm not with you, whether it's a weekend or overnight. You make me stronger, better. Can you see yourself with me, building a future, as a family?"

Her mouth fell open. In quiet moments, she'd had a daydream or two of a future with Curtis. Those days were far off, though, and marrying him happened in a hazy time frame. She wasn't used to getting what she wanted. The world kept tumbling forward with bewildering speed.

"My kids," she started. "I mean, wow. My head is spinning. Oh, I'm doing this all wrong." She grasped his hand and tried to corral her thoughts. "Even after everything you know about me—Brian, my family, all those things I told you about wanting to kill my husband—you still want me?"

He gestured to the rumpled bed. "I wouldn't be here with you if that mattered. You're an amazing person. Far better than you realize. Anyone else would have been beaten down by all the circumstances you've dealt with, but you just get tougher."

Tears sprang to her eyes. "Because of you." She leaned her head against his shoulder, too choked up to say more.

Curtis hugged her close. "Take some time and

223

think it over. No matter what, I'm here for you. And I'll build this house, whatever you decide." He gave a faint chuckle. Meredith heard the hurt beneath his laugh, and her heart contracted. Why couldn't she just say yes and be happy?

****

She lay in her own bed later, limbs heavy with fatigue, and her musings flickered from Curtis' proposal to her visit with Raymond. Her brow contracted, hating how her cousin intruded on more pleasant events. The coffee-time visit had been so…uncomfortable. It may have made sense to tell her cousin, yes, she had the ring and sold it. What could he do? The fact was, she didn't want to find out. If there was a possibility he had a real claim to the ring, she didn't want him causing trouble and demanding money already partially spent.

Her cousin hadn't given the impression he was lying, exactly. More like he was editing the facts and omitting crucial details. The conversation was a guessing game, with her not sure what questions to ask and answers sliding one way and then the other. She hoped Honey was right and he'd leave town before the full storm hit the valley.

What was wrong with her? She shouldn't be thinking about him. She rolled over and hugged her pillow. The man of her dreams made love to her, drew up plans for a house, wanted a future with her and she didn't leap into his arms and scream "yes!" Of course, she thought with a frown, he hadn't actually proposed. He never said the word "marriage." But a lot of people didn't get married. Maybe that was too much to ask.

Living with Curtis would be a solid life, nothing

fancy. But she'd never aspired to be rich. She didn't have a desire for pretty clothes, expensive restaurants or sparkling jewelry. An honest simple life, surrounded by good people—that's what was important. The riches she craved were what she had discovered in Hay City— the crisp smell of a first snow, lush green fields springing to life, laughter of her children, and the incredible joy she felt when Curtis riveted his gaze upon her when they were alone. These were the riches worth having. Let others hoard gold coins and fine jewelry, always looking over their shoulder and certain others sought their hoarded wealth. Somehow, through all the tragedy threaded through her life, she'd gotten exceedingly lucky.

Curtis was kind, handsome and good to the core. He'd be steadfast and good with her children. But he wouldn't get as much in return. He didn't understand all the ugliness and hurt in her life had damaged her to the soul. People don't start over from tragedy, they just keep putting one foot in front of the other. The residue of those days would remain with her forever.

She'd learned a thing or two about love in the past year. You don't use another person. You care about them and their happiness. You give more than you get. The fact was, he was too good for her and the scales were wildly unbalanced. At some point, she would drag him down. If she truly loved him, she would enjoy the status quo as long as it lasted. Their affair would fade and he'd be free to move onto someone else. Just as well he didn't propose marriage. She didn't need a ring in order to be cursed.

She punched her pillow and rolled over, knowing sleep wouldn't come for hours. The truth hurt.

Chapter Nineteen

Patrick burst into the office the next morning, mailbag swinging from one shoulder. The door slammed behind him as he stomped across the floor. "Meredith. I've been calling and calling. Then the office was locked up noontime yesterday when I stopped by. I even drove by your place after work and you weren't there either."

She leaned back in her chair, the ignored calls coming to her mind. The last thing she'd wanted to do was call him back and learn the ring was a fake. What was the fuss about this ring? It was a curse after all, in that it wouldn't go away. The last thing she wanted to do was return the money, some of it already spent.

"Oh. I'm sorry, I was out of town over the weekend, and walked down to the store for lunch yesterday. I've been really busy and…"

The mailbag hit the floor with a solid thud as his breathless words tumbled over hers. "You're not going to believe what I have to tell you." A ring case emerged from his pocket and he opened it on the counter. Even from across the room, she could see the ugly chunk of gold and the too-large stone. "This ring?" he said. "It's worth a fortune."

Hands on the desk, she pushed herself into a standing position and studied his face for any hint of a joke. A shiver ran through her. "My ring?"

"My friend sent it back, overnight mail, heavily insured. He can't buy it, he can't *afford* it. It's a good thing we're buddies because someone else could have cheated us. He'd never double-cross me though. He's one of the good ones in this world."

She surreptitiously pinched the side of her leg. No, not dreaming. Wrinkles furrowed her forehead as she crossed the small office to meet Patrick at the counter. She stared at the ring. "I don't understand."

He took a deep breath. "The gem is called taaffeite and it's very rare. Your stone is large and close to flawless, which makes it even rarer, so the value goes up exponentially. This is something a private collector would own. You were wearing it with blue jeans. To work in this office." His eyes lit up and he chuckled as though the entire situation were a joke. "Cats and dogs, I've been dying to tell you all this, but you just up and disappeared."

"I went to California," she said in a daze. "This ring is really worth a lot of money?"

She'd never heard of a gemstone called taaffeite, just as she'd never heard of spinel. Patrick was a rural mailman and perhaps never a jeweler at all. He could be making all this up. But there he was, full of confidence and exhilaration, his light brown eyes earnest. He'd have to be a terrific actor, and more than a little mean, to pull a prank like this.

"We could be talking a hundred thousand dollars, maybe double, triple that amount. Depends on the collector. This is a little out of my league so I'm not quite sure. At this level, prices aren't set—they fluctuate with supply and demand."

Her knees grew weak. Could it be possible she'd

sold a priceless jewel for eleven hundred dollars? Her grandmother must be laughing in her grave.

Patrick must have read the dismay in her face because he slid the ring case toward her. "I'm returning it to you, of course. Holding you to our little deal wouldn't be honest. I figured on making a couple hundred dollars at most as commission. I wouldn't fleece you. Tell me though, where exactly did this gem come from? My friend is anxious to know, too."

"My grandmother died and the ring was in a cardboard box, along with other items left to me. I was told not to expect anything of value so I assumed…"

The mailman eyed her, his eyebrows knitting together. "You're sure about this. I mean, the collector world is very small. If the ring came from, well, dishonest activities, people will know. I'm not saying you did anything fraudulent, of course—just whoever gave it to you. There would be folks out there who will be familiar with this ring and this particular stone."

"I'm not sure about anything," she said, tucking a loose strand of hair behind one ear.

Now it made sense why Raymond drove across the country, and why her grandmother's lawyer was so eager to be involved. There was a mystery behind the ring, starting with its value and ending with why it ended up in her hands. People were on the lookout for this valuable collector's item missing from her grandmother's estate.

Grimacing, Patrick laid one clenched fist on the counter. "Exactly what I didn't want to hear. Establishing provenance is important for high-end pieces. Just like fine art. Most people don't want stolen goods, if you'll pardon the suggestion. It's a liability."

She shook her head in a weary manner. Little could surprise her when it came to her family. They were an unsavory bunch. "I understand. Tell me, though, what would you recommend I do now?"

He chewed his bottom lip for a moment. "Someone in your family should be able to give you an answer, or whoever handled your grandmother's estate. All you really need to know is how the ring was acquired, and when. Establishing the chain of ownership goes a long ways toward settling a potential buyer's concerns."

Family or the lawyer. Raymond or Mr. Therald Holt, Esq. Both were unpleasant options. "I'll see what I can do."

"I'm assuming the piece would still be for sale…considering it may be a valuable family heirloom."

She set her mouth in a grim line and stared at the ring. Already, the responsibility of ownership weighed heavily on her. A stone worth so much would need a high level of insurance and to be secured away in a safety deposit box. Instead, since she couldn't afford either, it would go right into her jewelry box…or under her mattress, or hidden in a sock drawer. Snug though it was, her borrowed trailer could be peeled open with a can opener. Of course, she'd never wear a ring so valuable. There was no sentimental value attached to it whatsoever. It would be a burden and a curse, just like Raymond said.

She lifted her eyes and straightened her shoulders. "I want it gone."

He broke into a wide grin and expelled a relieved breath. "I know someone who deals with collectors of rare stones. I'll give him a call. I doubt they'll be familiar with this particular ring, but he'll give us an idea what the market's like. You can pay me back the eleven hundred dollars when you get a chance."

She closed the case and slid it toward Patrick. He raised both hands and backed away. "No can do. My blood pressure's gone sky high carrying this around. My advice is get it under lock and key immediately." He gave a nervous chuckle. "Some people would kill for an inheritance like this."

****

Not eleven hundred dollars but perhaps a hundred thousand dollars. The amount was so vast as to be unbelievable. She opened the case and stared at the ugly rock. Things were only as valuable as people made them. Her grandmother was a collector of expensive pieces of art and these were the things she valued, not people, and certainly not her own daughter. Her own values were just the opposite. This stone meant nothing to her. She'd take the money and repair her house so her children would have a decent home to live in.

If she was going to sell the ring, she needed to establish provenance. There were two people who might know the ring's background: her oily cousin or the impersonal lawyer. For a moment, anger bubbled up toward her mother for keeping so many secrets. She should have shared more about family while she was alive. Meredith's anger fell away as quick as it flared. How would such a conversation have gone? Her mother only wanted to protect a young daughter from ugly truths. She didn't expect to die so young, and may have wanted to wait a few more years before revealing painful information. As a mother, she understood the impulse to protect one's children. Someday, her own children would learn about their murdered father—but not now, not yet. Just like her own mother, she knew her children were too young to hear such terrible truths.

The office was still, with Curtis out on patrol and not expected back until the end of his shift. Her desk was clear of files except for the one she'd been reviewing on elections. No time like the present to dive into murky waters, while she still had plenty of privacy and quiet.

She considered her options and then picked up the phone. "Mr. Holt, please," she said to the receptionist, picturing the silent, disapproving woman at her desk. "Tell him Meredith Lowe is calling."

She could almost hear the clock ticking in his grand Fifteen Palms office. Had it only been two weeks ago when she was there, in the overly air-conditioned office high above the swaying palm trees? There'd been so much hope and joy during that visit—the trepidation in hearing her grandmother's words read and then her breathlessness at opening her mother's box. Not to mention an entire week with Curtis, the beach, and a warm winter sun. It was impossible to believe her life had become even more complicated since then. She'd learned her mother may have murdered her own step-father, she possessed a valuable gemstone, and gained a cousin. Her grandmother's only and last words to her, in the letter the lawyer read, were a lie. David Givens wasn't her father. Her grandmother's lawyer needed to cough up more than provenance for a piece of jewelry.

After a click, the dry, withered voice of Therald Holt scratched through the line. "Mrs. Lowe, I assume you received my letter and considered your legal obligations. You have something to send to my office?"

She took a deep breath. She couldn't let him sense her fear. "No," she said in a firm voice, though her hands were shaking. "I think you deceived me, you and my grandmother. You had me travel all the way to Fifteen Palms, with my children, and let me believe the wrong man is my father. Your actions have been reprehensible."

The immediate attack left him speechless only for a moment. "Mrs. Lowe. I represent your grandmother's estate. I'm not responsible for other family concerns. The late Mrs. Brittan tasked me with reading her words to you, nothing more. My legal duties were discharged to the letter of the law."

She nearly choked as she uttered the next words. "I'm Anthony's daughter. You lied to me this whole time. You were Leila's trusted adviser."

Now he was silent. She wanted to fly through the phone and shake the truth out of him. She waited for a denial but none came. She gripped the phone with both hands. "Did my mother kill him?"

There was a sharp intake of breath on the other end of the line. "There's no evidence of anything like that," he snapped. "Your grandmother's husband ran off."

She forced herself to speak in an even tone. "No one just vanishes. The last time anyone ever saw him was nine months before I was born." Curtis' advice on interrogating a suspect sounded in her mind. *Let them fill the silence.*

She waited. *One, two, three, four, five...*

"There's no evidence of anything," he repeated, regaining some semblance of poise. "There's no point in it anymore, is there?"

No point in knowing who your father is? Whether

your mother killed someone? *Let him fill the silence.*

She dug her fingernails into her palm to keep from asking another question. *Let him speak first.*

He cleared his throat. "I'd be willing to make a trade," he said, his voice tight.

Bingo.

"A trade?"

His breath sounded through the phone. "We played this game before, when you were here. You have something I want; perhaps I have information for you."

The lawyer would tell her what happened twenty-five years ago and she would hand over the ring. There was just the small detail that she had no intention of giving him anything. Whatever the story was regarding the ring, it had been left to her—not the lawyer or Raymond. She didn't care about its value or provenance, only what the man knew about her mother's past. She swallowed thickly and lied through her teeth. "Okay. I'll trade."

There was a moment of silence as he registered her admission and then a drawn-out sigh hissed through the phone. "Send me the ring. Once I get it, I'll call and tell you what you want to know. Nothing in writing."

Smart man. He was aware they were both lying. "Not a chance, Mr. Holt. You tell me first. Then I'll send you the ring."

They had themselves an old-fashioned stand-off.

Chapter Twenty

The dim winter sun disappeared behind a cloud and stayed there. Snow showers had sputtered on and off all day as sinister dark-gray clouds piled up over the western mountains. Those angry clouds would soon roil down into the valley and wreak havoc on the roads. Within twenty-four hours, locals forecast whiteout conditions. She forced herself to breathe slowly while her hands clenched and unclenched.

The lawyer broke first. "You asked three things: the truth about your father, the story behind the ring and what happened to Anthony. Pick one and I'll tell you everything I know. Then you send the ring and I'll enlighten you about the other two matters."

There was no time to savor victory. She reacted quickly. "Tell me two things—the last one after you get the ring."

"No. This is my final offer to take care of this between us, privately. Otherwise, we go to court. Can you afford a couple years of legal fees, my dear?" He was no longer off-guard. His defenses were up and he was on the attack, a savvy lawyer with decades of experience. "Remember I do this for a living. These private family matters might become public. And you have children…"

This was warfare and she didn't have a stockpile of weapons to use. This wily old trickster had the upper hand. "Okay, okay. We'll do it your way. Let me think a minute."

Three things: the identity of her father, the story behind the ring, and what happened to Anthony. She didn't trust the lawyer for a millisecond. Once he had the ring in his hand, she was certain he'd never take her calls again. So, she had to make the best of the next few minutes. She frowned and studied the floor. It was easy to discard one of her questions. If she was getting rid of the ring, what did it matter how it happened to be with her mother's belongings? She'd always wonder, but she could live with not knowing. It came down to the identity of her father and whether or not her mother murdered Anthony.

Think Meredith, think. If her mother murdered Anthony, she reasoned, then he *would* be her father. There could be no other reason for lashing out in a violent way, so unlike her gentle, loving personality. If her father was someone else, there could be no correlation to Anthony's disappearance. The much-younger husband of her grandmother simply took advantage of household turmoil to make his exit.

She wavered and then arrived at a decision. "The truth this time. Did my mother kill Anthony Noble?"

A rattling sigh came through the phone line and then silence. Finally, in a grudging tone, he spoke. "There was never any evidence of that. Leila...your grandmother...paid a private investigator to find her husband. She was furious. Leila was quite a woman in her day." He chuckled, and his admiration was evident. "As far as I know—and I do believe I *would* know—she never heard from him again."

"The private investigator found nothing? No clues

of any kind?"

"Anthony vanished, as though he never existed."

"It's strange," she mused, "you didn't ask me why I'd suggest he was murdered. Or that my mother was the one who did it."

His breath rattled dryly through the phone line. *Check*, she thought. But instead of answering, he questioned her. "What makes you believe there was a murder? What did your mother tell you? I can't believe she never said anything at all."

It was time to lay everything out on the table. No more holding back. "She never told me anything. My mother wrote a letter to David Givens just after she left home. She said she killed someone, but didn't say who. We made a deal, Mr. Holt. The answer in exchange for the ring."

His tone changed to one of resignation, the tone of one relieved to get a secret out in the open. "I'll be honest. We—Leila and I—discussed the possibility. I knew your mother since the time she was born. I watched her grow up. This was a small town back then; everybody knew everybody. There's no way little Laura killed anyone. There wasn't one shred of evidence. Anthony was just here one day, gone the next. Laura ran off a couple of months later. She might have been pregnant. Again, no proof of anything."

Not a murderer. Just a disturbed pregnant runaway with a drinking problem. The timing added up. "Me. I'm proof."

"Laura left a note. Nothing confirmed at the time, you understand. But, yes, your assumption is likely."

"Anthony," she prompted, hoping to keep him talking now that he'd started giving her useful information. "People don't just disappear."

He made a sound of assent. "This was before the internet so perhaps it'd be different today. Maybe Leila did a cursory search over the years. Far as I know, she stopped watching out for him long ago. She closed off her heart to family and focused on giving back to the community. Your grandmother was very generous."

Her grandmother's charitable giving was the last thing she wanted to hear about. "I don't think I'm getting my fair share in this trade. I'll say it again—you weren't surprised at my question, about murder. You and my grandmother considered the possibility. Why?"

There was a slurp and clatter, as though he took a sip of coffee or tea and then set down the mug. It was late in the day, though. Perhaps old Mr. Holt knocked back a late afternoon gin or bourbon. But no, he was surely buying time. Calculating what to say.

"Laura was pregnant with you, wasn't she? It made sense the father was her little high school friend, David. Your mother called once, and made some wild accusations. Just like in the letter you mentioned, she talked about killing someone. This is why Leila wanted to set the record straight in her letter to you—just in case your mother claimed someone other than David was your father."

"Someone like Anthony," she said.

"The ring," he snapped. "We agreed to one question now, two questions later."

She straightened in her chair. "You'll tell me why my mother left me the ring, why my grandmother let me have something so valuable."

He hissed, the sound of fury. "We had an agreement."

"I'm breaking it. The story of the ring. Now."

"All I'll tell you now is the ring was part of Leila's private collection, kept in a safe. I know Anthony wore it on his little finger from time to time."

She almost yelled. Without realizing it, the lawyer had established provenance by declaring the ring was part of her grandmother's private collection.

He made a scoffing sound. "Anthony. Ridiculous man. Leila's biggest mistake."

"Not her biggest one," Meredith said softly.

"Enough now. We'll talk more after I've received the ring. Send it insured and registered."

She didn't bother arguing that her first question was never put to rest. The lawyer pleaded innocence of any knowledge of foul play concerning her mother's stepfather's disappearance. He would do the same with the last question, for sure. Wily old Therald Holt, Esq. was a dead end.

****

The office floor was polished to a high shine, the bookcase dusted, and files reorganized by the time Curtis arrived in the office. The night before and his disappointment at being put off didn't show in his expression. He greeted her with a quick kiss as usual, and launched into a narrative about his day as he dropped into his chair.

"Car full of city fellows dressed in brand new camo got themselves stuck in the snow within sight of the highway. Appears like they were headed for a weekend hunt. Only thing, no licenses, no idea what they were doing, with a storm on the way. I'm sure one of them would've gotten shot if I didn't turn them around and send them home. They were happy enough I didn't call the game warden on them." He shook his head and logged onto his computer. "I'd better get their license plate number out statewide in case they try again, somewhere else. That's a car full of trouble."

Within seconds, he was immersed in his work. It would be unfair to interrupt with her own troubles. He was potentially saving lives. Her own day's adventures involving a ring worth a fortune and a less-than-revealing conversation with the lawyer would need to wait. Even though her nerves were jangling with impatience to tell him her news. Lives weren't at stake. Just my sanity, she thought wryly.

The next hour crept by and slowly, his shoulders lost their tension. Through the corner of her eye, she eyed the side of his jaw and its late afternoon stubble. For a moment, she allowed herself to daydream about pressing her lips against his jaw, soft kisses that would come to rest against his firm lips.

He glanced at her and she blinked, wondering if she'd sighed. "I can stop by tonight, pick up some chicken for dinner," he said, eyebrows raised and his eyes anxious. "Unless all of you are sick of me."

Relief surged through her. She was forgiven for not giving him an instant answer the night before. "We'd never be sick of you. I'll mash a few potatoes and pull a salad together."

"I'll bring ice cream, too."

"Chocolate?"

"What else is there?"

They smiled easily at each other. Curtis rolled his chair back from his desk, the old wheels squeaking, and his paperwork abandoned. "Anything interesting happen around here today?"

She gave a short laugh and then filled him in. Patrick's revelation about her ring and then the lawyer and his evasion of all her questions. "Mr. Holt can sue me but there's no proof I ever had the ring. I could have been lying to get my questions answered. I'm not giving it back."

He nodded, thoughtful. "True, there's no proof. Only a few people have seen it. And they won't talk. Hay City people are pretty loyal to their own."

Their own. She belonged here. This is what mattered.

"I feel like I'm spinning in circles with all these questions and half-answers," she said. "Maybe this is as close as I'll ever get to the truth."

He leaned back in his chair and stretched out his legs. "Some things are worth fighting for." His gaze was steady and serious. "Especially family."

She looked at him with gratitude for understanding. "I wanted the truth about mine, but maybe…maybe the truth should remain buried." She took a deep breath and then exhaled, wishing it was just as easy to let go of the past. "I'm coming to believe there's the family we want to know and, well, the family we avoid."

His expression was solemn as he said, "We all have decisions to make, some harder than others."

They sprang from such different backgrounds, but one thing was the same: their commitment to family. Well, except for her former husband, of course. He'd broken all their vows. She shoved remembrances of Brian away.

"Meredith," Curtis said, swiveling his chair to fully face her. "You aren't your family's past."

She gave him a quizzical look.

"I've been thinking about this," he said, his eyes dropping to study the office's shiny wooden floor. "I can't say I relate to what you're going through, with your family. You have my support for whatever you want, or need, to do. I know we come from different backgrounds and have had different experiences."

His gaze rose from the floor and fixed on her. The temperature in the room seemed to rise ten degrees, and she absently tugged off her fingerless gloves. This was the crux of the matter—what worried her about their relationship from the very start. Their differences.

"I'm not going to tell you opposites attract or some other nonsense," he continued. "There's no secret formula for why people fall in love. This is what I know for sure—we aren't our families. We aren't our pasts. We aren't products of where we come from or what's happened to us."

We are though, aren't we? she thought. He didn't understand. She opened her mouth to say this, but something in his face stopped her.

"We are how we respond to the events in our lives." He appeared to be struggling to articulate this philosophy, but his meaning started to become clear. "People have choices, every day. I told you before that you have grit. You aren't a *survivor*; you're a fighter."

"Curtis," she whispered. He'd taken her frustration at being stymied in finding answers, and flipped it around to another theme.

"I'm not in love today with the woman you used to be, not even who you were yesterday," he said as he rose from his chair. He crossed the distance between their two desks in a couple of strides and then knelt before her. "I'm in love with the woman I see in front of me now, and who I know you'll be in the future. Whatever you decide about your family, I want to be at your side."

He fumbled in his pocket and revealed a plain gold band. "I'm a fighter, too, so I'm asking you again, properly this time. Meredith, will you marry me?"

Her throat worked. She tilted her chin up and gazed into his eyes. The love and acceptance in his returning gaze took her breath away. In the past weeks, she'd traveled over the rainbow and back. She'd been chasing ghosts when living, breathing people were in Hay City.

Time to swim, a voice in her head whispered. She swallowed a lump in her throat. "I set off to find my family and the most important people in my life are right here. You're more than enough. You, Jamie and Atticus—you're everything."

"Everything?" he prompted.

"Yes," she said softly, and then laid a hand on his. "Yes, yes, yes…"

He stopped the words as his lips met hers.

Chapter Twenty-One

The wind blew icy daggers into the office that afternoon, ruffling the papers on Meredith's desk. She grabbed at the files she'd found tucked in the back of the supply closet, with a plan to organize them, but several papers escaped her grasp. She shot an annoyed glance at the person who'd just thrown open the door. Raymond. Still in town despite the whiteout conditions expected by nightfall. She exchanged a knowing look with Curtis.

Her cousin's jet-black hair rose in one piece with the gust, individual strands sprayed into a solid sheet, and then settled again into perfect place. His nose was reddened by cold and his lips were tight in a grim line. He closed the door in a hurry and jammed his hands deep into his coat pockets.

"I don't know how you people live here." His hard eyes scanned the room, taking in Curtis at his desk. "I haven't been warm since I left Florida, and there isn't a decent restaurant to be found in five hundred miles. Don't get me started about the motel room. The bathtub used to be lime green. I think."

She stayed seated. If she didn't engage him in conversation, perhaps he would go away. But they were fated to have this one last conversation. Each of them was in urgent need of something the other possessed. Curtis scraped back his chair and stood by his desk. She knew the insults to his town would rile him.

"You're free to go," he said. "Now, anyway. Stick around a few more hours and you may end up getting snowed in for the rest of winter. Haven't you been following the weather reports?"

Raymond's eyes widened, and he set folded hands on the counter in a business-like manner. His glance darted between them and settled on Meredith. "Nothing illegal happening here. This is a private family matter. We have unfinished business."

She picked at a thread in the fingerless gloves she wore in the office because of the chill seeping in through the single-pane windows and cheaply insulated walls. Being a public servant placed a special emphasis on the word servant.

Avoiding his eyes, she unlocked the bottom drawer of the desk, withdrew something and then stood. After a moment's hesitation, she crossed the small office in a few strides and faced him at the counter. Her throat convulsing, she thrust out a small box. "Here. This is what you insist is yours. Take it."

Without a word, Curtis edged up close and stood behind one shoulder.

Raymond's eyes widened and he held the box gingerly before opening it. "It's been a long time," he said in a gentle voice, as though to a lover. One finger stroked the gemstone and then he snapped the box closed. His voice brightened and turned brisk. "Well. I guess all's well that ends well."

She stared at her cousin. Trouble would come from the lawyer, but let him chase down this slippery fellow. Therald Holt had more resources at hand and, anyway, the two of them deserved each other.

Curtis cleared his throat. "I imagine you'll be on your way now."

"As fast as I can pack my bags." Her cousin chortled in triumph. "Within the hour."

She took a shaky breath. "Tell me about him. My father." The name quavered on her lips. "Anthony."

He almost succeeded in hiding the wince, but not quite. His hands trembled as he tucked the box into his jacket pocket and he took a step backward. "I knew him well. Both," he said. "Anthony...and your father."

Her mouth opened to say something, but her voice failed her. He took another step backward toward the door, with one hand still in the pocket with the box. "Anthony wasn't your father. I told you before he wasn't that kind of man. He just wanted a good life, a comfortable life. That's not a crime, is it? He gave as good as he got, married to Leila."

His tone turned bitter as his other hand touched the doorknob. His knuckles went white as he clenched the cold metal surface. "I served as her escort, flattered her, catered to her whims, took her insults. What did it gain me in the end?"

Her head swam with his words. "You...are... Anthony Noble."

"I was the only support for my brother, Raymond. Leila didn't want him around the second time, but family is family, and he needed a place to stay when he got out of jail again. No one could ever say Anthony Noble didn't do right by family." He pursed his lips. "Raymond didn't want money; he needed a home. We always did our best to keep him away from Laura, given his background. In retrospect, I guess, bringing him into close contact with a minor was a mistake." His tone was regretful, but not enough. Not nearly enough for the damage that resulted.

"His *background*." Goosebumps prickled up her arms and she shook her head at the implication, a tear slipping down one cheek. The words he linked together so easily were too horrible to believe: jail, a minor, a mistake. "Your brother—" she gulped at the next word "—*raped* my mother and you helped him get away."

"I didn't help him after...after what he did. I haven't seen Raymond in twenty-five years."

"So you stole your brother's identity in order to ease your own disappearance?"

"Not easy when your brother has a criminal record," he griped. His upper lip curled. "Hard to get a job or find a place to live. Good thing I had friends to help. I suppose this makes you my step-granddaughter and my niece, or something along those lines, but I don't suppose we'll see each other again."

Her knees trembled at his dismissive tone. All along, this man had known everything, yet all he cared about was a piece of jewelry, willing to trade the truth for a rock.

Behind her, Curtis offered a steadying hand on her shoulder. "Where's your brother now?" he demanded. "You can't be sharing a name, all these years."

"Dead. Laura killed him, for sure. The body never materialized, but there was this crazy teenager claiming he attacked her. She said she killed him. Maybe I'd have done it for her if I'd gotten to him first. He ruined my life too, you know." His voice grew hard in complaint. "Leila blamed me and she was out for blood. I had to get out of there. Florida law, you know, allows you to divorce a missing spouse. That bitch took care of the situation right quick to make sure I wouldn't have claim to her estate. When I think of all I lost..." His voice trailed off. Then he twisted the doorknob. "The ring will make up for some of it."

"Why did she leave me the ring?"

Anthony shrugged. "She *did* promise to leave me the ring. I swear I'm telling the truth. I imagine she knew it would flush me out into the open, if someone else ended up with it. Especially someone who shouldn't have it. Guess Leila has the last laugh." He patted his pocket. "Or does she?"

The door opened and he was gone. She stared blankly at the door and then her shoulders went slack. "Raymond," she said, before her face crumpled. Curtis' arms were about her in an instant and he held her while she sobbed.

Her mother had been a confused teenager, her life darkened by a neglectful mother and criminal step-uncle. No one protected her when she needed it. The young teenager didn't see a way out of her situation except through a bottle, and finally by running away.

A gust of wind rattled the window and, as though a spigot opened, giant snowflakes painted the sky white. All was quiet except for the sound of her sniffling. She wiped her eyes and leaned back against the counter. Her chest ached with the truth of Anthony's story. But there was still one last mystery unlikely to ever be solved. Those words: *I'm a murderer.*

"Did she kill him? Am I never going to know for sure? People don't just vanish."

"Raymond had a record," Curtis pointed out. "He may have found it pretty convenient to change his name and disappear. As difficult as it is, some missing persons remain in the unsolved file." He paused. "Maybe your mother wasn't being literal. Maybe she was referring to killing off her old life, the life she was leaving behind."

He was being kind in giving her another possibility to consider. She recalled David suggesting something similar. In her heart, she knew the truth. No one searched too hard for Raymond. He never surfaced again. The man surely was dead and the body too well hidden. Whatever manner her mother used to kill him and dispose of the body, she'd paid for the crime with an escape into alcoholism and homelessness. The penalty for his murder was her own life. Meredith searched her heart. It would take time to accept this version of events, but she had all the time in the world. She stepped forward and laid her head against Curtis' shoulder, and he drew her close once more.

"I'm done with searching for answers," she vowed. "Whatever happened, belongs to the past."

Out the window, a curtain of snow fell. Anthony better get on the road quick, she thought. She never wanted to see him again.

"I was never going to leave Hay City," she murmured. "Not this valley or these mountains. Not my friends or my house." She swallowed, knowing the truth of her next words. "Not you."

He blew out an exaggerated sigh of relief. "You had me worried for a while. I thought I was going to have to follow you to some big city and do some more convincing. I wasn't sure I could offer you enough of a life in this little town. With me."

"I couldn't imagine you in a city," she said. "You belong here."

His arms tightened around her. "With you."

She tilted her face up to his. "I'm ready for my future. Starting today."

Chapter Twenty-Two

Two folding tables and a mish-mash of chairs rested in the tall grass, stomped down by the spring morning's hubbub. Forty people or more milled about her old one-story house, now stripped bare of furniture, appliances and other belongings. Windows were lined up against a tree and priced individually. A deep vibration and then a roar resounded from a large yellow bulldozer, and then it rumbled toward the house, bumping over the gravel driveway.

"Right! Right! For God's sake, you're going to hit a tree." Deli-boy hopped up and down, his face almost purple, as he directed the bulldozer's driver.

The driver, a grim-faced Crusty, swung right too far and then over-corrected left. Weaving his way erratically, the equipment finally struck its goal at an angle and a wall buckled under the impact.

April twentieth rolled around, otherwise known as Demolition Day in Hay City. The event was stacking up to be everything Honey promised. Food, neighbors, and chaos. For a hundred dollars, people could operate the bulldozer for ten minutes, smashing it into walls of her house and leveling the leaking, decaying, crumbling eyesore. For twenty dollars, neighbors were provided with a sledgehammer and they could swing away at interior walls—when the bulldozer wasn't in motion, of course. The food part was well represented with three tables laden with pasta salad, stacks of thick sandwiches, gelatin salads, vegetable trays, cookies, and chips and dip.

Honey sat enthroned on a cushion-covered chair, an old-fashioned metal money box on her generous lap, and served as the grand ringmaster. Her sharp gaze surveyed the work and made sure no one climbed up on the bulldozer, lifted a sledgehammer, or loaded scrap materials in their vehicle without paying first.

Occasionally, she barked out commands to those near her and they hustled to obey. The woman sold off old single-paned windows, rotten flooring, and scrap lumber like a carnival huckster, and shamelessly pawned off items of questionable value. Next to her sat a newly pregnant Gemma, with her long auburn hair plaited in one single braid down her back, and holding her eight-month-old baby, the child she'd had with Brian.

By the end of the day, her home would be leveled and the grounds scraped clean. There would be no sign a building existed since no one ever bothered to place a proper foundation underneath. Over the decades, the house sagged tiredly in the middle like a well-worn couch cushion.

Bumblebees buzzed nearby and a red-tailed hawk circled above. The scent of a profusion of grasses, flowers, and newly plowed fields filled the air. Spring arrived in a hurry once the snow melted away, as though nature was aware it had limited time to conduct the business of renewal and growth.

Stacey left the month before, saying David and Ariel needed her for lambing season. They'd hugged and promised to visit each other as often as possible.

"I taught Dad five recipes and now he thinks he's a chef," Stacey said before she drove away. "Last week, he left the house for the first time in two years. Says he's going to buy a bicycle. I should have moved to California long ago."

The grinding of shifting gears screeched from the bulldozer, which now backed away from the house. Crusty's arms flailed as he worked the levers.

"Time's up," Deli-boy cried and hopped up on his family's bulldozer to wrest the controls from the ponytailed man, who was preparing for one more go. "You only paid for twenty minutes, not twenty-one. Go see Honey if you want more time."

"My turn," called out a teenage girl, who wore heavy army boots below a plaid skirt. She clambered up next to Deli-boy after Crusty stomped away. The girl pecked Deli-boy on the cheek and whispered something in his ear.

He blushed beet red and stroked a few wiry whiskers still struggling and failing to be a goatee. "I'd better help you." He placed his hands over hers to guide the controls and they giggled maniacally together as the bulldozer rammed into a wall of the house, then backed up to strike it again.

Crusty strode across the grass, his face breaking out in a grin. "Love is in the air," he pontificated, as he observed the two teen lovebirds bent on a mutual task of destruction. He turned to Meredith and Curtis, who stood to one side watching the event. "Speaking of love, you got a ring on this gal's finger, now you best set a date."

Curtis' chest filled out as he took a deep breath. "June twenty-third. We'll leave the next day for our honeymoon. Jamie will be out of school. We plan to take a drive as a family to Bodega Bay for our honeymoon. Visit Stacey, David, and Ariel." He gazed down at Meredith and then across the grass where the children played with half a dozen others.

She tucked her arm in his and leaned into his shoulder. "We'll pour the foundation next week, and then I suppose I'll learn how to drive a nail straight."

"You'll do fine," he said, his gaze returning to her. "We can get the frame up before we leave, and the rest done by fall. Family and friends are all set to help out, but in stages. We'll have everything in place before the first snow falls."

With the house crumbling in front of her, she could finally visualize the new one to come. The final blueprints called for three bedrooms, two baths, a small living room and a large bonus room. As the reality of a new house sank in and their discussions became more in-depth, sketches were revised and then revised again as they balanced simplicity with the mutual desire for more children. Curtis insisted on a large eat-in kitchen where their family could gather, entertain and build memories for future generations. The kitchen would include a deep garden window facing east so they could watch the sun rise over their morning coffee. They'd debated whether the main porch should be at the front or back of the house, and finally decided to build a wrap-around porch.

Phase two would involve building a new garage with attached workshop and shed, as well as building a large vegetable garden. Curtis' ideas ran rampant and he sketched out a phase three, four, and five, before she called a halt. "Let's plan to wing it a bit too," she'd suggested, and then he wrote those words down.

Jamie trotted up, half dragging her younger brother. "I think Atticus needs to go potty."

"I can handle this," Curtis said, and led the two-year-old to a cluster of bushes away from the demolition and neighbors' eyes.

The five-year-old stared after them critically. "Mom says we're not supposed to pee in the bushes."

Crusty leaned down and addressed the girl. "How do you feel about having the sheriff as your new dad?"

She shrugged, a bored gesture. "I thought he already was my new dad." The girl directed a serious gaze up to Meredith. "Rio called Laf a 'laugh riot' at school. I'm not sure I like him saying that."

She dropped to her knees and grabbed her daughter's hands. "That was yesterday. Do we raise a fuss about yesterday?"

Her five-year-old blinked, and then swept a hand over one shoulder as she recited the next words, as though from a lesson drilled into her: "We brush it off and move forward."

Meredith smiled her approval and let her daughter's hands go. "Exactly." She spun Jamie around to face the other children and gave her a gentle prod. "Go forth and conquer."

The girl ran back to the other children, her unruly black curls bouncing like springs.

"Your child won't have any problem conquering the world," Crusty remarked.

A shout went up as an entire wall toppled and crashed. One interior wall remained and two young men argued with Deli-boy over the right to knock it down. The teenager had a desperate expression on his face as he sought Honey's attention to mitigate the dispute, but the woman was deep in discussion with a local farmer.

"I'd better see what my plump chicken is up to over there," Crusty said, eying Honey. "I sense another plot being hatched as we speak." He strode across the grass and Meredith found herself alone for a moment.

Surveying the sight before her, she considered where life had taken her over the past year. Murdered husband, new friends and home, falling in love with the local sheriff, discovering the identity of her father and most of the mystery behind her mother's life. Giving away a valuable asset resulted in all these good friends and neighbors rallying to help her with a new house. Sometimes, the best course of action was to toss out the bad in order to allow the good to rush in.

I'm a strong woman, Mama. She spoke the words in her mind, and hoped her mother could somehow hear them. *And I'm worthy of a good life.*

One mystery remained unsolved. Those haunting words: *I'm a murderer.* If anyone alive knew what her mother had meant, they were going to the grave with the secret. Had her mother killed the missing Raymond? She still couldn't believe such a terrible thing could be true, but hadn't she, herself, once contemplated murder? People could only push you so far before you started considering escape options. Some people would murder for love, others for money, others for family. A young woman, trapped and feeling alone in the world, might murder an abuser if the opportunity arose. There were limits for everyone. She closed her eyes and pictured what may have happened, but nothing came to her. How would a teenager overcome a full-grown man? How would she dispose of the body so it would never be found?

As for everything else, what may have occurred was speculation, but she'd worked up a theory. It was likely *she* was the reason her grandmother never let her mother return home, and never wanted to acknowledge their connection. Her DNA proved Raymond's crime, and linked her mother to the man's disappearance. A child was both accusation and proof of motive for murder as well as her grandmother's foolhardiness in marrying Anthony. Her grandmother didn't hate her. She'd been afraid of her. In death, however, her grandmother left one clue—a ring. It drew Anthony out of the shadows to unravel the mystery of her birth. This might not be exactly the way it happened, but this was a story she could live with.

She'd created her own mantra to deal with her past. A little sweep of a hand on her shoulder and a few magic words: "We brush it off and move forward."

Curtis sauntered back and aimed the toddler in the direction of the other children. Atticus' legs, those of a sturdy two-year-old and no longer wobbly, hurried across the grass to join the fun. Curtis met her gaze and her heart filled. His light-brown hair shone in the spring sun and his two-day stubble reminded her of the night before spent enclosed in his arms. She was the luckiest woman in the world. She could live with some mysteries unsolved; she'd write her own story.

He nudged Meredith playfully and she nudged him back. There was no other way to say it other than to say this felt right, like a final puzzle piece snapping into place and filling out the picture. He made her whole. Her children loved him too, and his acceptance of them as a part of her meant everything. Here, in this unlikely nowhere town of Hay City, she'd discovered her life.

As the final wall collapsed, neighbors sent up a cheer. The two men in the bulldozer who shared the controls raised their fists in triumph. The house wasn't a house anymore.

So many changes in such a short time, she thought. But renovations of all types are good. Very, very good.

Epilogue—The Denouement

Raymond gripped her steadily by one arm and held her wet tangled hair back while she heaved the contents of her stomach into the sand.

"All okay now?" It was as though the past half hour hadn't happened. The assault—the rape. "Let's get you home."

Laura straightened and stumbled, then wrenched away. He let her go, easily keeping at one side with his strong gait. There was no point in running now. She just wanted to go home, to her room, and the bottle that would make this night disappear.

They walked together for a few moments, like two cozy companions out for an evening stroll. They emerged from the dunes and skirted the edge of the swamp. Home and her mother was to the right. Safety and sleep behind a locked door. Tomorrow, all this would go away, just as a nightmare fades when dawn arrives.

"We need to talk before I take you home." He stood a few steps in front of her now, facing her and forcing her to a stop in the shelter of a tree. Behind him, the swamp trees dripped their branches to the water. "If you say anything to your mother, or my brother, there'll be trouble for you. Leila won't believe you and Anthony will never take your side against me."

The truth of this stung. For the first time, she

spoke, her voice bitter. "My mother will call the police. You'll go back to prison."

He chuckled and spread his hands out at his sides. "I'll say I found you partying with a group of kids, swimming in the surf, in this storm. I mean, look at you; you're a mess." Before she realized what he was doing, he grabbed one of her hands and forced a ring on a finger. "What will your mother say about you getting into her safe? Taking things that don't belong to you?"

She gasped when she saw the ring. "You're a thief as well as a rapist." Her voice shook with disgust and rage. She wanted him dead.

"Anthony has many charms. He'll forgive me and convince your mother you're lying. She'll be grateful I rescued her ring. You'll end up labeled a naughty, nasty girl."

It was true. Her mother was besotted with her new husband, twelve years younger than her. Her mother didn't have relationships; she had acquisitions. This included her husband and daughter. They were required to fill their role when called upon.

Tears blurred her vision and she brushed a dirty hand across her face. Gritty sand scraped at her eyelids. She blinked, cocked her head and grew still. Her features softened and her eyes grew thoughtful. She drew a lock of loosened hair over one shoulder, glancing to make sure she had his attention. There was an ache in her scalp from where he'd gripped her hair. In some cultures, rapists were executed. Here…he was right, no one would believe her. "I suppose you're right. I suppose it wasn't all bad."

He appeared startled and then a leering smile came to his lips. "You liked it."

Julie Howard

Her gaze, steely now, flickered to the swamp behind him and back. Her jaw stiffened and the words were an effort. "Maybe."

The rain strengthened anew and now Laura stilled her breathing. He barked out a laugh, victorious.

"That's my little rab..."

The alligator lunged at him mid-sentence, cutting off his words. It was a huge beast; its dagger-like teeth seized both his legs in one bite and hauled him down. Laura backed away rapidly, scrambling to stay upright in the sand. Her throat tight, she gasped for air. The alligator loosened its grip for a fraction of a second, and lunged a second time to seize him at the hips. Laura spun and bolted from his screams. When she was at a safe distance, she peeked behind her.

The swamp waters churned at the edge. Crimson red pooled where her step-uncle once stood, diluting to tea rose and then a lovely shade of coral before turning clear in the pouring rain. She dropped to her knees, catching her breath, and stared at the swamp until she was certain both her attacker and the beast were gone.

The roiling swamp calmed gradually, but Raymond's screams echoed and echoed in her mind. He was right about one thing—her mother would never believe her, not about the rape or the alligator.

The rain ceased as though a spigot turned off. Humidity rushed in, heavy on her shoulders. Mosquitoes buzzed about her head and beetles clicked. The swamp lurked, alive in a thousand ways. It would be easy to believe the past hour had never happened. She sat staring at the dark water until it was past imagining Raymond would emerge dripping and bloody, but alive. I did that, *she thought, horrified at what she'd witnessed.* I wished it into happening. I'm a murderer, just as certain as if I'd drowned him myself.

The word "murderer" swam in her mind and blocked out everything else. "I'm a murderer," she whispered, just to hear the words out loud. "Judge, jury and executioner."

Sometime later, she headed home, clutching at her dress' torn shoulder strap and twisting the ring on her finger. Her mother would be furious at the ruined dress. She'd be furious about a lot of things. This could be the beginning of the end.

A word about the author...

Julie Howard is the author of the Wild Crime series and a paranormal mystery, *Spirited Quest*. A former journalist and editor, she is a member of the Idaho Writers Guild and founder of the Boise chapter of Shut Up & Write. She also is editor of *Potato Soup Journal* literary magazine.

Sign up for her newsletter at:
www.juliemhoward.com
to obtain information on new releases, sales and more.